Sweetened with Honey

A Farm Fresh Romance

Book 3

Valerie Comer

GreenWords Media

Dedication

For Jen

Beekeeper, Farmer,
and Treasured Daughter-in-Law

Books by Valerie Comer

Farm Fresh Romance Novels
Raspberries and Vinegar
Wild Mint Tea
Sweetened with Honey
Dandelions for Dinner (Spring 2015)

Christmas Romance Novella Duo
Snowflake Tiara
(with Angela Breidenbach)

Fantasy Novel
Majai's Fury

Acknowledgements

I'm thankful for the many people who've helped and encouraged me while I wrote *Sweetened with Honey*.

Jim, you are always my best friend and confidante. Thanks for your help with this story and for encouraging my dreams every day.

Thank you to my kids, Hanna and Craig, and Joel and Jen, for your love of fresh, seasonal food, and for teaching my little granddaughters to appreciate it, too.

A shout-out to my cousin Sylvia! Thank you for brainstorming the medical parts of this story, then reading my manuscript and helping me find ways out of the corners I painted myself into. Any medical errors that remain are my fault, not yours.

Thanks to Melanie and Sara for reading the manuscript and making suggestions. I appreciate you both so much.

I'm so thankful for the CIA—no, not that one! The Christian Indie Authors group has been a constant source of information and inspiration. Thank you!

Nicole, I think you're on my permanent thank you list. For your encouragement, your advice, your brainstorming... for being you. Thanks.

To the many fans who read, enjoyed, and reviewed *Raspberries and Vinegar* and *Wild Mint Tea*. Thanks for bonding with the gang from Green Acres and being eager to get your hands on this third volume in the Farm Fresh Romance series.

And to Jesus. Thank you for being my salvation, my hope, and my inspiration.

Chapter 1 --

*S*ierra Riehl had done a lot of strange things while studying natural medicine, but this seemed right up there with applying leeches to let blood. Straight out of medieval times.

"Are you sure you want to do this?" She set the jar containing two honeybees on the table in her naturopathy office.

"I think so." Her friend eyed the bees crawling up the side of the glass. "I've read a lot of reports that say stings really help. My rheumatoid arthritis seems worse every day."

"I know. That's the only reason I'm agreeing." Probably not what she should say out loud — and not what she would, if

Doreen Klimpton's symptoms hadn't taken over so quickly. Her once-vibrant friend had shrunk in on herself in recent months.

"Where are you going to apply it?" Doreen kept her eyes on the jar as she settled her bony frame in the reclining chair. "Are you going to sting me twice?" Her thin fingers gripped the armrests.

"Maybe." Sierra slipped a lab coat over her lilac dress. "I plan to start with one as a test. If things go well, we can do a second one. Or not, as you wish."

Doreen nodded. "I can't believe I'm doing this." She took a deep breath. "Getting stung on purpose."

Sierra couldn't, either. Yet, since she'd taken up apiculture, she kept hearing old beekeepers say they never had arthritis. The venom from the many stings they inevitably incurred in the line of duty kept their joints at ease. Unprovable at the moment, but she'd be glad of the side benefit as she aged, no doubt. She'd never expected her boss to test the theory.

Doreen closed her eyes. "Do it already. The anticipation must be worse than the sting."

"You're sure you don't have allergies?" Sierra had asked before, but man, all she needed was to see Doreen go into anaphylactic shock.

"I was tested. It should be fine."

Sierra took a deep breath. Should she swab Doreen's hand as though she were giving a needle of some other kind? Probably. She reached for a cotton pad and a bottle of alcohol and wiped the area at the base of Doreen's thumb.

Needles normally went into tissue-laden areas like biceps, not bony parts. But it wasn't a needle. A bee's stinger wasn't nearly as long as most of those.

Just do it.

She unscrewed the lid, grabbed a bee with a pair of tweezers, and put the lid back on. Did she have the bee in a decent grip? It looked like it. "Last chance to refuse treatment."

Doreen turned her face toward the window, where a late September breeze fluttered the mini-blinds. "I'm ready."

Sierra held the bee's rear against Doreen's hand. A sharp intake of breath revealed the insect had reacted as predicted, releasing its venom.

A man's voice came from the doorway. "What is going on in here?"

Sierra whirled, dropping the tweezers and the bee.

"Oh, Gabe!" Doreen struggled out of the deep chair. "It's so good to see you. I wasn't sure you were ever coming home." She tottered across the room and flung herself into Gabe's arms.

Whoa, working in that Romanian orphanage had treated Gabriel Rubachuk right. He looked leaner — better — than Sierra remembered.

Gabe's piercing blue eyes met hers over Doreen's head. "You didn't answer my question."

Sierra thrust her chin up. "Applying bee venom therapy for her rheumatoid arthritis." Speaking of bees, what had happened to the one she'd used? Not that it mattered much, since they could only dispense venom once before dying.

His laugh echoed harshly in the small room. "Are you some kind of quack?" He looked down at his former mother-in-law still in his arms. "Didn't the doctor prescribe medicine for you, Doreen? Isn't it working anymore?"

"I don't like how it makes me feel." Doreen sniffled against his chest, clutching him close. "And it doesn't work as well as it did at first. Don't be angry at Sierra. I asked her to do this. I researched it online."

Gabe shook his head. "You can't believe everything you find on the Internet. Anyone can pretend they're an expert." He eyed

Sierra. "I thought better of you. Anything for a buck?"

That stung. She pulled herself to her full height. Not that she was tall enough to intimidate a guy like him. "I'll have you know there's plenty of evidence to support the articles Doreen found. Even when I was in school, venom was noted as relief for several types of arthritis and multiple sclerosis. Besides, people get stung all the time. It's less invasive than the pinprick of a needle."

What Sierra didn't know was how the toxin affected Doreen. She touched the older woman's shoulder. "Can I ask you to sit back down, please? I'd like to have a look at the site."

Doreen released Gabe, who patted her back awkwardly, then resumed her seat. She laid her hand on the armrest.

Sierra scrutinized the area. A fiery mound the size of a nickel surrounded the white prick mark. That didn't look good. "I'm afraid you'll need to stay with me a while longer, until the swelling stops spreading."

"If she's allergic to the sting, get her to a real doctor." Gabe loomed closer. "They can give her an antihistamine shot. What's it called, an Epipen?"

The scent of his aftershave filled the air. Who knew those commercials for Old Spice would make it trendy again for guys under fifty?

Sierra's nose twitched as she put a bit of space between them. "An Epipen isn't an antihistamine. It's—" She parked her hands on her hips and sighed. "Oh, never mind. Just get out of my office and let me do my job. I'm perfectly capable of monitoring Doreen and dispensing a countermeasure if needed. For now, it bears watching, but impeding the venom will also nullify the good it's doing against her arthritis."

"I'm not going anywhere until Doreen comes with me." Gabe leaned against the beige wall, muscular arms crossed over his striped button-up. "Then it looks like I'm taking her to urgent care."

Lifting orphans must've provided a great workout. Sierra pulled her gaze back to his face. "Now who's overreacting? I've been keeping bees for two seasons. A lot of people have a quick reaction that subsides just as fast." Though most of Doreen's hand now looked puffy.

If only Gabe weren't in the room, blocking Sierra's ability to think. Of all the ways she'd dreamed they'd meet again, this wasn't one of them. He would come into Nature's Pantry and commend her for the way she'd helped Doreen pull his health-food store into the black while he'd been off in Europe. Or he'd stroll in at Green Acres Farm to see his buddy, who was married to her best friend.

In either case, his eyes would light up at the sight of her.

Yeah, she'd been dreaming. It would never happen. He'd never see her as anything but the woman whose father's semi-truck had rolled right over his wife's car, killing her and their unborn child instantly. Such a shame Bethany had swerved from the deer that jumped in front of her car and hit the semi instead. She probably would've survived the deer.

Sierra had hoped three years away would be long enough for Gabe to heal up and move on. Just her luck he'd now see her as a quack... or worse, a con.

oOo

Dread of returning to Galena Landing, Idaho, had dogged Gabriel Rubachuk for three years.

Staring down Sierra Riehl while she fussed over Doreen came as a welcome distraction. Something to focus on besides the apartment that had once been his home. Besides the shock of seeing Bethany's mom half-crippled and in obvious pain.

"It's so good to see you, Gabe." Doreen's sad eyes found his. "When did you land in Spokane? I thought you'd let me know when you were coming home."

How could he explain? Bethany had been close to her mom, but what linked him to her now? Just the health-food store. He and Bethany had bought it from her as newlyweds, but Doreen had taken over running it when he bolted for Romania to help in his parents' mission work after Bethany's death.

"I wasn't sure." It sounded lame. He'd had a pretty good idea when he bought the tickets, after all.

"Looks like the swelling has stopped spreading," Sierra said. "How are you feeling?"

Doreen looked down at her hand.

Looked inflamed to Gabe. A twinge of regret crossed his mind. He'd known her RA had flared, but it hadn't brought him back to the US. He'd just ditched her along with all his other responsibilities.

"It's kind of hot and itchy," she ventured.

Sierra nodded. "That's to be expected. I know we'd talked about doing both hands today, but I'd rather wait and see how this one fares."

Sting her again? No way. Gabe pushed off from the wall, mouth open in protest.

Sierra pinned him with a glare as she tucked a strand of long blond hair behind her ear. A curl sprang loose immediately. "This is none of your business, Gabe. You are interfering with my ability to provide quality care to a patient who came to me voluntarily."

"But she—" She what? Wasn't capable of making decisions about her own health care? Ouch.

"Furthermore, you're trespassing."

Gabe shook his head. He knew the answer to this one. "You

are. This is my building. My store downstairs. My apar—" He choked on the word. "My apartment up here." He allowed his gaze to rove the area. This would have been the baby's room. He tugged at his shirt collar as breath nearly failed him.

"You left Doreen in charge, and she leased this space to me." Sierra's gaze softened. "I'm happy to let you have it back, Gabe. We just didn't know when you were coming. Last we heard, you were thinking of staying overseas until the New Year."

He'd returned to sell the business. What he'd do then, he didn't know. Sticking around in the town that held all his memories of a happy marriage seemed a bad idea. Maybe he'd go back to school. Get a degree in something useful. Who knew what?

"It's okay. I-I'm not sure I can handle living up here anyway." He took a deep breath and let it out slowly. "Thanks for helping Doreen."

"Gabe's right," Doreen said. "He doesn't need to stay here for now. He can live with me."

His head was shaking before she'd even finished. "No, that's okay. No need to rearrange your life." The only thing worse than this apartment was Bethany's former bedroom in her mom's house and the kitchen where he'd taught her to bake chocolate chip cookies when they were thirteen.

"But—"

"Steve and Rosemary are expecting me. I'll bunk out at the farm with them for a few days until I figure out what I'm doing." Besides running again. "No need to put anyone out."

Doreen pushed out of the chair. "You're staying with Nemeseks? They knew you were coming, and I didn't?"

He liked Doreen fine. Respected her. Hated to see her in pain. How could he gently remind her that she didn't have a claim on him anymore? "We've stayed in touch since they came home from Romania. Being out at the farm will do me good."

Their son Zach had been the other integral part of his growing up years. He and Zach and Beth hung out lots as a threesome, but Gabe had plenty of memories of his buddy that weren't dependent on Bethany. Yes, staying with Zach's parents was the best idea.

"I needed to see the store before I drove out there. Looks good. Well stocked." He backed toward the door. "Thanks, Doreen."

Tears glistened in her eyes.

He'd bet they had nothing to do with her arthritis or the bee sting.

"That was Sierra." Doreen's voice trembled. "I haven't been up to much lately."

Gabe managed to get the words out. "Thanks, Sierra." Just his luck he was beholden to her, of all people. Yeah, he knew he'd left Doreen in a bind with the business. He'd lost a wife, but she'd lost her only daughter. Why had it seemed okay for him to run and push her to take on his responsibilities on top of her own grief? He'd been blind.

Blinders still helped him cope.

"You're welcome." Sierra's jaw tightened, and she looked ready to say more. She shook her head and turned away.

He couldn't stand it. "What?"

"Nothing."

With women it was never "nothing." He hadn't been married for five years without learning a thing or two. But did he really want to push it? No. Not with her, of all people.

He stared hard into her blue eyes. She needed to keep her distance. Not to be sweet to Doreen when he wasn't. Not to take care of the business he'd abandoned. Not to be happy and carefree in this place filled with his painful memories.

Sierra took a step backward, her eyes widening as her lips pulled into a straight line.

Good, maybe she was getting the message.

"I don't feel so well."

Gabe took a step closer as Doreen's head lolled against the back of the deep chair, but Sierra got there first. "Doreen? Are you okay?"

"She's passed out. That's it. I'm taking her to urgent care."

Sierra glared up at him but stepped aside. "There's no need. Give her a moment."

Gabe gathered Doreen into his arms. She hardly weighed a thing. "You've done enough."

Chapter 2 ---

*D*oreen opened her eyes and tried to focus on Gabe's face. "What's going on?"

"It's okay, Doreen. You just fainted." He managed to get the car door open. He'd need to get his old car on the road later today, then get the rental back to Spokane airport. Someone would have to give him a ride. He hadn't thought that one through.

Gabe settled Doreen into the passenger seat and tugged the seatbelt in place around her.

She pushed against his hand, but her strength was no match for his. "Where are you taking me? I don't understand."

He hesitated. "Urgent care in Wynnton."

She blinked and shook her head. "No. I'm okay."

Could've fooled him. She looked weak. Confused. He cast a glance at her hand. The swelling wasn't any greater, though. "I think you need to have that looked at." The nerve of Sierra, actually stinging Doreen on purpose. He rounded the car and slid into the driver's seat.

Doreen sat up straight. "I'm not going to Wynnton, Gabriel. And my car is right here. I'll drive myself home."

So much for swooping in and saving her. Now what? She wasn't in any condition to drive. That part, at least, was clear. "You need someone to keep an eye on you."

"Sierra can do that." She reached for the seat belt buckle. "No need to put yourself out."

Gabe put his hand over hers. "It's not putting me out." But her point was well taken. He'd only been back in Galena Landing for half an hour and he'd already made a mess. Did he want to alienate everyone he'd ever cared about?

No, of course not. "Let me take you out to the farm, then. You can visit with Rosemary, and we'll see how you feel after a bit. I can bring you back to town when you're ready."

She searched his face then leaned back into the seat, pulling her hand from under his. "Fine."

Gabe put the car in gear and headed toward the Nemesek farm. It wasn't all about him. He needed to remember that. He'd left the day after Zach's wedding to Jo, but their lives had gone on. They had a little girl now, over a year old.

He gripped the wheel. If it had been made of a lesser material, he would've crushed it. His own daughter would be nearly three. Running. Talking. Playing. He and Beth would probably have had another by now. How could he watch his buddy as a dad, when his own child had been ripped from him months before her birth?

Time. It was supposed to be a healer. He'd thought it had helped. Thought he was ready to face Galena Landing long enough to tie up business ends and leave again. A few weeks, right? A month or two at most?

He pulled into the senior Nemeseks' driveway. Zach would have to wait. He turned the ignition off, aware of Doreen's worried gaze on him. He tossed her a smile — or something that might pass for one — and opened the car door.

Voices, laughter, and the squeal of a child sounded in the distance. He swung toward Green Acres Farm just visible between the trees heavily laden with purple plums, and caught a glimpse of Steve's truck. Everyone was next door?

Gabe leaned into the passenger window. "Give me a sec. I'll see if anyone's home." He took the veranda steps two at a time and knocked on the screen door. No reply. He stuck his head in and hollered, "Steve? Rosemary?" Silence.

He returned to the car. "Sounds like they're next door."

Doreen nodded. A moment later they pulled in. A large house stood at the end of the driveway. A long low building, stuccoed like the main house, stood where the old mobile home had been, last he remembered.

Life had moved forward at Green Acres.

Half a dozen people, working in a large garden, looked up to see who'd arrived. Gabe took a deep breath. He exited the car and hurried around to help Doreen. His first responsibility was to her.

"Gabe!" Jo screamed.

Gabe shut the passenger door behind Doreen just as Jo blasted into him. "Man, it's good to see you." She hugged him fiercely around the middle.

He patted her shoulder.

The others crowded around. Zach slapped him on the back then enveloped him in a man-hug.

Gabe blinked back hot tears. Maybe part of him still did belong here.

Rosemary approached, a toddler wedged on her hip. "Gabe. So good to see you." She slipped her free arm around him.

Gabe hugged her back, but his gaze was filled with the curly-haired cherub.

"I'd like you to meet Madelynn Grace." Rosemary shifted the

child, who leaned against her grandmother's shoulder and eyed him thoughtfully.

"She's beautiful," he managed to get out. He jerked his gaze to Zach's. Hated the look of sympathy he found there. "Congratulations, man."

"Thanks." Zach reached for the child, who went to him willingly. "She's pretty awesome."

Gabe nodded and took a deep breath, just as a wet nose touched his hand. "Domino?" At Zach's nod, he bent down and patted the Border collie. "He's sure grown."

"Welcome home, Gabe. I'd like you to meet my husband."

Gabe turned toward Claire. Of the three gals who'd bought Green Acres Farm several years ago, he knew her the least. Of course, he'd heard about her marriage from Rosemary's emails.

"This is Noel Kenzie. Noel, meet Gabriel Rubachuk."

The guy had a strong grip. "Good to meet you, Gabe. I've heard a lot about you."

"Likewise." Gabe looked at Claire. She seemed relaxed. Happy. That boded well for their relationship.

She smiled at him. "Thanks for bringing Doreen out for a visit. You two are staying for dinner, I hope? Noel's on the barbecue tonight."

Noel laughed. "Not literally. Thinking steaks, for the record. Potatoes. Green beans. Tomatoes." He pointed at the garden. "There's no shortage of food, so you're more than welcome."

This gang was like a family. Some things never changed.

"Of course you're staying," Jo put in. "Rosemary made a peach cobbler, knowing you were coming."

o0o

Sierra pedaled up Thompson Road. She'd gotten out of shape living in town since Claire and Noel's honeymoon, but she'd moved back to the farm just a few weeks ago when they'd finished painting her side of the new duplex. Her clinic could be moved to the other half with only a few days' notice.

But was Gabe staying? He acted like a trapped animal, not a guy who looked ready to step back into normal life in northern Idaho. He'd be bolting again pretty quickly. She'd bet on it.

The other shoe had finally dropped. She'd somehow built up hope he'd pick up the first one and lace it on her foot, like she was some kind of Cinderella. It was silly. She knew it was. She hadn't known Gabe without Bethany except for the few weeks after the funeral.

How had she ever gotten him stuck in her head? Probably from listening to Doreen as they worked together. She'd helped Doreen grieve and find new hope in life. When had she transferred those thoughts to Gabe?

Seeing his cold expression when he saw her was a slosh of ice water into her face. She might have built up a crush on him, but he certainly hadn't done the same for her.

Her reality had been thoroughly checked.

It sounded like party time at Green Acres. Jo and Claire had pulled the troops together for picking and canning tomatoes. Sierra'd be doing her share later. She and Claire had chosen recipes for the homemade ketchup and barbecue sauce they'd be creating tomorrow.

Sierra turned her bike into the driveway. Coming home to Green Acres on a late September day was a balm to her soul. Her true friends. Her calling in life. Peace. Satisfaction. A sense of belonging.

She didn't need Gabe. There were other men in Galena Landing, like Tyrell Burke. Sierra dismounted in front of the duplex and removed her helmet. All those people, and her hair probably lay plastered to her head. She'd take a minute to freshen up before facing them.

A few minutes later she rounded the main house then climbed the few steps to the back deck, where Noel adjusted the settings on the gas grill. He grinned and snapped a pair of tongs in her direction.

Sierra heard Gabe's voice. She stopped, one foot on the bottom step. What happened to taking to Doreen to Wynnton? He couldn't have gotten back already. Where had he parked his car?

Part of her screamed to go around the house and in through the larder door, but Noel had already seen her. Besides, she couldn't avoid Gabe forever. Sierra took a deep breath, sent up a quick prayer, and stepped into view.

Her gaze went straight to his, but Doreen wasn't beside him, nor was she anywhere on the deck. Just the guys. Zach snapped the ends off a bowlful of green beans as he visited with Gabe.

"Where is Doreen?" Sierra demanded, a hand wedged on her hip. She couldn't help it.

Gabe's jaw hardened as he turned to face her. "Inside."

Sierra's eyes narrowed. "Did you take her to Wynnton?"

He averted his gaze, a flush creeping up his neck. "No. She convinced me she was okay."

"You might've let me know."

"You're right." Gabe tugged at his collar. "I'm sorry."

He probably wanted to hear, "that's okay," from her, but she didn't have it to give. She shot a few more daggers at him then stepped over Domino into the house.

"Whoa," Zach said as she shut the door with perhaps more force than necessary.

Whatever.

Valerie Comer

The aroma of roasting tomatoes and eggplant wafted her way. Lunch seemed forever ago, like maybe last week.

Claire glanced up from behind the peninsula. "Hey, Sierra, you're home! Would you mind grabbing the beans from Zach? Hope he's got the ends all snapped off. Supper's in ten if he's ready."

Sierra froze. Did she mind? Yes, she did. Could she say it? Not so much. She pivoted and headed back to the deck. Best to get this over with as quickly as she could.

"Zach? Done with the beans?" She didn't have to look at Gabe. No need. "Claire is ready for them now."

"Slave driver," Zach muttered.

Noel laughed. "She is that, but I'm starving, man. Hurry it up already. I can't put the steaks on until those beans go inside. Chef's orders." He moved the potatoes around the grill.

"Yeah, yeah, almost done." Zach's hands hadn't stopped. "Sit down a minute, Sierra. You've had a long day, I'm sure."

Because she'd been rude to Gabe? She refused to look at him even now. "Pretty busy," she allowed, sitting on the swing beside Zach. She reached for a handful of beans that needed snapping.

"I've got 'em," Zach said. "You don't have to do everything."

"Just trying to help." She made short work of the ones in her hands, and a minute later, Zach finished the rest and slid the bowl toward her. "Thanks."

Sierra took the beans into the kitchen. "Is Doreen around?" she asked before anyone else could either put her to work or tell her to stop doing it.

Jo laughed. "She and Rosemary are in the larder organizing our empty canning jars."

The larder was one of the best things in this straw bale house they'd built together. It bore witness that they were serious about food security with its two large chest freezers and ample sturdy shelving for dozens of canning jars. Maybe hundreds. Sierra had lost count.

The two women's voices came clear as Sierra neared the doorway.

"That's forty-two quarts of tomato pieces," Rosemary said.

"Seems like a lot," Doreen answered.

Sierra grinned and walked in. "We'll need at least double that, but there's plenty ripening in the garden yet."

Doreen, seated on a kitchen chair with a clipboard in her hands, looked up in surprise. "Double?"

If Doreen had ever canned, it had been for just her and Bethany. The number of people who poured through Green Acres at mealtime would boggle her mind.

"We go through at least two quarts a week, and that's on top of the ratatouille and pasta sauce we'll prepare before canning."

Doreen shook her head. "I can't imagine."

Sierra reached for her friend's hand. "May I see how you're holding up?"

"It's fine. See?" Doreen held it out. "The swelling hasn't spread any further, and it isn't as hot and itchy as it was a couple of hours ago."

"That's good. Breathing okay?" Though if Doreen had allergies, those would have kicked in by now.

"All is well. I told Gabe I didn't need to go to urgent care, so he brought me out here with him."

Sierra smiled. "And you were right." She'd said the same thing, but had Gabe listened to her? No.

"Food's up!" called Claire from the kitchen.

Sierra could do cheerful. She'd even include Gabe in it. No way was he going to see how much he rattled her. If Jo or Claire got wind of it, though? She'd be toast.

Chapter 3

Gabe grabbed the bowl of barbecue-baked potatoes Noel handed him and followed Zach and Madelynn into the straw bale house. The tot peered at him over her daddy's shoulder.

He couldn't help himself. He scrunched up his nose and winked. After warping his face into a few more expressions, he was rewarded with a little giggle.

"She likes you." Jo took the toddler and buckled her into a wooden high chair. "You accomplished a miracle in just a few minutes."

"Find a seat, Gabe." Claire made room for his bowl of potatoes and the steaks Noel carried. She pulled out a chair around the corner from Noel.

Gabe hesitated. Probably everyone had regular places. Didn't they run this like a community? He touched the back of the chair beside Zach, hoping he wasn't stealing anyone's seat. But Jo sat beside Madelynn.

Zach reached for his hand as others around the table did the same. He glanced to the other side. Sierra? Great. He couldn't very well make a scene and, besides, it was just a convention. His own family had held hands over grace all his growing-up years.

He laid his hand palm up on the table, and she placed hers on top. From somewhere in the distance, Steve prayed a lengthy prayer of thanksgiving. Gabe should probably be listening. Instead, he stared at the hand on his.

A hand that knew work, but was still soft. Fingers that tapered to manicured purple tips, much shorter than what he remembered of Sierra. Bethany had once commented those nails wouldn't last long on the farm. She'd been right, but they still looked nice.

Madelynn shouted, "Amen!" and everyone laughed.

Gabe pulled away both his gaze and his hand. No doubt Steve had been thankful for all the usual suspects on a farm in autumn. Abundant harvest. Plentiful food on the table. Friends.

Sierra handed him the platter of steaks. He helped himself and passed it to Zach. The tantalizing aroma of barbecued meat rose to his nostrils, and his stomach growled.

Zach's elbow caught his ribs. "Hey, Rubachuk, when did you last eat? Pass the food over here, everyone. This guy is starving. To the death."

"I hit a drive-through in Coeur d'Alene." That had been, what, five hours ago? Six?

"Yeah, but that's not real food. You know better, Gabe." Claire glowered from across the table.

He laughed as he took a potato. The bowl of sautéed green beans was right behind it. Man, those smelled awesome. And then tomato and cucumber salad. The burger, fries, and soft drink in the car hadn't tantalized him as this did, even though it'd been three long years since he'd had the option of American fast food.

"One of the jugs is full of iced mint tea and the other is raspberry vinegar, Gabe. Which would you like to drink?" Sierra asked.

"Uh." His memory shot straight back to childhood visits to

the Nemesek farmhouse next door. "Raspberry vinegar sounds good."

She poured him a glass of the sparkling red juice.

"Thanks." He took a sip, and it tasted like his memories. Two young boys playing hard, running with the Border collies through the pastures and up the hillside, climbing into their tree house... no, he didn't want to remember the tree house. That's where he'd gone to grieve when Bethany died. Zach had found him. Been a brother to him.

Focus on his best friend. Focus on today. He blinked the food on his plate back into view and picked up his utensils.

"Anyone need anything from the city Thursday?" asked Sierra.

Jo glanced over. "You're taking Tyrell to the airport?"

Sierra nodded. "Yes. His flight is at two, so we're out of here between nine and nine-thirty. There's plenty of time afterward if anyone needs me to run an errand."

"Why isn't he leaving his truck in Spokane?" Claire wanted to know.

"It's in the shop. His cousin is picking him up Monday."

Gabe's insides clenched. An answer to prayer... but was it? With Sierra, of all people? Man. But he was low on options. He gritted his teeth. "Could I get a ride back with you? I have to return my rental to the airport."

She glanced at him, her blue eyes guarded. "Sure. There's no reason why not."

That was rather unanimated, but he guessed he couldn't expect enthusiasm after how he'd treated her in the clinic this afternoon. "Thanks. I'll go down to the DMV first thing and get my old car insured. I assume it's still in your garage, Doreen?"

She nodded from across the table.

"Where's Tyrell going?" Claire put in. "I must have missed

something."

"He's off to a beekeepers' convention in California for the weekend. He's learning about the opportunities for hauling his hives to the almond groves."

Claire's utensils clattered to the plank table. "He's transporting his bees to California? Sounds about the opposite of local food to me."

"Whoa," Jo put in. "You've got to stop seeing this guy."

Sierra had a boyfriend? Good. Excellent, in fact. It would be so much easier to ignore her or talk to her or, well, anything if she were attached. Like Claire. No problem, right? She was married. Gabe could just be a friend to her as a member of the Green Acres community and it was no big deal. Like Jo.

Yes, so much simpler if Sierra had a boyfriend. Hopefully it was a serious relationship.

"You aren't considering sending our hives as well, are you?" Zach leaned forward on the table.

"Of course not. Don't overreact, you guys." Sierra swooped her hair back over her shoulders, giving Gabe a clearer view of the side of her face. "Tyrell has over three hundred hives. It's his business, and he has to run it like one if he hopes to keep it going and stay in the valley. We're on a small scale here, with just enough for us and our friends and to sell at Nature's Pantry." She turned to Gabe, eyes wide. "That is, if you don't mind if we continue."

"Uh, no. That's fine. Carry on as you have been." What else could he say? He wasn't ready to tell this bunch of people he planned to list the store. Next week was soon enough to talk to a Realtor. He'd have to go over the books with Doreen in detail first, but she'd expect that, no matter what.

"Okay, good. We have customers who prefer a one-stop shop. We don't sell tons through there, but enough to be worthwhile."

"Now, Sierra, don't downplay it." Doreen leaned across the table. "We sell a few jars a week. You see, Gabe, Nature's Pantry has turned into this little hub for locally sourced food. We're selling all kinds of vegetables and fruit in season and have several people interested in producing more for us."

Over the past months he'd stopped reading Doreen's emails after the words, "the store is doing well." He should've read the details. How could he sell now, when she'd worked so hard to build it up?

oOo

Sweat dripped off Sierra's nose. What she wouldn't do for a draft of cool air about now, but Tyrell had told her often enough of the need to keep the heat turned up in the extraction shed. The warmer the better to keep honey flowing smoothly as they rotated each wooden frame through the process.

Claire flinched as bees circled her head.

"They're unlikely to sting," Sierra told her friend.

"I don't know how you get used to it. Why can't I wear a bee suit or at least a screen hat?"

Sierra laughed. "You can if you want, but you'll totally cook." She picked up another frame and ran a comb across the partially sealed cells of honey. "And I'm not kidding when I say you are unlikely to get stung."

"He did." Claire jerked her head toward Tyrell, who operated the steam decapper at the other end of the frame holder about eight feet away.

And Tyrell had made a big production of it, too. "He forgot to check the handles of the super before he lifted it. You'd sting someone too if you were nearly squished. It's like yelping if someone surprised you by grabbing you."

"I wouldn't."

Sierra rolled her eyes. "Well, most people would." Of course, calm, cool, and collected Claire wouldn't react that way. She'd freeze for a couple of seconds while she gathered her wits. Sometimes it was frustrating to be the only squealer in the group. No one understood.

She turned and slid the scraped frame into a niche in the huge centrifuge. The aroma of warm honey flooded the air like a cozy down comforter. The drone of dozens of bees on top of the machines only added to the sleepy sensation. Soon the bees would find their way to one of the escape hatches at the peak of the translucent corrugated roof panels. They'd started the day with hundreds in the workroom. She counted it all good they were down to so few. Still, every time Tyrell cracked open a new stack of supers, a few more bees escaped from their confines.

Claire swatted at another bee. "I don't know how you can stay so calm. Everyone knows bees sting everything in sight."

"You're mixing them up with wasps and hornets." Sierra did her best to keep her voice from sounding like she'd told Claire this a hundred times. Which she had. "Honeybees don't hate everyone in the world. They only sting to protect themselves — so don't squish one — or to protect their queen, and she isn't in here."

"How do you know?" Claire set a frame in the extractor and reached for another one.

Sierra shrugged. "Because they're not glomming onto one spot. If you ever see a big bundle of bees, you'll know there's a queen at the center of it."

"Is that extractor full enough to run yet?" yelled Tyrell over the hum of the steam decapper.

"We need eight more frames first," Sierra called back.

"More scraping and less yakking!" He winked.

Sierra grinned until she caught the thin set of Claire's lips. "He's only teasing."

"Just remember I'm here to help you, not him."

"Aw, he doesn't mean anything by it." Sierra pointed at Claire's frame of honey. "You need to get the comb right into the corners so every cell is open."

Claire's jaw twitched.

Her friend better not quit on her. It would take more than twice as long if Tyrell had to help score the cells as well as decap, and he wouldn't let her forget it. Tyrell was nothing if not efficient. He'd hired a crew to extract the honey from his hundreds of hives, but Sierra couldn't afford to do the same. She could manage the twenty Green Acres owned with a little help from her friends.

Claire held up the frame for inspection. "Better?"

Sierra looked it over carefully "Yes."

"Good." Claire plunked it into the extractor and reached for the bottle of water hanging from the belt loop of her jeans.

Sierra didn't glance at Tyrell. He'd expect them to get the last few frames in and grab a water break while the extractor spun. Although there was no shortage of frames on the rack to scrape for the next go 'round.

When she'd participated in extraction days last year, it hadn't seemed so daunting. The eight people in her class had worked together over two days under the watchful eye of Tyrell's dad, who'd taught the course.

This year she was lucky Tyrell could take the time to help her and Claire at all. Of course they'd had to wait until his own honey had been processed, but that was only fair as it was his building and equipment, and he derived his sole income from beekeeping. He'd already shipped numerous barrels to bulk buyers.

A few minutes later Tyrell adjusted a few of the frames, then gave the extractor a tentative spin. Evidently satisfied, he started the motor before rounding the machine to pull Sierra to his side. "How's it going, doll?"

Did he have to call her that in front of Claire? Sierra pulled away from his hug. "Doing great. How many more stacks of supers?"

"We're about half done." Tyrell grimaced as he took in the row of frames the girls had yet to score. "Or at least *I'm* half-done decapping." He gave her another squeeze then peered into the whirling extractor.

The breeze from the extractor wafted a sweet scent over Sierra. She inhaled deeply. Was there anything sweeter than honey? Could be she'd eaten a little too much of it in the past year, but it was a hard habit to break. Honey had become a staple in or on everything from homemade mocha to baked goods to toast.

"Where do I put them now?"

She looked across at Claire, who held up another scored frame. Sierra pushed the row of frames back a little on the rack to create space. She picked up another frame herself. Enough daydreaming. This was no time to lose momentum.

Chapter 4

*T*yrell folded Sierra's hand inside his massive one as they strode from the parking garage at Spokane International Airport to the terminal. She glanced up at him and found appreciative eyes peering out from under his black cowboy hat.

"You're a doll, Sierra. All the men in the terminal will be jealous when they see such a pretty girl kissing me goodbye at the gate."

A little tug to free herself from his grip did nothing but cause him to chuckle. "Aw, come on. You like it. Why else did you wear that dress I told you I liked a few weeks ago?"

Sierra's cheeked flamed. She'd forgotten his appreciative whistle in the church parking lot. This was a dress she felt confident in. She knew she looked good, and she needed every ounce of poise she could muster for three hours with Gabe in her car. She'd never dreamed Tyrell would take it personally.

Tyrell slid his arm around her as they stepped into the pedestrian crosswalk. She shifted slightly, but he didn't seem to notice. What was happening here?

Sure, she liked Tyrell, but that wasn't the same thing as wanting to marry him. She'd be twenty-eight in a few short weeks and didn't have time to date someone she wasn't serious about. She constantly felt like a fifth wheel — not that Jo, Claire, or their guys made a deal of it. It's just that, well, she *was* the fifth wheel.

The terminal doors swished open and they headed for the nearest overhead display. "Flight's on time. Good." Tyrell snapped his carry-on handle into the closed position. "Shall we grab a coffee before I have to go through security? We've got a few minutes."

She didn't want Gabe to come up on them together, and he'd be here anytime. She needed a break between to gather her poise and prepare for the return journey. This was crazy. How had she gotten herself in this predicament with both men in her passenger seat today?

Sierra smiled up at Tyrell. "You know they have better coffee and more options up in the hub. Besides, I'm meeting Gabe any minute."

His brown eyes darkened as he turned her toward him and clasped his hands behind her back.

Her hands braced against his forearms as she tried to keep some distance.

"Sierra, be careful with him. I know he was a local guy, but he's been gone for years. Your heart is in Galena Landing, and he'll probably want to keep moving on." He leaned closer.

The mint on his breath caressed her forehead. She pushed back, needing air.

"I'll be back in a few days, doll. I'll miss you every moment in between."

How could she answer? She hadn't dreamed his thoughts had progressed this far.

"Sierra?"

She looked up just in time to see his mouth coming for hers, too quickly to avoid. His lips pressed against hers more gently than he'd seemed capable of. She couldn't respond, but did she even want to?

Tyrell pulled back, his brown eyes deep pools.

No, she wasn't ready, biological clock or not. Sierra managed a sort of smile. "Have a good flight, Tyrell. If you learn something new about beekeeping, let me know."

"I will. See you Monday." He dropped a kiss on her forehead and released her then pulled his carry-on handle up and strode toward security without a backward glance.

Sierra stared after him as he turned the corner, out of sight. What had just happened? Had she agreed to something?

Someone cleared his throat behind her, and Sierra whirled.

From less than six feet away, Gabe raised his eyebrows. "Ready whenever you are."

The flush she'd felt a few minutes ago had nothing on the raging inferno that engulfed her throat and face now. This would be a good time for one of those sinkholes they had in Florida. Something — anything — to swallow her up.

But no. The tiled floor of the airport stayed solid beneath her feet. Gabe was still just a few feet away from her, arms crossed over his button-up shirt.

Sierra gathered her hair in one hand and tossed it over her shoulder. "You've turned in your rental?"

He nodded.

"Well, then, let's get going. My car is out in the parking garage." She tucked her thumb behind her purse strap and headed for the automatic doors.

Silence followed her. Was Gabe there or falling behind? She glanced back and nearly stumbled. Right there.

Gabe caught her and held on until she regained her balance then let go immediately.

Her arm chilled. "Sorry about that. I'm not usually so

clumsy." She definitely didn't want to give him any hints about what his presence did to her.

"No problem." He stepped up beside her as they crossed the pedestrian walkway.

A few minutes later they were both buckled into the old VW hatchback. Sierra stuck the key in the ignition. "Any other stops you need to make?"

Gabe shook his head. "You?"

"No one needed anything. Guess it's a straight road back to Galena Landing."

"Let me buy you lunch," Gabe said. "Know anywhere good?"

Now that he mentioned it, she was hungry. "There's a good diner just across the state line." She stopped the car to pay the parking attendant.

"Sounds good."

She pulled the car into traffic heading away from the airport. "Yep, it's a fun spot where they try to do as much local as they can. By local, in this case, they mean regional. Their beef comes from a ranch in Oregon."

He shook his head. "You guys really eat, sleep, and breathe this local food stuff, don't you."

Didn't sound like a question to her. "We do."

"I don't get it. I'm after quality. I'm after organic, if I can afford it. Local just seems to limit it too much."

"A lot of small farms use organic practices but aren't certified. And a lot of the big ones like Jo's stepdad's business, Jimmiesin Farms, are just in it to see how much money they can make by walking the line as close as they can."

"I suppose."

It was going to be hard returning control of Nature's Pantry to him if he didn't get with the program she and Doreen had been building. Sierra glanced over her shoulder and merged onto

I-90 as an eighteen-wheeler shifted over into the other lane.

A sharp intake of breath from the passenger seat caused her to look at Gabe's white face. "There was plenty of room."

He flexed his fingers but didn't look at her.

Probably thinking of the crash that took Bethany in completely different circumstances. She'd built up fantasies of this man that had nothing to do with reality.

Time to get him out of her head.

oOo

Seeing Tyrell Burke had flung Gabe straight back to high school when jocks ruled the corridors. Thankfully Burke had been a few years ahead of him and his bunch. They'd managed to avoid him and his kind for the most part.

What might Sierra see in a guy like that? Could Burke actually have grown up a little? Oh, he'd matured all right, but he still looked the same, only with broader shoulders and even more swagger.

Gabe got out of the car and followed Sierra to the Side Street Place entry. How come he'd never noticed this café before? Sierra was right. Traffic whizzed by on I-90 behind him, within clear view. Maybe it was new since he'd left for Romania.

Sierra reached for the door handle. Man, he was forgetting to be a gentleman. He strode the few steps and pulled the diner door the rest of the way open.

She smiled at him over her shoulder. "Thanks." Sparkling blue eyes. Really, she was rather pretty in her own way. Blond hair curled where it hung below her shoulders. A bit of makeup, but not a lot.

Pink lipstick. Was it smudged where that guy had kissed her?

He jerked his gaze toward the diner's interior. Better to

examine the decor of the building than the woman. He followed Sierra to a booth beside an oval window and slid onto the padded green vinyl seat. "So, what's good?"

Sierra opened her menu. "Everything."

Gabe glanced over the options. Burger on sourdough? Onion rings stacked inside? Sold.

A few minutes later they dug into their meal.

Sierra wiped her mouth with her napkin. "I don't imagine you've had time to go over things at the store yet with Doreen."

He shook his head. "We're meeting Monday evening. She didn't want to do it during store hours."

"Too busy." She laughed. "I know she'll want to go through everything point by point and not get too distracted by customers."

The word "really?" was on the tip of his tongue, but he bit off a bite of his Frisco-style burger instead. Amazing food. "I had no idea." He should have read Doreen's emails in greater detail. Inspiration struck. "Why don't you tell me what you think made the difference? It was easy for one person to do everything the store needed a few years ago."

"You started it with the organic seeds rack." Her blue eyes met his. "That got some people starting to think. Doreen asked the Burkes for local honey, and Jean Donaldson asked if we could handle her egg orders for convenience. Someone else started up a home business making pickles and relish." She shrugged and stabbed French fries with her fork. "It kind of grew from there."

His mouth soured. Now what was he supposed to do? It would be easier to sell a thriving business. Hmm. He tried to keep the words light. "Doesn't sound like you ladies need me around at all."

Sierra stared at her plate and bit her lip.

What in the world was that supposed to mean? "You're

obviously doing a fine job."

"It's been hard for Doreen with her RA. I'm sure she's relieved you're back to take the helm."

Gabe set the burger back on the plate and forked an onion ring out. "Yeah. I didn't realize how bad it'd gotten." He hadn't wanted to.

"I'll have my clinic moved out by the weekend so you can have your space back."

"About that…"

"No, it's fine. I haven't gotten as much clientele as I'd hoped, so a part-time office at home will be better. Then I'll be around to do my share of work at the farm. You'll be in charge at the store, and Doreen and I can phase out."

"But I'm not sure what I want to do."

She paused, coffee cup halfway to her lips. "What do you mean?"

He shook his head and stared out the window. Traffic on the interstate zoomed by. "It's been a tough few years."

Sierra's gaze softened slightly. "I know, but…" She hesitated, searching his face.

What clues was he giving her? Could she read his mind? He kept his expression as blank as he could.

"Forgive me if I'm too personal," she said at last. "But it's been more than three years since Bethany died."

Gabe winced. Even now, the words sounded harsh. Cruel.

"For everyone else, life goes on, Gabe. You can't stay in a time warp forever."

He shoved at his cup, sloshing coffee over the edge. "You think that's what Romania was for me?"

Sierra sopped up the coffee with a wad of napkins. "I didn't say that."

Then what had she meant? "I'll have you know there's more

need in places like Romania than here. I could make a real difference there. Orphanages are full of unwanted kids who crave someone to love them and care about them. It's not a time warp. It's a whole different world with its own set of real actual problems."

Her voice took on an edge. "I didn't say it wasn't real or that your presence served no purpose."

"Sure sounded like it."

"Look, like it or not, you've got responsibilities in Galena Landing. You own a building and the business within it. Your mother-in-law—"

Gabe leaned in. "I don't have a mother-in-law. Don't you get it? Doreen is..." What?

"You're wrong, Gabe. She's still part of your world. You knew it even then, because you asked her to run the store."

"I bought it from her. There was no one else qualified to take over."

"Oh, come on. You'd bought it five years before. You think she could just step in? It wasn't that easy. You had a whole new way of doing things she struggled to figure out."

If he let himself think, his conscience would bite him.

Thankfully, Sierra kept right on going. "You may not feel like you have ties to her, but you do. No matter what you do with your life, she'll always be your first mother-in-law."

Heat shot up his neck and across his face. "My *first* mother-in-law? Who said anything about remarrying?"

Those pink lips had looked almost alluring half an hour ago. Now they pressed in a tight angry line across her face while her blue eyes hardened. "How old are you, Gabe?"

"It's none of your business."

She shrugged. "You graduated with Zach, and he turned thirty in August. I'm assuming you're the same or will be soon."

"Your point?" He crossed his arms.

"My point is that you've probably got another fifty or sixty years ahead of you. You don't have to get married next week, but can you really close off that part of you forever?"

The words stabbed. Pain oozed out of the wound. Alone for that many years without Bethany by his side? But who could ever take her place? No one. It was disloyal even to consider it for an instant.

Chapter 5 ---

*S*ierra shouldn't have to apologize to Gabe, should she? They'd finished their meal with only the bare minimum conversation. Gabe had insisted on paying, saying he'd called it in advance. Which he had, but only because he'd beat her to it.

She shot him a sidelong glance in the car.

He sat with arms crossed across his pinstriped button-up, both feet planted on the floorboards, staring straight ahead, chiseled jaw clamped. A little mousse in his hair created loft that hadn't been there the other day.

Okay, so she had some thinking to do. Re-evaluating. Somehow she'd built ideas up in her head about Gabe. Three years of her life wasted when she could have been married by now. Not that Galena Landing boasted that many eligible bachelors.

Tyrell Burke. He was fun. Nice enough. Could she marry a guy like Ty? How would she know? She'd never given him much chance. She'd subconsciously compared him to a guy on a pedestal.

The pedestal was empty.

She sighed. "Look, I'm sorry for being so blunt with you in

the diner. It's none of my business what you do with the rest of your life."

"You're right."

Well, that had gone over well. Still two hours on the road to Galena Landing though. She could crank some music or a Deconstructing Dinner podcast and ignore him, but...

"Talk to me, Gabe. Tell me about Bethany. Tell me about Romania."

"Why?"

"Why not? Seems like you might need to get things off your chest."

"And you're some kind of psychologist?"

She grinned. "Not so much. Just someone who's known you for a while. Someone who cares." She shouldn't have added that last bit.

"No reason you should care."

Something snapped. "Gabriel Rubachuk, give it up already. You can close yourself off all you want, but you can't stop people from caring about you. I knew you and Bethany before. Not long, perhaps, but enough to have had a glimpse into your relationship. You had a good thing going from what it looked like."

"We did."

"A person can't live in the past, Gabe."

He turned, his blue eyes blazing. "Don't you think I know that? I spent three years in Romania working with abandoned kids. Contrary to what you think, I didn't spend all my time moping and whining about my hard lot. I found work to do. Good work. Hard work. And I did it."

At least he was talking.

"Sure I thought about Beth and our baby. She'd be nearly three now, you know that? But being there helped me heal."

He didn't sound healed.

"It's Galena Landing that's so difficult. You say to leave the past behind. Well, maybe that's just what I should do. Sell my store and go someplace else. Someplace that doesn't shackle me to painful memories."

Her head was shaking before Gabe stopped speaking. He couldn't mean it. "Bad idea."

"Says the not-a-psychologist."

Touché. "There's more than one way to deal with the past. You can run from it, or you can face it and heal. You ran once, Gabe. Now it's time to face it."

He straightened, the seat belt seeming to be all that restrained him. "I did not run. My parents are missionaries there. I joined them in their work."

"It was okay to run. Everything was fresh and raw. But it's been three years. It's time to face reality."

"I'm not a fan of reality." Bitterness oozed from his voice.

"Then why didn't you just stay in Romania forever? Why come back at all?" She kept her gaze on the road but could feel the burn from his eyes. Wait. He'd already said. "To liquidate?"

He gave a terse nod. "I didn't mean to tell anyone yet. Please keep it in confidence."

Sierra's hands tightened on the steering wheel. Anything she could think of to say was bound to be wrong. *Oh, God, please.* This guy needed a hug from heaven or something.

Gabe glanced her way. "Maybe you'd like to buy it. You've been working with Doreen, so you know what it entails. It's right up your alley."

He couldn't be serious. "Me?" She turned a shocked face to him. "No, I have no desire to own a store."

"Then why did you start working there?"

"To help Doreen out. She needed someone to make sense of it and get some income happening, so I leased the upstairs until I could get my clinic built. I'm happily out of the building by the end of the week."

"But you'd be perfect."

Sierra's teeth clenched. She'd wanted to be perfect in his eyes, but not as someone who helped him escape. Even if she wanted Nature's Pantry — and she didn't — she wouldn't make it that easy for him. "Not interested."

"You don't think it's a viable business? You and Doreen proved it is."

He needn't sound bitter. "That doesn't mean I want to own it."

"Do you think I grew up telling everyone I wanted to own a health food store one day? Not a chance. I was a normal boy, dreaming of being a pilot or a cowboy or a pro basketball player."

Endearing. But she couldn't let him think he'd win this one with nostalgia. "Your point?"

Gabe shrugged. "The opportunity came along, and I took it. It was a good choice."

"Then keep it."

"Sierra, I—"

"Don't make any hasty decisions, Gabe. Really. Give it six months. Get to know the business the way it is now. Make sure if you sell out and move on that it's what God wants you to do." She glanced at him. "Have you asked Him to guide you on this?"

He stared straight ahead, a tic pulsing in his throat.

She didn't stand a chance of winning his love. She might as well go for that jugular she could see. "Or are you determined your way is best? I don't have to be a psychologist to know you're hurting. Running won't help, Gabe."

By chance she glanced his way just as he turned to face her. The pain in his blue eyes crashed over her. Good thing traffic was sparse.

"Six months? I don't know if I can manage that long."

Sierra's heart lifted. He was actually considering her challenge? "I'm willing to bet it will do you a world of good."

"You're the betting kind?"

She laughed. "Not really. It's just a saying."

"How about if you buy the store in six months if I can't find another buyer and still want to leave?"

"I bet that won't happen."

oOo

Galena Landing couldn't appear fast enough to suit Gabe. They'd managed a few random sentences since Sierra's challenge, mostly about the weather and politics. Anything, so long as it was far removed from his personal situation.

Yet he couldn't get her words out of his mind. Could he do six months? Every cell in him screamed that it was five and a half months too long. Somewhere underneath, he knew he was trying to bolt again. Did that make it wrong? Did he even care what God had to say about it?

The tic-tic-tic of a signal light pulled him from his reverie as the car slowed.

He blinked, catching a glimpse of a sign for Cottonwood Road. He sat up straighter.

"Ah, you're awake?" Sierra asked. "Sorry, I forgot to mention I need to pick up the remaining boxes of honey jars from Tyrell's extraction shed. It will only take a few minutes."

She could've come back for it. They were only a couple of miles south of town. Oh right. The Green Acres girls used as little fuel as possible. Amazing Burke had managed to convince Sierra to drive all the way to Spokane. Maybe he'd paid for the diesel. But the way Gabe understood the girls' philosophy, it wasn't so much the money as the environment.

Besides, Burke was on his way to California. "Yeah, whatever."

This was about the last place Gabe wanted to see. But if Sierra married the guy, at least she'd be taken, and Gabe could remove her from his thoughts. Not that she was in them, of course. He'd do well to remember he didn't want to remarry.

Sierra pulled into a tidy farmyard. A 70s style split-entry house nestled in a mass of flowerbeds. Beyond it, a red barn sat surrounded by corrals. Sierra turned left just before the barn and backed up toward a low concrete building partially hidden behind some trees. She popped the hatch on the car before opening the door. "I'll just be a few minutes."

She came out of the building carrying a cardboard box. It thunked as it hit the car deck. She slid it forward before turning back to the building.

The box looked heavy. How many of those things did she have anyway? Gabe pushed his car door open.

By now she was back with another one.

"Let me give you a hand."

"Thanks. Everything in that corner is mine. Or rather, belongs to Green Acres."

The little hatchback sat considerably lower on its springs when they'd finished loading the last box.

Gabe couldn't help but be interested. "All this honey is from your hives?"

"Yep. We have twenty. We doubled the number this year because of the demand at Nature's Pantry."

"Cool." Gabe peered further into the dimly lit building. "How much do you get from a hive?"

She shrugged. "Anywhere from seventy to a hundred pounds, depending."

The bulky equipment in the room beyond made no sense to Gabe. He pulled the building's door shut behind them. "That's a lot of honey."

Sierra slid into the driver's seat and turned the ignition as Gabe climbed in. She flashed him a grin. "Well, you know that everything tastes better if it's sweetened with honey."

"Everything?" He raised his eyebrows. "How about fried chicken?"

"Okay, not everything. How about, if a sweetener is needed, honey does it better?"

"I've done just enough cooking to know you can burn honey faster than sugar."

"But why burn it at all?" She shot him a mischievous glance.

It was a temptation to get to know this Sierra better. One who didn't badger him to get on with his life but could banter with ease. Except he wasn't ready to think of a woman again that way just yet. Probably never would be. To say nothing of driving past her boyfriend's house while he thought it.

Gabe's jaw clenched and he jerked it toward the house. "How many hives did you say he operates?"

"Phil? None. He used to have around one hundred until Tyrell bought out his business last year and tripled it."

That wasn't Tyrell's house? Then what... where...?

"Oh, you mean Tyrell. Over three hundred. It's big business compared to what I do."

So they'd said at Sunday dinner. And weren't they, as a group, against big agriculture?

"Sorry, I thought that was his house. His parents live here?" Then where did Burke live, if he ran his business from his parents' farm?

"His dad and step-mom. Tyrell has an apartment at the back of the extraction shed. I'm not sure how he's planning to proceed."

"I thought you guys were an item?"

Her face flamed.

"It sure looked like it there in the airport." He suppressed a surge of jealousy again just at the thought. What was up with that? He remembered a fable from when he was a kid, a little story about a dog who barked and harassed the cows wanting to eat hay from their manger, even though the dog didn't eat hay himself. Why should it matter whether or not Sierra hooked up with Burke? It wasn't like Gabe wanted her.

"I took a beekeeping course from Phil, and that's how I met Tyrell. Of course, I also see him at church sometimes, but we're really just starting to get to know each other."

That kiss had looked mighty possessive in that case. But maybe Burke had been more aware of Gabe's presence than Sierra had been. Could the display have been for Gabe's benefit?

Like the guy had anything to worry about.

Chapter 6 --

*D*id these gals do everything together? Even after they were married?

Gabe couldn't very well reject the Sunday dinner invitation from Jo he'd already accepted, even though he'd managed to skip church. It hadn't crossed his mind she meant a group meal at the straw bale house with Claire and Noel. And Sierra.

No Doreen this time. No Steve and Rosemary. Just a cozy group of six adults and a toddler who made his heart ache.

"You're in charge of the salad." Zach clapped Gabe on the shoulder and steered him past the plank table and into the fully equipped kitchen.

"Me? I don't remember volunteering."

"Noel made the pasta sauce before church. He's adding fresh herbs now, right, bro?"

Noel looked up from the butcher-block island. "You got it. But you ought to give the poor guy a hand, Zach. Cooking the pasta doesn't take that much focus. Even for you."

Gabe jabbed at Zach. "Trying to make me do your work? Not fair, Nemesek. Not fair."

"Garlic toast, remember? Not just the pasta. I know my

place."

The aroma from the heavy pot on the stovetop smelled like heaven. And to think he'd planned to live on pasta from cans. Were these guys really going to make him learn how to cook? He supposed he should embrace it.

"When did you turn into such a kitchen boy, anyway?" he asked Zach.

Zach filled a pot with water at the sink. "Who, me?"

Noel snickered.

"Pretty sure you once thought it was women's work. Don't forget I roomed with you in college."

Zach carried the pot to the stove and turned the burner on. "Well, Jo's a lousy cook."

A voice from the other room hollered, "I heard that!"

So the women were within earshot. Good to know.

"You misunderstood, Jo! I said you were a *lucky* cook. Lucky girl to have me cook for you."

The women laughed. "I'd starve," said Jo.

"Hey, now." Zach tossed a bag of salad greens at Gabe. "These have been washed, so just rip them into that bowl. Even you can hardly mess that up."

It was an education seeing his best buddy as a long-time married man and father. Gabe had left the country before Zach and Jo returned from their honeymoon.

Something gripped Gabe's pant leg. "Dada!"

He looked down into a cherub face that quickly grew confused then puckered and cried.

Zach scooped the toddler up and planted her on the island. "Hey, Maddie. Daddy's here. You got Uncle Gabe by mistake."

She sniffled.

"Rule number one." Noel chopped a pile of fresh herbs. "Don't wear the same color pants as Zach. That's as far up as

Madelynn looks."

Gabe dumped the bag of greens into the bowl and began tearing them into smaller pieces. There must've been half a dozen different kinds.

"This cooking thing is all Noel's fault." Zach handed the crust of French bread he was slicing to Maddie, who gnawed it happily. "I was mostly getting away with staying out of the kitchen until he came along, but he put me in a bad light."

Gabe glanced at Noel. "You're a chef, too? I knew Claire was."

"Hardly seems fair to lock all that talent into one family, does it?" Zach asked.

"I heard that, too." Jo settled on one of the stools on the dining room side of the peninsula.

"No, I'm not a chef, but I was on my own a lot of years and took to cooking. Puttering in the kitchen relaxes me." Noel dumped the herbs in the pot and gave it a stir. He tousled Maddie's hair on his way back to the workstation.

"When they dragged me into this big happy family, they led me to believe Sunday dinner was Zach's responsibility. By the time I found out he didn't know which end of a knife to hold and couldn't cook his way out of a paper bag, the rules had morphed. It was guys' day in the kitchen. Period." Noel dipped his head and looked Gabe in the eye. "You better believe he had stuff to learn. The quicker the better."

Gabe chuckled, remembering all the wrappers, bags, cartons, and cans littering their student apartment. He'd done a bit of the cooking during his marriage to Bethany. She'd worked long hours as a nurse, after all. But he'd had a few default meals to rely on. Easy stuff.

"Chunk in some of those tomatoes, man. Over on the counter." Noel started peeling cucumbers, giving a piece to

Maddie.

It didn't take long until dinner was on the table. The rich aroma of tomatoes, basil, and garlic filled the air. This time Gabe ended up around the corner from Sierra, with Noel on his other side. There was just no way to avoid her in this gang, was there? And he'd have to touch her hand again during prayer.

After grace, chatter resumed and serving dishes passed.

Gabe took a bite of the pasta slathered in sauce. The stuff was crazy good, better than he'd ever had. Maybe his taste buds had been reawakened after being dead for years. If they'd ever been alive. "You need to teach cooking classes."

Noel laughed. "I think that's a compliment?"

"Man, yes."

"You his first paying customer?" Zach set more cucumber pieces on Maddie's high chair tray. The kid was already smeared with tomato sauce. No wonder her mother had stripped her to the cloth diaper before lunch.

Gabe sobered. "Might need to be. Otherwise it looks like a long bleak future."

"Oh, you'll meet someone and get married, Gabe. Not saying that knowing how to cook isn't still a good idea." Jo gave a pointed glare at Zach.

Claire chuckled. "A guy who cooks can be a powerful attraction to a woman."

Noel slid his arm across the back of Claire's chair and nuzzled her hair. She wrinkled her nose at him.

Gabe'd had it all and lost it through no fault of his own. But to open himself up again? He shot a quick glance at Sierra, remembering her challenge.

She stared at her plate, fork slowly twisting pasta in circles.

What, she wasn't going to join in ribbing him?

"Thanks." He tried to smile. "I don't see it happening, but I appreciate the advice."

"Wasn't advice." Jo glanced his way. "Advice sounds more like, 'Gabe, you should get out and meet someone and get married again'."

She'd never been one to mince words, had she? Seemed she hadn't changed much.

oOo

Sierra couldn't believe Jo's words to Gabe. They lingered in the air. So long as Jo didn't follow up with something like, "And oh, look, Sierra's still single."

Thankfully the silence held until Madelynn demanded "noo" and made the hand signal for more.

"Noodles," enunciated Jo as she forked pasta onto the high chair tray. "More noodles."

"Moh noo." Madelynn nodded enthusiastically. "Tank."

Sierra dared a breath. It was one thing for her to tell Gabe to move on and remarry, and entirely something else for Jo to say it in front of everyone. But why was it different? Jo had known Gabe better than Sierra had before.

Before.

The defining words for Gabe.

She couldn't do Gabe. She needed someone with less baggage. Somebody ready to lean into the future.

Or she could embrace the single life herself. No, she'd tried that after Claire and Noel's wedding. She'd moved into the apartment above Nature's Pantry to get away from all the starry eyes on the farm. While it was true the newlyweds didn't need her living in the same house as them, she'd bolted more out of selfishness than consideration.

But Galena Landing had proved to be either too far from the

farm, or not far enough. She'd missed the day-to-day life at Green Acres. She'd missed doing her part. When the gang decided the next building to go up should be a home and clinic duplex for her, she'd conceded.

Definitely a cozy space, with only the tiniest of kitchenettes. The girls had always planned to keep cooking and living communally even after they were married. Not that anyone expected marriage at the beginning.

Not that Sierra'd expected to be the last woman standing.

She shook her head and became aware of Jo's quizzical look. She blinked and refocused on the group around the table. This looked too much like three couples enjoying time together, but it wasn't. She and Gabe weren't a couple. He wasn't ready to consider a relationship, and no amount of daydreaming on her part was going to change that.

She'd been crazy to challenge him to six months. Hopefully he hadn't sensed the real dare behind the words. If she couldn't make him see her as a potential spouse — if he couldn't learn to love her — in six months, there really was no hope.

Only, there wasn't any to start with.

"Too much oregano, Sierra?" asked Noel. "Too little basil?"

"Um, it's fine. Great, really." She pushed her plate away. "I'm just not very hungry."

In fact, the discomfort she felt might not all be attributable to Gabe but the onset of yet another period. Whoever called those things monthlies was oh so wrong. Seemed lately she menstruated more often than not, and the cramping seemed to increase each time.

She'd rather think about other people's medical problems than her own. But maybe she ought to see a physician at some point. Next month, if things didn't improve.

"Why not put Maddie down for her nap here?" asked Claire.

"We can play Pictionary or something while the peach cobbler bakes."

"You're always looking for a sixth player," grumbled Zach. "But on the other hand… peach cobbler?"

"It's a wonder you all aren't fifty pounds overweight." Gabe shook his head, grinning. "The food around here."

Noel began gathering plates. "We work too hard to get fat."

"And the meals are well-balanced," Claire put in. "We don't usually eat this many carbs."

Except honey, of course. This definitely wasn't the time to mention she herself had put on a few pounds in the past year.

"Sunday comfort food." Noel reached for Sierra's plate then raised his eyebrows. "Unless you want me to leave it?"

She shook her head. "Sorry. I'm not feeling well." She pushed back her chair. "In fact, I think I'll pass on games and dessert. It looks like a perfect day to curl up with a good book." And a hot water bottle.

"I guess we'll play Blackout, then." Claire jumped to her feet and began gathering glasses. "I hope you feel better soon. Don't worry about a thing."

"Somebody I know needs a bath before her nap." Zach scooped Madelynn out of her high chair. "Did you have to smear tomato sauce in your hair, kiddo?"

"If you do the bath, I'll help in the kitchen," said Jo.

Zach nodded and left, a kicking bundle under his arm.

They kept a second set of everything at the big house. A crib in the spare room. A bathroom drawer full of cloth diapers and another with clothes. Communal living at its finest. Sierra stood, suddenly aware only she and Gabe were left at the table. "Well, I'll see you around."

"Look, if I make you this uncomfortable, I don't need to stay. It's your home, not mine."

Sierra grasped the chair back and looked at Gabe. "It's not you." She tried a shrug, but it hurt. It was all she could do to not wrap both arms around her middle and bend over. "Trust me, it's not about you at all."

His blue eyes clouded over. Was it that easy to tell what he was thinking? Could come in handy. "I didn't mean it that way."

How many possibilities were there? She raised her eyebrows. Hopefully her eyes were as chilly as his. "You're not that important to me." Liar. And did she have to be cruel to him to get some distance?

She would've loved to flounce out of the house with a carefree wave, but she didn't have it in her. Instead, she focused on getting both feet moving toward the door at regular intervals.

Sierra pulled the door shut behind her... or tried to.

"Hey." It was Jo. "You okay?"

"Not really. Period coming on with a full load of cramps."

Jo pulled the door shut behind them both. "Didn't you just have one?"

"It always seems like it, doesn't it?"

"For a minute, I thought I'd said something wrong." Jo laughed. "I shouldn't have said that to Gabe, at least not in front of everyone."

Probably not, but this wasn't a discussion she wanted to have with her best friend. Not now, not ever.

"But it had to be said. It's time he started moving forward, you know what I mean?"

"Jo, I'm dying here. Gabe's love life isn't any of my business, and I can't even pretend to be interested when I'm in this much pain."

"Sorry. You're right. Want me to walk over with you?" Jo cupped her hand under Sierra's elbow.

Sierra shook it off. "I'm not an invalid. Quit trying to avoid doing the dishes and get back in there. I'll be fine."

"That obvious, huh?" Jo laughed. "Call me if you need anything, okay?"

"Will do." But the things Sierra needed, Jo was in no position to supply.

Chapter 7 --

*D*oreen peered at Gabe over her reading glasses. "But I sent you all the statements regularly." She indicated the accounting software visible on the computer monitor. "I even learned how to use this program and emailed the files to you." The stack of ledgers on the corner attested to her preferred method.

Everything was too hot. The wooden chair he sat on, the once-homey apartment, and his face. Definitely his face. "I didn't study them. I see now that I should have, but everything seemed so distant." He swallowed hard. "I needed to keep it that way."

How could he fit back in Galena Landing, even for a few months? Had he actually promised Sierra? And if he had, did it really matter? Some promises should never be made to start with.

He'd kept the big one. 'Til death do us part. Bethany had, too, but her death had released him. Clinging to her and the memory of their years together seemed all that kept him sane some days, but maybe it was an illusion. He wasn't sane anyway. Maybe he should let her go. Maybe Sierra and Jo were right. He had to move on. Somehow.

"Gabe?"

He blinked and Doreen's face snapped into focus across the table. "I'm sorry. What did you say?"

She removed her glasses, folded them, and set them on the

ledgers. "Gabe, I'm really concerned about you."

She could get in line.

He jerked to his feet and paced the space that had once been his dining room. His and Bethany's. He swung to face Doreen. "Do you know what I liked about Romania?"

She raised her eyebrows. "What?"

"No one said, 'Gabe, I'm really concerned about you.' They didn't probe my feelings or tell me to move on. They said, 'can you shoot some hoops with the kids?' 'Can you go pick up food from the market?' 'Can you figure out what's wrong with the email program?'"

"So you just shoved your feelings into a back corner and tried to keep busy enough to avoid thinking about them."

Gabe jammed his hands into his pockets. "Basically. Is there any other way to cope?" Man, he shouldn't have asked her that. Not Doreen of all people. Not when he'd ditched her, leaving her to do his job as well as deal with the death of her only child.

She met his gaze steadily. "I think you know the answer to that. You always have a choice."

"Doesn't seem like I've had an option in any of it."

"I know Bethany must have told you about her father." Doreen took a deep breath. "He was a police officer who died in the line of duty when she was only two."

Why hadn't he ever thought about the fact that Doreen, too, knew what it was like to lose a spouse? He racked his brain for something to say. "You guys lived in Sacramento."

"We did. I didn't know how life could go on without Paul."

He slumped back into the chair. "But you had a child. Someone to focus on." And he didn't. Their baby's life had been snuffed out with Bethany's.

"Some days that seemed more of a curse than a blessing."

Surely he hadn't heard her right. How could she say such a

thing? About his Bethany?

"I couldn't run away." Doreen's gaze held his. For once he could see the anguish deep inside her.

Gabe nodded. She hadn't had the luxury of abandoning everything as he had.

"What I'm trying to say is, losing your life partner, your other half, is horrendous, no matter the circumstances. Whether you have five children, one child, or no one to remember your beloved by. It's something no one should have to go through."

And then she'd lost her daughter, and he'd been no help at all.

"Doreen, I... I don't know what to say. I've been a jerk. I've been so swallowed up in my own problems, my own pain, I haven't thought of you. Haven't thought of others."

A half-smile formed. "That's the first step. Looking past your own grief. Remembering you're not alone."

Did he want to know what the second step was? Taking any of them only seemed to be the last nail in Bethany's coffin. Like he was really saying goodbye to her forever.

"How's your relationship with God, Gabe?"

His gaze shot back to her face. "Okay, I guess."

"That doesn't sound promising."

He pulled back to his feet. "He could have prevented that accident. He could have kept her alive. Why did He kill her?"

"God didn't kill her."

"Give me one good reason she had to die."

Doreen shook her head. "There isn't one."

"See?" He flung his hands out to the sides. "God just lines up His pawns on the board and sacrifices them without a second thought." He had vague memories of throwing those words at Zach in the days after the accident.

"Not exactly. God has a plan for everything."

"Then you're saying God killed her. That He wanted her to die and leave me alone. That He wanted me to suffer without her for the rest of my life. Some God. That's an even worse belief."

"I can't pretend to know God's mind. The only peace I can find is to acknowledge that He sees the whole chess game, to use your analogy. That He has a strategy I cannot understand."

"You say that. You who lost a husband and your only child."

"I cling to it."

"Then you can't have loved them as much as I loved Bethany." The harsh words sprang to his ears, and he cringed. So unfair. So cruel. He knew it. And yet… wasn't it true? How could Doreen sit there and spout nonsense about God's plan as though it mattered more than their own lives and hopes and dreams?

Doreen stared at him, tears welling in her eyes. She brushed her graying hair from her face with the back of her hand then clicked the mouse to close the program. "We'll finish the books another day." She slipped her glasses on, grabbed her light jacket from its hook on the wall and headed for the door.

"Look, I'm sorry."

She stopped with her back to him and her hand on the knob as though waiting for him to continue. But what else could he say? After an instant, her shoulders drooped even more and she slipped from the room.

He should call her back and apologize as though he meant it. She didn't deserve his harsh words. She'd been a good mom to Bethany and accepted Gabe into their circle as a teen. Why couldn't he bridge this gap?

Her soft footfalls sounded down the stairs. A moment later he heard her car start up then crunch across the gravel parking lot. Silence.

Gabe looked around the dining room that had been converted into the business office since he'd left. The small kitchen looked just as it had when Bethany stood at the stove making dinner. If he closed his eyes, maybe she'd be right there, proving he'd had a bad dream.

A three-year-old bad dream. Not likely.

The baby's room pulled him like a magnet. Bethany had asked the ultrasound technician for the baby's gender. He'd wanted to wait and be surprised. Thank God she'd insisted. What if he'd never known they were to have a baby girl? His daughter. Bethany had wanted pink walls. She'd even bought the paint.

Sierra had moved her stuff out sometime in the past few days. The walls were as beige as they had been for the life of the building. What was that, forty years? He jerked the closet door open. Cans from Benjamin Moore sat on the shelf amid piles of boxes.

Boxes of what? Had Sierra left something behind to pick up later?

He opened the top one and lifted out a baby sleeper hardly any bigger than his hand. White with ruffled pink edging and an embroidered rosebud.

Gabe clutched the piece of clothing to his chest as he sank to the floor.

"Why, God, why?"

o0o

She'd forgotten her coat in the back of Nature's Pantry. It was nearly dark as she headed back from Tyrell's bee yard. What was Sierra going to do about him? He was a nice guy and he seemed to really like her. They both loved life in Galena Landing and, since Tyrell had moved back to the area, he'd become a regular attendee at the church. He even taught Sunday School.

There wasn't any reason to keep him at arm's length, which

he often managed to circumvent as he swooped in for a quick hug or a kiss. No reasons at all, except for his big business beekeeping ideas. And the slight fact that he didn't make her knees wobble.

She pulled along the curb in front of the store and turned off the car. She ran to the door, unlocked it, and let herself in. At the back of the store, she opened the closet and grabbed her jacket and shopping bag.

A muffled sound from upstairs caused the hairs on the back of her neck to prickle. The store's parking was behind the building, and she hadn't even wondered if anyone might be here. Doreen would have gone home hours ago.

Gabe?

Or maybe a burglar. Not much crime in Galena Landing but, hey, you never knew. It would only take a minute to tiptoe up the back steps and see what she could see.

Sierra fingered the cell phone in her pocket. She could call for help pretty quickly if she needed it. She opened the door to the inside stairs and listened. A man's voice. Desperate.

She began up the long flight, craning her ears to hear the second voice as she avoided the steps that creaked. One must be giving orders if another was begging. The other person must be speaking very quietly.

Finally at the top of the steps, she slowly turned the handle and opened the door just a crack. A sliver of bright light slanted through. The voice was clearer without the door between.

Gabe?

In distress?

Was there something she should know about him, some reason someone would blackmail him? She pushed the door open a smidge further, but she couldn't see anyone. Gabe still sounded distant, like his voice came from her clinic or the bedroom. She'd lived up here, but it had always been his and Bethany's. She'd never forgotten.

Sierra tiptoed across the combo kitchen and dining room she and Doreen had used as shared office space. Light shone from the clinic… from the nursery.

"Oh, God, give me a reason to live."

Her heart lurched. There was no intruder. Just Gabe in his own space, grieving.

She was the intruder, frozen in the middle of the space. Should she carry on and let him know he wasn't alone, that there were plenty of reasons to live? Or sneak back the way she'd come, and not let on she'd trespassed and overheard?

Their relationship was tenuous at best. It couldn't even be called a relationship. Best to leave and pretend this never happened. She turned, and her jacket caught a stack of ledgers on the edge of the table. With horror she watched them slow-mo to the floor. They would crash any second.

She whirled back to the doorway across the space as they hit with a resounding splat.

"Doreen? I'm sorry. I shouldn't have been so insensitive. Please forgive me."

He expected her to speak. Expected her to be Doreen.

"I… It's Sierra. I thought I heard something up here and came to check." She took a deep breath. "I'm leaving. I didn't mean to bother you." She grabbed the pile of ledgers and smacked them back on the table, farther from the edge, then scurried toward the back stairs.

"Sierra?" His voice was clearer. Nearer.

She yanked the door wide before daring a glance back.

He stood, blond hair disheveled, his shirt partially untucked, his face wet.

Tears?

Anyone else, she'd be over there in a second, seeing if she could help. It was her nature. But not Gabe. She'd show too much.

"Sierra, I-I was just about to leave. If you had something to do here in your... office, go ahead."

"No, it's okay. I only needed my jacket from downstairs." Her gaze fell on the work spread out on the table. His words clicked in. "Doreen went over the books with you?" Monday night. How could she have forgotten?

He wiped his sleeve across his face and moved closer. "She was here. We didn't get too far in the books."

The guy looked miserable. "Oh?"

"It's all so hard. I can't handle this."

Common sense fled. "You think it's any easier for Doreen? You're not the only one hurting. She lost her husband years ago and then her only child. Her only hope for a grandchild." Sierra's hand flew to her mouth. Way to go for the jugular.

Gabe's face blanched. "You think I don't know that?"

Well, she'd gone and done it. Might as well finish this off. He already wouldn't ever want to speak to her again. "Stop being so selfish. You're not the only one who's ever lost their love. Think about her. Think about other people for once."

"What do you know about it?" His face hardened as he took a few steps toward her.

No way would he hurt her. Not the way she was hitting him with words.

"Did you lose a spouse? A child? Anyone at all? Tell me how you have the right to tell me what to do and how I should act. Tell me what stakes you've got in this."

She stared at him. The loss of her favorite aunt to cancer wouldn't have any power against his pain. It was completely different than a spouse or a child. She knew it, even though it had hit her hard as a preteen. "No, I don't have any experience in your kind of grief."

"Then get out. Don't tell me what's right and what's wrong. Leave me alone."

She bolted for the stairs.

Chapter 8 --

*E*ight forty-five Tuesday morning, Gabe let himself in the back door of Nature's Pantry. The two people he wanted least to see in the world would probably be here any minute. He'd acted like a spoiled kid last night. He knew it, and they knew it. But it was time he got a handle on the inner workings of his store so he could sell it. Until then, he'd do anything he needed to do to save face. He was on hold. Once he was free of Galena Landing, he'd figure out his new life.

The one without Bethany in it. Without their baby, their dreamed-of family. Without any reminders of all their years together.

Three years away hadn't been long enough, but he knew now it didn't matter. Ten years wouldn't have been any better, and even he knew it was completely unfair to leave the store up to Doreen that long.

Or Sierra.

Her voice sounded from the storefront. Bah, he'd hoped she wouldn't be in. Didn't she have a farm to run and a naturopathic practice? Wasn't that enough to keep the woman busy... and out of his business?

The woman.

She couldn't get married soon enough to suit him. Tyrell Burke. The guy had been a jerk in high school, but that was years ago now. What was holding him back from asking her? If not him, why hadn't she chased some other man down by now? Her friends were both married. She should be, too. She was pretty enough and nice enough — most of the time.

The door opened, and Sierra burst through. She stopped dead in her tracks, eyes wide, as her hand flew to her chest. "I didn't know you were here."

Gabe took a deep breath. "About last night."

She shook her head. "I'm really sorry. I way over-stepped."

Yeah, she had. "True." Sort of true. He forced a smile. "Truce?"

Her blue eyes jolted up to meet his. "Truce?"

"Yeah. I need you and Doreen to show me the ropes around here again. I-I don't know what I was thinking last night. Cutting off my lifelines. I'm sorry I got so angry."

"But... it was me. I was all wrong."

He kept the smile in place as best he could. "It took two of us." To tango. He gave his head a fierce shake to get that image out. "Look, I'd really like to get along. I owe you a ton of thanks for stepping in. For taking care of my store. For looking out for Doreen."

The wild look in her eyes softened. "It's okay. If you can forgive me, too."

"Of course." He stepped past her into the once-familiar space, noticing the vitamin section had shrunk and the organic packaged foods had stayed about the same — sparsely populated. On the far wall, racks had been rearranged and bins added for fresh produce. "Can you get me up to speed? Do you and Doreen split the hours, or what?"

She hesitated. "She did it all at first, and I'd come by and see her. After a few months I started putting in some time on the clock, then we split the hours, but recently…"

"Recently?"

She glanced at him. "When the RA flared, I kind of just took over for the most part. She's kept up the books and comes in when I can't."

"So I'm asking the right person, then." He tried to keep a light tone even as his heart crushed at Doreen's pain.

"Today we get freight, like every second Tuesday, with the dry goods." She waved toward the shelves.

So they weren't half-empty because no one bought food here? "Okay. So what time does the truck come?"

"Usually late morning." She straightened health and cooking magazines on a rotating rack. "Doreen will be in around ten to man the front counter while I do the freight. She can't really lift the boxes."

Gabe definitely needed to sell the store. He should have come back a year or two ago to do it. He couldn't tell Sierra that, though. Not when she'd tried to elicit a promise he'd wait six months. That would put it well into spring before he got it on the market. Much too late for him, even though it was probably a better time to find a buyer.

"Well, for the next day or two, treat me like a novice employee you're training. Don't let me sit around. Tell me what needs doing and keep me busy."

She looked at him uncertainly, twisting a long curly lock behind her ear.

"I mean it."

"Okay. Well, here's the float if you want to open up the till. We always count it at closing so there's two hundred in it."

He gave her a half-salute, took the divided drawer from her, and headed behind the counter. She turned the neon sign on and flipped on the lights before following him.

Gabe edged over, unsure what she was doing. She crouched and turned on a stereo system sitting on a lower shelf. Nature sounds mixed with classical music wafted through the store.

She glanced at him as she stood. "If you don't mind, that is."

"No, it's fine." Why hadn't he ever thought of that? He'd run rock in his day, but not all the older people liked that kind of music. This was probably more welcoming, more in tune with the type of business. "I'm the hired help, remember? I don't get an opinion."

His eyes caught on hers, so close to his. She was only a few inches shorter than him, taller than Bethany had been. Long blond hair with curls that flowed past her shoulder blades. Face with the perfect amount of makeup, pink lipstick. He jerked his gaze to the cash tray in his hand. Every woman had lips. It wasn't like he needed to start staring at them.

She reached past him to turn the cash register on, her arm brushing his sleeve. Some floral essence tickled his nose as he stepped back to break the contact. He took a deep breath, hopefully silently. No way did he want her to know she affected him at all. She was just a woman he worked with now... for a little while.

Just a woman he worked with.

Just a woman.

He backed up another step.

She'd said something, but he couldn't remember what.

oOo

So he wanted a truce. That was probably better than being at each other's throats for six months if, in fact, he stuck to her challenge. Had he promised? She couldn't remember. Seemed like he'd been vague. Had that been on purpose?

"Have you added any new categories?" Gabe pushed the cash drawer into the register, brushing her arm in the process.

Old Spice again. It had never smelled so good on her Great Uncle Orville. But there was more to the scent than that. Orville stank of cigarettes and garlic at the same time. Gabe... not so much. Fresh, clean.

Oh, great, now she was practically sniffing him, his crisp shirt collar inches from her nose. Wait, he'd asked something. Something about the till. Right.

"Stuff that's in on consignment is under this button. Perishables go here." She reached past him and tapped. This behind-the-counter space had never been intended for two. "And local stuff we buy outright is in this one."

"But some is on consignment?"

She crouched to pull a ledger from a low shelf. "A few things, yeah." She flipped it open and ran her finger down the entries. "Like these."

Gabe's breath tickled her ear as he peered over her shoulder. Every molecule on her back strained toward the warmth from his body.

Trapped. Right in a place she'd been dreaming of, but not for the right reasons. Not because Gabe wanted to be close to her, but because he needed to read something she'd carefully placed so he had to work for it.

"What kind of produce do we carry?"

Sierra turned slightly. Man, he was right there. He could only be closer if they were actually holding each other up, but it was hard talking to him without looking at him. She backed up half a step, all there was room for. "We, um, carry quite a bit this time of year. We've got potatoes and carrots and parsnips in those bins, and the farmers will bring in more when we need them. Onions, leeks, and garlic. Apples."

He nodded.

She glanced up at him, the space between them negligible. His eyes were like the bluest Idaho sky, the Gulf of Mexico, and chicory blossoms all rolled into one. He'd never be caught dead with hair as long or mussed up as Noel seemed to prefer. The peak of Gabe's hair begged to be touched. Was it natural? Was it gelled?

His gaze met hers in a shock of recognition. His nostrils flared slightly.

What had she put on this morning? Rhapsody? Did it go with Old Spice?

The door jingled as it opened, breaking the spell.

Sierra blinked and tried to pull back, but Gabe was still in her space. She backed right into him. "Excuse me."

"Oh." He moved off a few steps, still staring at her.

Sierra tore her gaze from him and escaped the confines of the area behind the counter. She pasted a bright smile on her face and turned to view the customer who'd just arrived.

Jo. With a knowing smirk, she glanced from one to the other and hoisted Madelynn on her hip.

Great. That was all Sierra needed. Jo, of all people to witness... whatever that had been. She glanced back at Gabe. What *had* it been, anyway?

He ran his fingers over the keys on the till, apparently memorizing each category.

"Hi, Jo! What can I do for you today?" Had she sounded shrill to any ears but her own?

Jo produced a jar with two honeybees in it. "You left this on the counter, and I had to run some errands, so I brought them. I thought you were giving Doreen another treatment today. How's she feeling after the one last week, by the way?"

Sierra froze, even more aware of Gabe than she had been with him breathing down her neck. "She's doing well. The swelling and itching subsided in a few hours last time."

"Does she think it helped?"

Tap-tap-tap.

Probably Gabe's fingers on the counter, but Sierra wasn't about to turn around and check.

"A little early to tell, but we're hopeful."

"Oh, good. It sounds so wonky, you know? But it would be awesome if it made a difference for her."

"Yeah. Thanks for bringing the bees. I knew my bike bags were missing something."

Anytime would be good for Jo to shut up. Not that she ever took a hint.

Maybe this time. Jo glanced over at Gabe. "Getting back in the saddle, then?"

"Sort of." His voice was tight. Tighter than she'd heard it yet today. All that talk of stinging Doreen on purpose was no doubt bringing back the emotions of their first fight after his return. The first of many.

Jo's gaze, alive with curiosity, shifted back and forth between them for a moment.

Sierra folded her arms across her chest and glared Jo down. "When you've done that, Gabe, we need to make sure there's room for a pallet in the receiving bay. If you wouldn't mind."

"No problem." He strode across the worn wooden planks and into the back, the door thudding shut behind him.

Jo's eyebrows shot up. "Who's the boss here?"

"I am. Until he's learned the ropes the way Doreen and I

have been running things for the last few years."

Madelynn struggled to get down, and Jo shifted her to the other hip. "Well, that's handy for you, I'd say." Jo grinned. "Anything I should know about your working conditions?"

Sierra narrowed her gaze. "Like what?"

Jo thrust her chin toward the back of the store. "Like you and Gabe? You seemed a bit lost in each other's eyes when I came in."

Keeping solid eye contact was key to making Jo believe her, but it was impossible. Not only that, but the flush swooping up her neck and across her cheeks surely gave her away. "Trust me, nothing is going on."

"Uh huh. You've got that Queen of Denial thing down quite well, I'd say. But denial doesn't mean it's true."

"Give it up, Jo."

"I don't think so. I seem to remember a few years back, and I'm pretty sure I owe you one. Or possibly a lot more than one. Wasn't it you who—"

"Shush! It's not just me." Sierra glanced toward the back door, but it stayed firmly shut. How well could someone hear through it? She lowered her voice. "Remember Gabe's in mourning. Don't be mean to him."

Thankfully Jo followed suit. "It's time he remembered life."

Sierra caught her friend's gaze. "Guess that will be up to him, won't it?"

The door to the store's receiving bay opened and Doreen limped through. "Did you bring the bees?"

Gabe leaned against the doorway behind her, arms crossed.

Jo held up the buzzing jar. "Nope, she forgot them, but I had to come to town anyway."

Doreen reached for the jar and held it to the light as she watched the two bees zipping around the enclosed space. "I can't believe I'm going to do this again. After we've unloaded freight?"

Sierra nodded, not daring to look at Gabe.

Chapter 9 --

Gabe slashed the plastic wrap holding the boxes on the pallet. If only Sierra would leave him alone to do this, but no. She'd set the clipboard down to yank the wrap away.

"I wish there were some other way to keep a pallet together," she muttered.

It did seem the guy in shipping had made twice as many rounds of plastic as would have been required, but Gabe wasn't going to give Sierra the satisfaction of agreeing with her. "They never know how many times they'll have to move a pallet around in the back of the truck."

She shot him a peeved look. "What'd they do before wrap-on-a-roll?"

Hadn't been since before he bought Nature's Pantry. He shrugged and stuffed an armload of dirty plastic into a trashcan.

Sierra pulled a sheaf of papers from between two boxes at the top, opened them, and clipped them to her board. She scanned the list and grimaced. "They shorted us Cora's Mac and Cheese for like the third time."

"Who's Cora?"

"New GMO-free convenience food company."

"Oh." Gabe lifted off the top box. "Sesame oil, case of twelve." He set it on the cart.

"Got it." Sierra made a mark with her pen.

New companies, new products all over his store. Vegetable bins. A cooler with milk in glass bottles and packages of cheese. His store. Ha. Sure didn't feel like it.

But whose fault was that? Nobody's but his. Unless it was Sierra's father's.

No. He'd promised himself and God he wouldn't go there. Eyewitness accounts agreed that the little red car — Bethany's — had swerved to miss a deer. She'd been on her way home from a twelve-hour nursing shift in Wynnton, the last before a few days off. Her coworkers said they hadn't caught a break all day. Run off their feet, all of them. If it hadn't been Sierra's dad's eighteen-wheeler on the road right then, it would have been someone else she'd hit.

Gabe was the one to blame. He'd been tending this no-account store and not making enough money to give Bethany the escape she needed. She'd been counting the weeks until maternity leave.

Bethany's life insurance had given him enough to pay his own expenses in Romania. He'd run away and, inexplicably, the store started making money. He'd finally dug into the bookkeeping program last night, trying to make sense of them on his own. Nature's Pantry was firmly in the black, and he couldn't even take the credit.

That was probably Sierra's fault, too. Why did she have to be here, in his face? Oh yeah, he'd asked her to treat him like a new hire. She was doing it, too. Lost in his own thoughts, he'd still been announcing the contents of each box he moved while she checked them off.

Gabe reached for the clipboard. "Here, I'll get what's left.

Why don't you take the rest of the day off?"

Her blue eyes bounced to meet his. Startled. "But this is only the beginning. Everything needs to be shelved. Of all the days of the month, this is the one that needs extra staff the most."

Probably true, but he couldn't back down now. Somehow those words had erupted from his mouth. "I've got it."

"What happened to me getting you up to speed? What happened to me retraining you?"

"Doreen can do it."

Sierra plopped one hand onto a curvy hip. "This is her treatment day."

Right, those stupid bees. "Sting her another day." He leaned closer. "Or never."

Her chin rose, and her eyes flashed. "That is absolutely none of your business. She is in enough pain you cannot make that decision for her." She leaned closer, too. "You abdicated that right. If you ever had it."

Her lips were right there. He wouldn't have to move more than a couple of inches to taste them.

Her blue eyes widened. Her perfume filled the air, removing all the oxygen he'd been breathing.

"Sierra, I—" He what?

She backed up a few steps, gaze locked with his, clutching the clipboard to her chest with both hands. She slipped on a remnant of plastic wrap and, before he could reach her, fell into the metal trashcan. It tipped forward as she crashed to the floor, the rim bashing the back of her head. The clipboard clattered away.

"Sierra!" Gabe knelt and swept the hair away from her face. "Are you okay?"

She blinked and rubbed the back of her head as she struggled to sit. The can had given her quite a wallop. She'd probably have a good-sized bump and a headache to match.

"Yeah, I'm fine." She turned away from him and pushed herself to her feet, ignoring his outstretched hand.

"What happened?" came Doreen's voice from the doorway. "I heard a big crash."

"Everything is fine, Doreen." Sierra righted the trashcan. "I slipped on some plastic wrap and knocked the garbage over. No problem."

Concern swept the older woman's face. "Are you sure? It sounded like more than a metal can."

Gabe couldn't hold back the words. "Sierra fell."

The door to the store swung shut behind Doreen. "Oh, no. Are you okay, dear?"

"I'm fine." Sierra glowered at Gabe. "No need to worry." She smiled tremulously at Doreen. "Thanks for the concern, though."

"But—"

She silenced him with a glare.

Why wouldn't she admit to Doreen how hard she'd fallen? Pride? Not that he knew anything about pride, of course. That'd never stopped him from saying anything in the past.

The front door jingled. Doreen turned. "I'll see who it is." She cast another worried look over Sierra and returned to the storefront, minus the confident stride she used to have. Was the pain in her joints really that bad?

Sierra's floral scent invaded Gabe's space again. He shut his eyes for an instant, letting it filter over him while he tried to pull himself together.

"Don't you ever," Sierra whispered, just inches from his face. "Don't *ever* worry Doreen about anything that isn't absolutely necessary. Do you hear me?"

o0o

Gabe backed up a few steps.

Good. Sierra needed the space. That whack to her head had addled her thinking for sure. There wasn't a chance in the world she'd read that expression on his face correctly.

Gabe, the guy who apparently lived to antagonize her, had looked like he was going to kiss her there for a minute. She'd been kissed a time or two in her life. She knew the look. The gaze fixed on her mouth, the pursing of his lips.

Although her head screamed — correctly — that someone had hit it with a large metal trashcan, it was obviously wrong about Gabe. No way was he going to get the satisfaction of sensing her response to his touch. His lips.

If she knew the signs, so did he. He'd been a married man. Sierra'd be crazy to think he didn't know what a woman begging a kiss looked like. So she'd keep her eyes off his face, thank you very much. She'd keep her distance. Maybe if she couldn't smell Old Spice, he was far enough away.

She retrieved the clipboard and the packing sheets that had been bumped off in the crash. "Where were we?"

Gabe sighed. "Here's a box of Cora's rice cakes, cheddar flavor. Hasn't everyone got the memo that rice cakes aren't really good for them?"

"The fad lives on." Sierra turned to the second page and marked off the item. "Next?"

Man, her head hurt, but if she put her hand up to feel the bump, Gabe would send her away for sure. And why, again, was that a bad thing? He was so stubborn he deserved to flounder. It wasn't like she had nothing to do at the farm.

Claire and Noel had headed to the backcountry with a hunting group from California. Jo was home whacking up pumpkins for processing... at least if Maddie allowed it. That's where Sierra should be. At the farm helping Jo. Not here where she was so obviously unappreciated.

"Did you get the caramel-flavored rice cakes?"

Sierra blinked and refocused on the packing sheet. "Um, here they are." This was going to be a long, long day.

oOo

He'd sent them both home early after allowing Sierra to stick the bees on each of Doreen's hands. Doreen hadn't been up to a full day of work even without the stings. Too bad he hadn't really noticed until Sierra pointed it out in that obstinate way of hers. And Sierra obviously had a painful head.

Much as Gabe hated to think it, it was a good thing she'd wiped out. He'd been seconds away from kissing her. He probably would've gotten his face slapped a good one for his thoughtless behavior. He'd have deserved it.

What had come over him, anyway? Sierra wasn't his type. His type had died with Bethany. But did he really want to spend the next fifty-some years alone?

He pulled the last package of Cora's plain rice cakes off the shelf and layered the new stock behind it. That's what his life felt like. Bland. A little crunch to make a person's taste buds think this was worth eating. Sodium-free. Gluten-free. Hypoallergenic.

Lowest of common denominators. Barely life-sustaining.

The door jangled as someone entered.

Gabe looked up from his spot near the floor.

"Gabriel! The rumor mill said you were home again, dear boy. So good to see you."

He clambered to his feet as the wizened elderly woman thumped over, cane in hand. "It's nice to see you again, Mrs. Bowerchuk."

Her gaze slid past him to the open case on the floor. "Oh,

good. Did you get in more of those rice cakes?"

Gabe picked up a package and held it out to her. "These are the plain ones, if that's what you're looking for."

She accepted it. "I didn't want to take the last one in case someone needed it more than I did."

Were they talking about the same product? How in the world could anyone *need* plain rice cakes? Had Cora laced them with crack at the factory? His gaze caught on the label. Organic crack, of course.

"They make other flavors, you know." Gabe tapped the shelf in front of each. "Salted…"

"Sodium is bad for my blood pressure."

"Caramel."

"I'm diabetic."

"Cheddar."

She shook her head. "I mentioned about the salt, didn't I?"

Gabe managed to get a smile on his face. "Well, then. Plain it is. Would you like more than one package today?"

"No, one is fine. I cut each in half so a package lasts almost two weeks."

His smile froze in place. "Fair enough." Fair? Who rationed out something this tasteless to make them last? Who figured they were worth it? "Can I help you with anything else today, Mrs. Bowerchuk?"

"No, this is everything for now, Gabriel." She started for the counter.

He followed her then rounded the end and rang up her purchase.

Her shaky hands counted out the bills and coins from a worn wallet. She pushed the package into her black net bag and headed for the door. "God bless you, Gabriel. It's good to see you home again."

Gabe opened the door and saw her out into the sunny October afternoon. Did she still live in the apartment over on Fifth? She looked ready for Galena Hills Care Facility where Jo still worked part time as a nutritionist.

Wilma Bowerchuk must be eighty-five if she was a day. Probably more like ninety. Plain unflavored rice cakes made her life brighter.

Gabe turned back to the boxes on the floor. Five flavors besides plain.

No, he did *not* want a life like plain rice cakes. He couldn't see Bethany wishing that on him. She'd want him to live a little, or maybe a lot.

If he had to be one, caramel was the best bet. Something with pizzazz. Something that tingled the palate.

Sierra would invent a new flavor that hadn't been tasted before. Something with honey. But look at all the cross words they'd exchanged since his return ten days ago. She wasn't interested in him. She was all about protecting Doreen and making sure he didn't wreck the business the two women had built.

Besides, Burke the Jerk had kissed Sierra, and she hadn't looked like she minded. If Gabe were going looking — and he wasn't saying he was — he'd look elsewhere.

Chapter 10 ---

Sierra wielded a heavy butcher knife over a massive chunk of pumpkin. If only her headache would simmer down. The pumpkin had been so huge even Zach couldn't lift it. He'd rolled it over to the compost pile before he'd gone off to a day of work at Landing Veterinary. He'd taken an axe to the squash, whacked it into manageable sized chunks, loaded them into a wheelbarrow, and pushed it right into the kitchen.

Jo tucked a loose strand of hair behind her ear, leaving an orange streak and a few pumpkin seeds in the wake of her finger.

Should Sierra tell her? Nah, she'd look just as bad herself in a few minutes, no doubt. "Where's Maddie?"

"Rosemary took her. She was so angry I wouldn't let her climb in the wheelbarrow."

"She keeps life interesting."

Jo shook her head. "That's one way to put it." She heaped chunked pumpkin onto a baking pan and set it in one of the wall ovens. "Now I know why the general population has gotten away from gardening and home processing."

Sierra leaned into her knife. Well, Claire's knife, part of the set

Noel had given her as an engagement gift. This was the thickest-skinned pumpkin she'd ever been privileged to tackle. When Jo didn't go on, Sierra glanced up. "Your great revelation is…?"

Jo reached for another baking pan. "Back in the old days, extended families lived near each other. They could share tasks, so no one felt the weight of doing it alone."

"You're saying our set-up isn't unique." Not that Sierra had ever believed they were the first group to live communally.

Jo laughed. "Not exactly. I didn't expect to become part of an actual extended family when we moved here, though."

"What you're really saying is it's handy to have Maddie's grandparents nearby when we've got a big day in the garden or kitchen." There'd be no extended clan here for Sierra. Doreen was the closest thing she had to a mother figure in Galena Landing. Her own family lived in Portland. Supportive, yes. On the spot? Not so much.

"You got it. The kid never sits still for two seconds. She's enough to wear a person out."

Sierra laughed. "Except Zach's dad. She'll sit with him and look at storybooks for ages."

"Steve's amazing with her. I wish I'd known him before he got struck with Guillain-Barré Syndrome. Zach says he was always busy puttering around the farm. You can tell he hates sitting around, unless he's got Maddie with him."

They chopped in silence for a few minutes before Jo glanced at Sierra across the butcher-block island. "So, what's up with Gabe?"

Sierra's gut, already tense, seized. "What do you mean?"

"You two looked mighty cozy behind the counter at Nature's Pantry this morning. Gazing into each other's eyes and all."

Sierra shrugged. "Just going over the new categories on the till and the new suppliers we've brought in since he left. Getting him up to speed."

"Right."

"Honestly. He's ready to take over, so I came home from town early. You should be happy. I'll be around more to help with everything at the farm."

"That look—"

"Jo? There's nothing going on with Gabe. I'm serious." She forced a laugh. "Now if we were talking Tyrell, it would be a different matter."

"Tyrell Burke?" Jo sniffed. "I don't see what you see in him."

"What do you mean? He's a nice guy. A Christian. A local beekeeper."

"How local a beekeeper can he be if he hauls his hives to California for almond pollination? Didn't you tell me yourself that half the problem with the bee population is most of the hives in the country are clustered together for a time? If anyone has any diseases in their colonies, that's a perfect chance to spread them around."

"I know, I know. It's not ideal. But that's how beekeepers in America make money to stay afloat. It's simply how the business operates when you get to a larger scale."

Jo pulled a pan of pumpkin out of the oven and slammed the door. "I can't believe I'm hearing this excuse from you."

Sierra clenched her jaw. "What?"

"You know what. It's exactly the kind of Big Ag mentality that's gotten the whole food system in such a mess. Delete almonds permanently off the grocery list. I won't support that industry."

The walnut and hazelnut trees they'd planted hadn't begun to produce yet. It took years to become self-sufficient in nuts. But there was no sense arguing with Jo when she got this way. She'd given up coffee cold turkey, after all. Sierra and Claire's consumption had gone down and they only bought organic fair trade, but still. Sierra was pretty sure Zach drank coffee at the clinic.

"Relax, Jo. It's one reason I don't want to run more hives than we do now. This much honey we can easily sell locally, and Noel's happy to make mead with the extra. It's only part of the whole farm's income, so it's manageable."

"Diversity. That's another thing." Jo went off on a tirade about monoculture and how bad it was for the environment.

Sierra didn't bother to stop her. They were in total agreement on the topic, and it kept Jo from pursuing her inquisition about either Tyrell or Gabe. Sierra brought the two men up, side by side, in her imagination. Tyrell all but swaggered into place. Confidence wasn't a bad thing, though. It was nice to be around somebody who knew what they wanted, had made a plan to achieve it, and worked his plan.

Unlike Gabe. Sierra had no trouble cutting him a bit of slack for the tumult of the past three years. But still, he'd always lacked the confidence that was part of Tyrell's innate being. Gabe didn't have big dreams. He'd been satisfied with a small business in a small town, with a contented wife and a baby on the way.

What about her? She'd obviously had big dreams, too. Her and Claire and Jo. She didn't know any other group of women who'd decided to buy a farm and grow their own food. They'd created goals and followed through. So she was probably more compatible with Tyrell than with Gabe, no matter what Jo said.

That Zach and Noel had come along to share their dream was a bonus, according to Jo and Claire. Sierra wasn't so sure. Yeah, it was great that her friends were happy, but it made her the odd girl out. If she married Tyrell Burke, she'd move off Green Acres, but only by a few miles. She could still see her friends and work the farm with them. Or maybe they'd buy her share eventually.

If she married Gabriel Rubachuk… well, first off, there was zero chance of that. But if she did, who knew what would happen? The contented small-town guy had disappeared to some European third-world country for three years and now talked of moving away permanently. What kind of life was that for someone whose roots dug deeper into the Galena Valley every day?

No, Tyrell Burke was by far the better choice.

"Earth to Sierra. I'll bet a pumpkin pie you're thinking about Gabe."

Sierra summoned up a grin. "You'd lose. I was thinking about Tyrell." She rubbed her belly. "But why don't you let Claire make the pie instead? Then it would be edible."

oOo

He'd been back in Galena Landing for nearly two weeks and had managed to avoid dinner hour at his host house nearly every night, just in case it turned into another group meal. Rosemary had pinned Gabe down this morning and made him promise to show up.

Well, if he was going to fit back in, even temporarily, he should make an effort. Zach's parents and his had been close friends, so Gabe had known them well even before they'd shared experiences in Romania that year.

Why was he so reluctant to spend time with them now? Partly the framed portraits of Zach's wedding and the family pictures that hung on the living room wall. Partly the slightly worried crease on Rosemary's forehead whenever she looked at Gabe. Partly the reminder, when he looked at Steve, that a man couldn't plan out his life and assume it would run smoothly. Who expected to contract a neurological disease like Guillain-Barré, anyway?

Gabe drove his old car into the Nemesek driveway and parked near the plum trees. Starlings had swept through and cleaned off the trees a few days before. Only a few leaves remained, opening a clear view of the straw bale house next door.

He should probably brace himself and move back into his apartment. Everyone would worry about him less. He laughed, the sound harsh in the still autumn air. It should have the opposite effect.

Gabe rounded the house to the veranda. He couldn't remember anyone using the front door once in all the times he'd been to the farm over the years. The sound of voices and laughter filtered around the corner.

He stopped. Not a quiet meal with Steve and Rosemary then. Madelynn shrieked. Zach and Jo must be here, unless Rosemary was babysitting. He closed his eyes, straining to hear. Surely Sierra was next door. She wasn't part of the Nemesek clan.

At any rate, it didn't matter. He'd been invited. He was here. It would be beyond rude... and a bit revealing... if he left now.

"Rubachuk!" Zach's fist came up as Gabe stepped onto the veranda.

"Nemesek." Gabe rammed his fist against Zach's.

Jo rolled her eyes before grinning at Gabe.

"Hey, we've been around a while," Zach said easily, his other arm draped around Jo on the porch swing. Domino lay sprawled at their feet. He raised his voice. "Mom, Gabe's here."

"Good!" she called from inside. "Want to light the grill? Everything else is nearly ready."

Zach disengaged from his wife, strode over to the gas grill, and opened the lid. "Don't you ever scrub this thing?"

"Yes. Last time I lit it."

"Uh. Where's the brush?"

"Let it get hot first, Zachary. Some things you have to do when the time is right."

The words trickled into a parched spot of Gabe's soul as he sank into a wicker chair.

Madelynn pressed her face against the screen door from inside the kitchen then started bashing at it.

"No, Maddie!" Jo sprang to her feet. "Be gentle with Grandma's door. You don't want to break it."

"Break?" echoed the tyke, still pounding.

Jo rescued the child and set her on the veranda floor. Maddie ran to Domino and jumped on his back. The startled Border collie strained to get to his feet, but Maddie wasn't budging.

Gabe reached over and rubbed Domino's ears. "It's okay, buddy. Be nice to her. She won't bite."

She wouldn't bite Gabe, either. He eyed the little one for a few seconds. "Hey, Maddie, want to come see Uncle Gabe?" He patted his pockets. What could he entice her with?

"No!" she yelled, yanking on the dog's ear.

Jo pulled her off Domino's back. "Be nice. Gentle."

Maddie wriggled to get down.

"It's never-ending," Jo said to Gabe. "She never stops. Ever."

The pang was less than it had been. Maybe because he couldn't imagine parenting a tornado like Maddie. Surely his and Bethany's daughter would have been calmer... not that there was any way to know.

"Grill's hot," hollered Zach. "Now where's the brush you told me about?" He hunted around in the porch cupboard.

The screen door opened, and Sierra came out holding a platter of raw burgers. She didn't glance Gabe's way but set the plate down on the table near Zach, who'd found the brush and was scrubbing off the remains of the previous meal. She pivoted for the kitchen.

Gabe released a breath. Okay. Sierra was here after all. He'd survive.

A moment later she reappeared at the door carrying a tray loaded with a pitcher of raspberry vinegar and glasses. She went down the steps, over to the picnic table under an awning, and began unloading the tray.

Probably there was more where that came from, if seven people were eating outside. Gabe walked into the kitchen. "What else needs to go out, Rosemary?"

She wiped short graying hair from her face. "Thanks, Gabriel. These salads can go. Sierra can load the condiments and buns on the tray next time. Then plates and cutlery."

He nodded and lifted the salads. Sierra, on her way in, opened the screen door at his approach. A moment later he held the door for her as they crossed paths again. By the time the burgers were cooked, they'd transferred everything to the outdoor table. He hadn't even had to look her in the eye once. So far, so good.

Zach's dad was the last to sit down. He glanced at Gabe as he lowered himself gingerly into his chair. "So, how was your first full day back in the store?"

"Good." Gabe refused to look at Sierra. "A little busy putting away freight around the customers, but not too bad."

Steve nodded. "Busier than it used to be, I'll warrant. Doreen and Sierra have worked hard."

So he was cornered. He managed to come up with a smile for Sierra. "They have, and I'm thankful. How's your head?"

Her hand slid to the back of her skull. "I'll have a bump for a few days, but it will be okay."

"Oh?" Rosemary looked up. "What happened?"

"I slipped on some plastic wrap and fell. No big deal."

"And here I asked you to come in and help with supper. You should have told me."

"No, really. It's fine."

"She's got a hard head," quipped Jo.

Sierra shot her friend an unreadable glance.

Gabe took a deep breath. "I'm planning to move back into the apartment this weekend." He focused on Steve. "I'm so grateful you allowed me to stay here for a bit, but it's time I stood on my own two feet."

Rosemary touched his arm. "Only if you're ready, Gabriel. We're in no hurry to see you leave."

"I can't avoid it forever." Much as he wished the opposite were true.

"Sorry we took over your dining room for a store office." Sierra reached for the mustard. "We can get that moved downstairs again, if you'll give a hand with the desk."

"That old office under the stairs is no bigger than a closet." It had been enough when he was running a failing solo business. Now, he wasn't so sure.

"We can make it fit. Upstairs was easier when two of us were going over reports together. There isn't room for two chairs downstairs."

And he was alone. One more reminder. Not that Bethany had taken a hands-on approach to Nature's Pantry. Maybe if he'd encouraged it, things would have been different.

Gabe blocked his brain. He couldn't go there. The what-if spiral could drag him way down. He knew. He'd been there.

"Besides," Sierra went on. "You won't want Doreen or me intruding on your personal space to look something up." Then her brow furrowed. "Though I guess that won't be a problem once you're up to speed."

"Hey, Rubachuk, you might want to splash some fresh paint around that apartment before you move in." Zach put his hand on Jo's shoulder. "My woman here is an expert. She'd love to paint your place."

"Ha." Jo shifted away from Zach's touch. "Not by myself, I wouldn't. But a bunch of us could make a day of it. What colors do you like, Gabe? And don't say beige. That isn't a color."

"Well, not pink." Gabe glanced at Jo. "Anyone need some of that, there are three cans in the closet." He managed to get the words out without choking. "Maybe you'd like it in Maddie's room?"

She shook her head. "Already done in green, with everything matching. No pink for my kid."

Surprise.

"I haven't painted the spare room in my duplex yet," Sierra said. "I could take the pink off your hands. It's definitely better than the drywall mud smears it's got now."

"Sure. It's all yours." The perfect place for it... somewhere he'd never have to see.

"Saturday good for everyone?" Jo looked around. "It will be nice to get a break from gardening and canning."

"I'll keep Madelynn," Rosemary offered. "I'm not up for ladders."

"That's a huge help." Jo grinned at her mother-in-law. "Though I'm sure she'd love to finger paint. Or, you know, foot paint."

Gabe's head reeled. Had he agreed to all this? Really? "How about shades of blue?"

Jo narrowed her gaze at him. "Blue would be okay, but only if I can do the wall that runs through the dining room and living room deep gold, like honey. I think that will keep it from being gloomy."

Yeah, he had enough trouble with depression without inviting it in on purpose. Gold wasn't a color Bethany would have chosen. She hadn't ever complained about the beige walls. Gabe shrugged. "Sure. Whatever."

Sierra glanced at her watch and pushed her chair back. "Sorry, I have to run. Saturday's good though."

"Where are you off to?" asked Jo.

"I have a date with Tyrell."

What was the unspoken conversation going on between the two women? Gabe could almost read it, but not quite. He should be glad she was going out with the other guy. He really should.

But he wasn't.

Chapter 11 ---

Tyrell gave Sierra a hand up into his gleaming truck, and she sank into the sumptuous leather seat. A moment later he grinned at her as he snapped his seat belt into place. "Hello, doll."

Sierra smiled at him. "Hi, yourself." Maybe if she didn't show her annoyance at the nickname, it wouldn't be worth his while to keep using it.

"Just wait until you see the boat. She's a beauty. Almost as pretty as you." He glanced her way as he navigated back onto Thompson Road.

"That's great." She'd worn jeans and a fitted sweatshirt tonight, a pleasant enough evening for October. Could get cold on the lake, though.

"Done much boating?"

"My uncle had a sailboat moored at Lincoln City. We went out with him a few times."

"A sailboat?" Tyrell laughed. "You can't water ski behind that and, besides, it's a lot of work. I'll take a speedboat any day."

"Oh, my uncle loved the wind. Bragged how little he had to spend on fuel for his boat."

Tyrell winked. "Money's not a problem for me, but I didn't

mind getting a deal on this baby at the end of the season."

It wasn't a problem for Uncle Ward, either. Money hadn't been the point.

The truck came to a stop at the small marina near Lakeside Park. Tyrell bounded around to open the door for Sierra. "After you, my lady." He gestured toward the dock.

One shiny speedboat stood taller and broader than the others. Sierra's gut sank. That had to be Tyrell's. Why did he have to have everything bigger and better than anyone else?

He slung his arm around her shoulders and pointed as they walked to the dock. "There she is."

She'd been right. She took a deep breath.

"Isn't she a beaut? The former owners just had her registration number on the hull. I'm thinking of giving her a name."

Sierra could feel the whisper of his lips beside her ear. She pulled away slightly. "Oh? What kind of name?"

"The Sierra doesn't sound quite right. Sorry, doll."

The *what*? He'd actually considered naming his boat after her? This was crazy. "I'm glad. Sierra's a good name for mountains, a desert, or a woman. Not a boat." Please, not a boat.

"What's your middle name?" He released her to untie the mooring.

Sierra stepped further away, wrapping both arms around her waist. "Ann."

"The Ann." Tyrell held the thick rope in his hands and tilted his head to look at the watercraft. "The Ann." He shook his head. "It doesn't have the right sound. Let's think on it a bit. Maybe The Singing Ann."

"I don't sing." Church on Sunday didn't count, did it? Certainly no one would ever ask her to join a worship team.

"The Dolly Ann?"

Sierra cringed. "Boats don't really need a name."

"Here, let me give you a hand in."

When she was settled as far away from the steering wheel as she could get, Tyrell pushed off and clambered aboard. He made his way to the cockpit and started the engine.

It was quieter than the flapping of sails in the wind, she'd give it that, but how much fuel would it go through in an hour?

Once they'd puttered out of the sheltered marina, Tyrell opened he motor, and the boat leaped forward, bow high. He beamed at Sierra from the cockpit. "Isn't it great?"

She nodded, flipping her hair so it streamed behind her instead of whipping her face. Across the valley beyond Galena Landing, the sky turned orange as the sun impaled a mountain. Aside from the motor and a few southern-bound Canada geese flying overhead, silence reigned. The pain meds for her head had finally kicked in.

Peace. A balm to her soul. She could get used to this.

"Are you cold?" Tyrell called out. "Come over here, out of the wind." He waggled his eyebrows and held out an arm.

Peace. Could she ever attain it with Tyrell nearby? Why couldn't she simply settle in and enjoy being close to him? He was a nice guy. He went to her church. Sure, he was a little on the touchy-feely side, but he hadn't made any improper overtures.

She'd much rather stay sitting in the stern with the wind howling through her hair than snuggle up behind the windshield, but was that being rude? She'd told everyone it was a date, but she wasn't acting like it.

Sierra needed to give him a chance. She didn't want to spend the rest of her life alone, and Tyrell was a better catch than most. With one last flip of her hair, she stood and made her way to the shelter of his arm.

oOo

The evening light faded from beyond the Nemesek veranda. Jo had long since taken Madelynn home to bed. Zach's parents had retired, urging the guys to stay and visit as long as they liked.

Gabe took a sip of his coffee. Decaf, given the hour.

Zach glanced his way. "So, how are you really doing, man? Hardly seen you around since you got back."

"I've been busy."

Zach chuckled. "If I didn't know better, I'd say you were busy avoiding me."

Gabe shrugged. "Not you so much."

"Then who?"

"Everything. Everyone."

"And you look at me and see everything you lost." Sympathy shone in Zach's eyes.

How to deny it? Gabe couldn't. "Well, yeah. But it's not just that."

"I've been praying for you, man." Zach leaned his elbows on his knees.

"I appreciate it."

"There for a while you were the one praying for me. Praying I'd find my way back to God."

"I'm not *away* from God." Not precisely.

"Yeah." Zach didn't sound like he quite believed that one. "Anyway, I'm here if you want to talk."

"I just don't quite know how to pick up and start over, if you know what I mean. In theory, it sounds like it should be simple."

"Coming home is a good first step. Getting back into your own place will be tough, but I think the paint job will help, don't you? Move the furniture around, or get some new pieces if it helps."

"Paint will make a difference." Probably. Maybe. "I hate to make everyone give up a day for that, though. Everyone's so busy, and I'm intruding."

"Oh, man, you are definitely not intruding. It was our idea. Haven't you figured out yet what we're all about here? Community. We work together. We play together. No one has to carry a burden alone."

Gabe'd had a community of sorts in Romania at the orphanage. The directors, the various workers, the children. He nodded slowly. Not that Zach could see in the near-darkness. "Well, I appreciate it."

"Noel and Claire will be back from their guide trip on Saturday night, but I think we can handle the paint job without them, especially with Mom taking Maddie. Jo and Sierra painted most of the big house and the cabin. They're efficient."

Another day spent in Sierra's company, whether he wanted to or not. So long as she didn't bring Tyrell Burke with her. Gabe took a long swallow of coffee.

"If you don't want to talk to me, how about Pastor Ron? He's a good guy."

"I'm not sure there's anything anyone can say, Nemesek. I know all the words. I know I have to accept things the way they are. I mostly have, but sometimes things catch me wrong."

Zach angled a look his way. "Like seeing my daughter."

"Yeah." It didn't hurt as much as it had, though. "Things like that. She's a cutie, but you know that."

"She is. She's also as stubborn as her mother. Some days the only reason we win is because we're bigger than she is."

Gabe chuckled. "She'll be fine, surrounded by as much love as you all give her." Not like the kids in Romania. There just wasn't enough of anything to go around. Not even love. He'd been making a difference there. It would've been easy to stay where he felt needed. But he'd known in his heart it was time to return to American soil.

Too bad he couldn't have brought an orphan or two with him, but the days of Romania allowing international adoptions were long past. And a kid… even an orphan… should get two parents out of the deal. Not a man struggling to find his way alone.

"You'll meet someone," Zach was saying. "You know Bethany wouldn't want you to stay single for the rest of your life. Did you guys ever talk about it? What would happen if one of you died?"

"Yeah." Gabe's mind slid back to that day, early in their marriage. "She wanted to talk about it. I didn't."

"I bet."

"She was like, don't be alone, Gabe. You know you can't take care of yourself. You need a woman in your life."

Silence for a moment. "What did you say?"

Gabe's laugh came out almost with a sob. "I said, how about if we agree to both live until we're a hundred?"

Sympathy shone from Zach's eyes in the dim light. "Guess it didn't work out that way."

"Guess not." Gabe took a sip. "I don't know why it still feels like I'm letting her down when I try to focus on the future."

"You're taking good steps now. Real feet-on-the-ground steps. It will get better."

"It has, but it's such a slow process. And honestly…" He took a deep breath. "Honestly, sometimes I don't want to move forward. I just want to curl up in a ball and never come out again."

"Still?"

"It was getting better. It's why I thought I could handle coming back. But now? I'm not so sure."

"What're you afraid of, man?"

Zach was a good friend. Even those challenging words came out with gentleness Gabe would never have dreamed his childhood buddy had in him.

"You don't need to prove to anyone how much you loved Bethany. We all knew it. We know it broke your heart when she died. Don't worry about what other people think."

Was that what held him back? Maybe. Maybe Doreen would think he hadn't really loved her daughter. Maybe others would wonder. But that was dumb. There'd never been anyone but Bethany for him since he'd been a teenager. The whole town had known.

Time to let go? Gabe fisted his hand in the darkness then released one finger at a time. "Thanks, man."

o0o

"I bought a few acres off my dad." Tyrell's hands held the boat's wheel, his arms hemming Sierra in.

She tried to pour enthusiasm into her reply. "Oh, that's great."

"I'll start building a house in spring. Big one. What style do you like? We can do big windows and a big deck. There's a great view across the valley." He nuzzled her neck, minty breath from his gum trickling over her.

A chill ran through her, and she shivered.

"A hot tub off the master bedroom. Made for two."

A hot tub sounded nice, but they wouldn't be two people forever. She'd be twenty-eight soon, and her biological clock was ticking. She shoved the thought of her miserable periods out of her mind. Sometimes pregnancy helped women regulate better. She could hope.

"We can build up the honey business. Hmm, maybe I should call the boat The Honeybee."

Sierra loved being in the apiary. The bees forced her to slow down and breathe deeply. But still, running hundreds of hives? What about all the other things she liked doing? She'd always meant to get Rosemary to teach her to quilt, for one thing.

He nudged her with his elbow. "What are you thinking?"

If he was going to talk about a future together, she guessed she could ask some frank questions, too. "How many kids do you want?"

Tyrell laughed. "Who needs kids? They're expensive, and the world is populated enough, don't you think?" He slid a hand down her hips. "Besides, we wouldn't want your beautiful figure ruined."

Sierra flinched and glanced up.

He met her gaze, startled. "Oh, fine. You could probably talk me into one. It would be fun trying."

Her face flamed in the near-darkness, and she ducked from under his arm then backed a few steps away.

"It's okay, doll. Whatever you want. What do you think?"

She took a deep breath. "About what?"

Tyrell frowned as he glanced her way. "About the house. About us."

Had she missed some kind of proposal? Sierra wrapped both arms around her middle. "What do you mean, about us?"

His teeth flashed as he grinned. "You and me. Cruising into the future together, just the two of us. Like this."

Sierra backed up another step, and the back of her knees caught the edge of a padded seat. She sank into it, her mind whirling.

Not that she expected the kind of marriage proposal that went viral on Facebook. She didn't know any guys who'd make a big production. But this? Was he even asking her to marry him, or what?

Her biological clock said, "Tick-tock." But he didn't want kids?

"I'm not sure, Tyrell," she managed to get out. "I think we should get to know each other better before making such a big decision, don't you?"

Chapter 12 --

*T*his isn't the kind of blue I was expecting." Gabe slammed his fists against his hips as he surveyed the row of cans, each with a daub of paint on the lid, on the plastic drop cloth.

Jo, dressed in jeans and t-shirt already spattered with multiple colors, popped the lid off one of them, confirming Gabe's suspicion. This wasn't blue. Call it turquoise.

"You said you trusted my judgment." She grinned up at him.

"Uh, yeah. I trusted you to get blue."

"You'll love it." She dipped a brush in and painted a quick splotch on the wall. "Perfect."

Gabe shook his head. Whatever. He was only going to be here for a few months, and it was definitely better than beige. Maybe having a fresher look to the apartment would help when he sold the building.

Jo tilted her head at him. "How much painting have you done? Are you any good at cutting in?"

He raised his eyebrows and pointed at the wall. "Do I look like I've got experience?" He smelled the floral scent at the same time Sierra chuckled from behind him.

"Zach can cut in for Gabe." Sierra tossed her jacket on a

kitchen chair. "So long as you mark which walls are which colors, so the guys don't make a mistake."

Good idea. He'd work with Zach, maybe in a bedroom. The girls could do the living room.

Jo frowned. "Zach might be able to suture a dog, but he can't cut in without painter's tape to save his life."

Uh oh. Gabe could see where this was going.

"We don't have time for tape," Jo went on. "Not if we want to do all the walls today. One color won't be dry enough before we need to start the other."

Sierra stared hard at Jo. "There's no need to kill ourselves doing everything in one day."

Looked like she wanted to be paired off with him as much as he wanted it. He was likely a poor imitation of Tyrell Burke. The guy had a flashy new truck and knew what he wanted out of life. Sierra.

Jo stuck her hands on her hips. "Are you kidding me? Who knows when I'll get Rosemary to watch Maddie for an entire day again? Nope. We've got too much to do to stand here arguing. We'll start in opposite corners and work until we meet up then switch to the next room. You cut in for Gabe, I'll cut in for Zach." She glanced around. "Wherever he got to."

Great. No one said "no" to Jo. Gabe glanced at Sierra. "If you've got other things to do, I'm sure we'll manage fine without you."

She narrowed her gaze at him. "I promised to help. I'm here."

Zach came out of the bathroom and flipped the fan on as he closed the door behind him. "Might want to do that room last."

The girls rolled their eyes, and Gabe stifled a grin. "Looks like you've got everything ready to go. Let's get started."

Sierra shoved a stepladder into one corner. "Same color on both sides?" she asked Jo.

Jo smeared a splotch of light turquoise on three of the four walls. "This is where the colors go."

Sierra nodded and popped open a second paint can. She poured some into a tray before selecting a brush from the array Jo had laid out. She carried the bucket up the ladder, set it on the rest, and dipped her brush in. With a steady hand, she angled her brush against the ceiling and drew a line along the top of the wall.

Zach busied himself removing electrical covers then taped over each outlet.

Nothing Gabe could do for a minute but watch, right? Somehow watching his buddy wasn't as fascinating as watching Sierra, several steps up the ladder with her back to him. Her paint-splotched t-shirt tucked into the waistband of an old pair of jeans, hiding little of her feminine curves. She'd woven her hair into a thick French braid that hung way down her back and curled at the tips. No shoes, her toes twinkled with her signature purple nail polish and… something else.

He stepped closer. A toe ring? Yeah, that figured. See, he should remember stuff like this. How different she was from Bethany, who'd rarely worn jewelry other than her wedding set. For her, dressing up included clear nail polish, not this purple stuff Sierra must buy by the case somewhere.

Maybe Bethany would have worn more bling if he'd given it to her.

Ouch. Where had that come from? They'd never had money for extras like that. Non-essentials.

Try telling Sierra purple nail polish was a non-essential. Gabe couldn't help the grin. He could make a good guess how that would go over.

"Gonna stare all day?" Zach's elbow caught Gabe's ribs.

Gabe blinked back to reality and caught the knowing look in his buddy's eyes. A heated flush crept up his neck. "Uh, I'm not sure what to do now."

Sierra turned. "You've never painted at all?"

Gabe pointed at the beige wall. "Does it look like it?"

She shook her head. "Zach…"

Zach laughed. "I've got it. Grab that roller, Rubachuk. Here's what you do." He showed Gabe how to load the roller then get rid of the excess before spreading the paint out on the wall. "Just be careful not to hit the ceiling or the wall that's gonna be yellow."

"Honey gold," corrected Jo, scooting her ladder over.

"Right." Gabe gave an experimental roll. This should work out okay. And the color might be greener than he'd expected, but it did look kind of refreshing. Time to get rid of his boring beige life and step into fresh turquoise.

Sierra stepped off the ladder and moved it out of her way. She loaded her brush and glanced at him.

Speaking of turquoise, why had he ever thought her eyes were blue? They matched the wall, and they looked good.

o0o

Sierra's breath hitched. Why did Gabe keep looking at her like that? His eyes, his expressions, his body language, all said the opposite of his scathing commentary. Which side revealed his true thoughts?

Her instructors had told her eyes were the windows to the soul. A cliché, but true nonetheless.

Gabe turned away, bending to fill his roller again. When he looked at her again, the softness had disappeared. He raised his eyebrows, his eyes cold as blue steel.

Was it hot in here or what? This was crazy. She strode across the room to open the few windows the apartment had. Sure, it was mid-October, but the day was bright and sunny, and she needed air.

Thankfully, Jo broke the uncomfortable silence. "Good idea, Sierra. Get the paint fumes out. At least low-VOC paint isn't as lethal as the old kind."

"Did anyone bring food? I'm starving." Zach, of course, always thinking of his stomach.

"Yeah, I brought lunch." Jo waved her brush at him. "And it's what, nine-thirty? Get to work."

"I'll grab some chips from downstairs." Gabe set the roller down. "Unless you'd rather have rice cakes."

"Rice cakes?" Unbelief laced Zach's words. "You are kidding me, right? That's a pseudo health food if I ever heard of one."

Gabe's gaze met Sierra's. "Some people like them. We seem to do a thriving business in all the flavors. Especially plain."

Mrs. Bowerchuk had been in then. Sierra couldn't help the giggle that tumbled out. "Gabe's right, Zach. They're a hot seller."

"What, if you're ninety?"

"I don't think it's a requirement." Gabe cracked a grin. "But it might help."

Now that was more like it. Loosen up a little, buddy.

"I think I'll stick with something less popular. Jo will kill me if it isn't organic, but I'm happy to pay for whatever you rustle up."

Gabe raised both hands. "Hey, it's on me. Unless you're thinking of working your way through a whole case of chips, in which case you're on, man." He disappeared down the back stairs.

"Can't you even work for half an hour without eating?" Jo smacked Zach's arm with her brush, leaving a turquoise smear.

Uh oh. Sierra could see where this would lead.

Zach lifted his arm and examined the paint. "If only I had

food, I'd have enough energy to get even with you for that, woman."

"Yes, I can see how weak you are." Jo raised her eyebrows.

Zach stepped closer and wrapped both Jo's wrists with one hand while he yanked the brush out of her fingers with the other. "Is that right?" He dabbed paint on Jo's nose.

Sierra took a deep breath and turned her back. Where was she on this wall again? Time to cut in along the baseboards, which, thankfully, were white and in reasonable condition considering how many years it had been since they'd last seen attention.

"Take this," said Zach. "And this." Something dropped.

No peeking. She didn't want to see how much fun a married couple could have procrastinating painting a wall. She crouched at the baseboard and carefully angled her brush along it.

Gabe's footsteps clattered up the stairs as Sierra reached to load more paint on her brush. Against her better judgment, the silence from across the room made her steal a look from under her eyelashes. Yep, Jo and Zach stood there, wrapped in each other's arms, kissing like there was no tomorrow, the brush on the drop cloth beside them.

"Get a room," Gabe said. "Later, that is. Here, have some chips."

Zach ran his finger along Jo's nose, grinning as he spread the smear one way, then the other. "Mmm. Chips." He released Jo and turned toward Gabe, who held out a basket with a selection of snacks.

Jo swooped for the abandoned brush and smacked his backside.

"If you two would focus on the wall, we'd be half done by now." Sierra's gut tightened painfully as she dipped her brush. Yes, she was happy for her friends. Really. But sometimes they were just a reminder of what she didn't have. No marriage. No adorable toddler. Even pulling Tyrell's face up did nothing to comfort.

"Want some chips?" Gabe's voice came from just beyond her shoulder.

She glanced up, glad he blocked the view of the scuffle she could hear behind him. Not like she needed the calories, but... why not? She chose a bag and tore it open. Salt and fat, the next best thing to chocolate.

Gabe picked up his roller and got back to work, mere inches from her. How was she supposed to concentrate with him right there? She climbed back on the ladder to cut in along the ceiling again. Across the room, Jo and Zach had resumed painting, banter now restricted to verbal.

"I don't know how you do that so evenly."

Sierra jerked, and a smear caught the ceiling.

"Man, I'm sorry for distracting you."

"It's okay. Toss me that wet rag. It'll wipe off easily at this stage." When she'd removed the blip, she glanced down at him. "It's all in the angle you hold the brush. And knowing how much paint to have on it."

"You need a good brush, too," Jo called out.

Gabe's gaze kept Sierra captive. Finally she found more words. "If you want to practice, the closets are a good place to learn."

He quirked a grin, and her heart flipped. "Where no one will see my mistakes?"

"Exactly. It does take practice."

"A steady hand," offered Zach. "Like with a woman. Always a fine line between messing up and perfection."

Jo dabbed paint in his hair.

"Thanks, woman." His roller found her pant leg.

"Give it up, you two. We'll be here all night." Sierra glared across the room. "Keep going like that, and we'll need another gallon of paint."

Gabe chuckled.

She shot him a surprised glance. Laughter out of Gabe? Who knew it was even possible?

"Looks like we have a lot of buckets. I don't think we'll run out any time soon."

Sierra shook her head at Gabe but couldn't help the grin. So nice when he wasn't glowering at her.

"How do you do that, man?" He half-turned to Zach.

His pivot caught Sierra off guard as his roller bumped her shoulder.

"Hey! Watch what you're doing!"

Gabe's blue eyes twinkled. "I was."

"You go, Rubachuk."

A mask pulled across Gabe's face at Zach's words. His gaze, still fixed on hers, hardened and chilled. His jaw flexed and he turned away to dip the roller.

Zach mouthed, "I'm sorry," to her over Gabe's bent head.

Who'd decided she and Gabe ought to be a pair, anyway? She shook her head at Zach and reloaded her brush. She was dating Tyrell, and he was obviously creating plans for their future together.

That's what she needed. A man who didn't have one foot in the past and both eyes fixed on the rearview mirror.

It was going to be a long day.

Chapter 13

"*G*abriel Rubachuk!"

Gabe barely made it through the double doors of Galena Gospel Church before Ed Graysen clapped him on the back.

"Ed! Good to see you."

"Likewise, brother. Likewise." The church elder peered deeply into Gabe's eyes before squeezing his shoulder. "I heard you'd returned, and I can't tell you how glad I am the rumor was true. Those junior high kids sure missed you."

The smile Gabe'd barely managed to bring up froze, the panic welling up his throat keeping it in place. "Oh, they've all moved up to the next class by now, Ed. It's been a few years."

"You had a way with that age group no one else has. We've been through several teachers since you left." The older man frowned. "And the fellow who's doing it now seems to need a lot of time off. Maybe you could team-teach with him or something like that?"

"Ed, I'm not sure I want to—"

"We can give it a bit of time. New term starts in January, after all. I think Tyrell is around for the next two months."

"Tyrell?" Gabe barely got the name out.

"Tyrell Burke. His family's been around here for years. You must've known him at some point? Though he's a more recent believer."

Gabe nodded. "He was ahead of me in school. I have vague memories of him." The historical memories were vague, anyway. The most recent recollections, not so much. "So he's been teaching the junior high class?"

"Yes, he took it over last winter when Dan North got pneumonia. But it's had its challenges." Ed's gaze slipped past Gabe. "Well, I shouldn't be telling you all that, I'm sure. Still, have no doubt we'll welcome you back with open arms."

"Uh, thank you. Don't go doing anything rash, though, Ed. I'm not sure what my plans are, long term."

The older man frowned as his gaze snapped back to Gabe. "What do you mean, son?"

"Just… I'm not sure."

"Well, I'll give you a bit of time. I can't go making these decisions without the board, though I'm certain they'll be in agreement. Do pray about it. I know I will."

Gabe nodded as the elder moved on to greet someone else. He was so not ready for this, but he also wasn't quite prepared to announce his intentions of leaving Galena Landing for good to the general public, of which the well-meaning elder certainly qualified.

"You okay, man?" Zach's worried face swam into focus.

"Nemesek!" Gabe stretched out his fist, and Zach responded. He had to get a grip. Enough already with people tiptoeing around him as though he were something fragile. That meant no more letting his emotions show. Another reason to shake off the dirt of this small town.

And leave the tweens to the likes of Tyrell Burke? The amount that bothered him was astonishing. After all, he was leaving Sierra Riehl in Burke the Jerk's hands. Acknowledging that stung, too.

Gabe didn't want her, so why did it bug him that Burke did? Why did Gabe see things in her eyes and mannerisms that seemed to invite more from him? But he didn't have more to give. Burke, apparently, did.

He heard Zach's voice. "How did Maddie do?"

Gabe blinked and gave his head a shake. Where had that come from? Why was Zach asking about Maddie?

Jo had appeared out of nowhere and slid her hand into Zach's. "She screamed bloody murder when I handed her to Jean, but she was playing with the toys before I got out of earshot."

Behind Jo stood Sierra, her back to him as she chatted with Noel and Claire. Her hair, curled at the bottom, swung below her shoulder blades, accentuating her narrow waist.

"You're coming for lunch after church, aren't you?" asked Jo.

"Uh, no. I was going to get things settled in the apartment."

She waved a hand. "It's Sunday, dude. Take a break. You're just afraid of guys' day in the kitchen." Jo leaned closer. "But they need all the help they can get."

Zach slung his arm across her shoulders. "I heard that."

"Don't deny it. No one will believe you."

Zach laughed. "Too true. But yeah, Rubachuk, definitely come over. I bet the apartment still reeks of paint anyway."

The other three drifted closer.

"We won't even make you work," Noel put in. "I put a pot roast in the oven before church. Plenty enough to go around."

Gabe forced himself not to check Sierra's expression as he shook his head. "No, that's okay. Really. I need to start out as I mean to carry on."

"Now you're just being stubborn." Jo parked her hand on her hip. "You mean to go on alone, ignoring the fact that you have friends who want to hang out with you? This is your standing invitation for Sunday lunch, and we're not taking no for an answer."

The piano music through the speakers faded away as the worship leader invited everyone to stand.

"Come on, man." Zach bumped Gabe's shoulder. "Lead the way. I'm pretty sure no one dared to sit on our bench."

So now he was somehow not only going to Green Acres for lunch, but sitting with them in church? How long before folks started speculating about him and Sierra? He led the contingent into the pew and glanced back, his gut souring. With Burke the Jerk at the other end of the line, grinning down at Sierra, the answer would be never.

Still, on his first Sunday back at church, it was better to be with friends than alone at the back, burning holes in the back of Burke's head.

oOo

She'd pulled the "not feeling well" card last week. Two Sundays in a row, when she'd been involved in everything else all week, would be too obvious. Besides, how could Sunday dinner be any worse than an entire day of painting Gabe's apartment with Jo and Zach yesterday?

It didn't escape Sierra's notice that no one, not even her, had invited Tyrell for lunch. She hadn't thought of it before, but maybe next time she should just do it and let everyone know where her allegiance really lay.

Good luck with that. She could barely convince herself when she was in Tyrell's presence. When they were apart, no dice. If only Gabe had stayed in Romania another year. Maybe even six months. Then she'd have had time to properly fall in love with

Tyrell and all this awkwardness need never have happened.

Tyrell didn't want kids. Gabe did. She'd seen him on the floor with Maddie.

"Don't get used to it," Zach was saying. "Noel is usually a slave driver. It's pretty rare he'll prep lunch all by himself before church."

Claire plopped down onto a leather love seat. "Let's play Pictionary after lunch, during Maddie's nap? Girls against the guys, of course." She waggled her eyebrows at Sierra and Jo.

That beat all the scenarios where Sierra got paired up with Gabe. Besides, once upon a time, the three best friends' brains had ticked almost as one. "I bet we could smear them."

Jo corralled Madelynn by the toy box. "Don't forget Zach and Gabe have known each other forever. They might do better than you think."

"I doubt it." Claire laughed. "Noel will throw them off. Besides, it's a fun game for a group this size."

Sierra closed her eyes for a second. Way to remind her she was normally a fifth wheel.

"Just trying to make Gabe feel at home, Sierra." Claire lowered her voice. "Unless that makes you uncomfortable."

She could lie through her teeth. "No, why would it?"

Jo snickered and glanced toward the kitchen. "You should have seen them yesterday."

Sierra glowered. "I have no idea what you're talking about."

"Ooh," Claire said with a grin. "That's the way of it, is it?"

"Shush," Sierra hissed. "That's enough out of both of you. No need to act like junior high. Been there. Done that." And senior high. And college. There'd never been a shortage of guys hanging around. Some of them had been morons, but there'd been a few decent ones in the mix. How come none of them had stuck around instead of leaving her lost in a place where making a choice between Tyrell and Gabe seemed like a sensible plan? Or, rather, between Tyrell and nobody, being as Gabe's smile was on and off like sunshine on a mostly stormy day.

Sierra's cell trilled with her younger sister's ring tone. "Excuse me a minute." She slid the phone on and walked into the sunroom, shutting the French door behind her. "Hey, Chelsea. What's up?"

"Happy birthday!"

Sierra shook her head. "It's not my birthday until next week, Chels."

Her sister laughed. "Yeah, I know. But in case I forget. Listen, do you remember Allison Hart? She was at college with you, I think."

Allison. Allison. "Is she the tall girl with long dark hair? I think she transferred into agriculture after the first year. Do I have the right person?"

"That's her. She called me to plan her parents' funeral a couple of months ago. I know, morbid, right? But she said she had no idea how to go about it."

"Just one of the many services you offer?" Sierra teased. "Not that it's funny her parents died. An accident, or something?"

"Their small plane went down in the mountains. Really ugly stuff. If you read the Portland Tribune, you might have seen it a while back."

"No, sorry. I missed it."

"That's okay. Anyway, I decided to help her out. She seemed so alone and needing a friend. I figured I could learn about funerals. Why not? An event planner gets called on for many things."

Chelsea always had a soft spot for the underdog.

"Good for you."

"Anyway, we got to talking about other things. She'd been

teaching organic farming practices through a rural education division but wants to become part of something bigger."

Sierra clutched the phone as excitement buzzed in her veins. "Oh?"

"I told her about what you and Claire and Jo are doing in Idaho. She seemed so wistful, but never figured she'd be able to buy into something like that. And I figured you guys weren't quite ready to hire instructors yet. Am I right?"

Boom. Sierra's gut sank. "No. I wish we could. She sounds ideal. Like the kind of person we want on staff someday." How long was someday going to take to arrive? They'd arranged some weekend workshops on straw bale building, gardening for self-sufficiency, as well as some other things, but nothing had taken off enough to propel them to the next level.

"Well, here's the deal. She just found out her father had a bigger life insurance policy than she thought. A lot bigger."

"I'm not following you, Chels. That's great for her, but why are you telling me this?"

"She and I would like to drive out before the snow flies so you guys can meet her. If you all click, she might like to buy in."

Sierra sank into a wicker chair in the sunroom. The autumn sun warmed the space quite nicely. In fact, she felt rather hot. "Are you serious?"

"Totally."

"Well, um. I don't know what to say. I'll talk to the others. Maybe you can get her to email us her credentials? But so much depends on personality. We've never talked about letting someone buy in whom we haven't known for years."

"Yeah, I get that. She does, too. All we ask is you give her a try. She's got no reason to stay in Portland with only a sister she's not even close to."

"I wish you lived nearby, Chels. I love it here, but I miss you and Jacob and the folks. I really do."

"Maybe if you take on Allison, there will be enough planning to do that I can move up there, too. I don't have the cash to buy in like she does, but I love what you guys are doing. And, I have to say, your weddings and events could use my touch."

Your weddings? It took Sierra a second to put the words in perspective. Not her own multiple nuptials, but the events hosted on the farm. Excitement built as she contemplated the proposed changes. "We could sure use you, girl. I even have a spare room in my new cottage, with pails of pink paint ready to roll on the walls."

"Ooh, that'd be awesome. Love me some pink."

Pink, ruffles, lace, and flowers. That about summed up Chelsea Riehl. Sierra chuckled. "What weekend are you and Allison thinking of coming? I can't wait to see you."

The French door opened behind her.

Sierra turned to see Claire beckoning. "Lunch is ready whenever you are."

"Listen, Chels. I've got to go. Get Allison to send me that email, and we'll go from there. Okay?"

"It's a deal."

Sierra tapped her phone off and followed Claire back into the great room.

"What was all that about?" Jo asked, strapping Maddie into her high chair as the guys set bowls on the table, tantalizing aromas floating in the air.

Gabe glanced her way then chose a chair at the opposite end of the table.

Well, if Allison and Chelsea moved to the farm, Sierra wouldn't need to feel like the odd girl out all the time. It wouldn't be the same as finding true love and a partner for life like her friends had done, but it would redistribute the ratio and make her feel less pressured.

Maybe one of them would capture Gabe's heart. Now, why didn't that make her feel better?

Chapter 14 --

Gabe sat at Doreen's kitchen table for the first time in over three years.

She bustled around the space, putting on a pot of coffee. "I'm so glad you're here. I have cookies in the freezer. Just give me a minute."

"It's okay. I didn't come here to eat."

"But they're your favorite. Homemade chocolate chip."

The recipe he'd taught Bethany when they were kids. His mom had been a from-scratch kind of baker back then, and she'd taught her boys their way around the kitchen whether they wanted to know or not. As soon as Gabe had graduated from high school, his folks had taken early retirement from their teaching careers and gone to Romania as missionaries, with only a few visits to Idaho in twelve years. And Gabe hadn't cooked much of anything since.

Doreen had been a single mom for years, working to support her and Bethany. She hadn't had time for kitchen indulgences.

"Thanks. You didn't need to do that." High honor, really.

"I know. Gabe, whatever happens in the future, you'll always be like a son to me. I hope you know that."

And to think he'd hurt her so badly, trying to protect himself. He stretched his legs under the table, trying to relax, as he watched her get a container out of the fridge freezer. She seemed to be moving fairly freely.

Gabe leaned forward. "How are you feeling these days? Is Sierra still stinging you?"

"Yes, we've done it three times now? Maybe four. It's early to say for sure, but I'm cautiously optimistic. She says we won't be able to do it over the winter, so I guess we'll see how I hold up."

"I'm glad it's helping." He couldn't believe how he'd ripped into Sierra that first day. In his defense, he'd been looking for something to attack. He'd felt so vulnerable when returning to Galena Landing and Nature's Pantry. Lousy excuse, though.

She set a plate of cookies on the table in front of him then sank onto the other chair. "I've been praying you'd come by."

He nodded, unable to meet her gaze. He'd felt the pull, knew he had to come. "I've been talking to God."

"That's good."

The coffee pot gurgled.

Gabe had been so mean to Doreen last time they'd talked away from the store itself. He'd been careful to keep discussions to bookkeeping the few times she'd come by since then.

He took a deep breath. "Look, I'm sorry. I really am. I said some cruel things to you the other day, things I had no right to say even if they'd been true. But they weren't. Can you ever forgive me?"

She reached across the table and covered his hand. Hers was thin with protruding veins. "I forgave you then and there, Gabe."

"But—"

"No buts. You lashed out, and I forgave you. You asked for forgiveness, but it's already done. In the past. Water under the bridge."

"How?" He dared to meet her gaze for a second then withdrew his hand and reached for a cookie.

"God has forgiven me so much more, Gabe. You know that parable Jesus told about the man who owed his master a huge debt? His master called him in and demanded payment. Do you remember what happened?"

Gabe's mind slid to the Bible story. "He begged forgiveness."

"And?"

"His master gave it. But the guy was a jerk." Understanding began to dawn.

"Yes, he was. But typically human. What happened?"

"Instead of being thankful, he found some guy who owed him a small amount and demanded he pay up. Refused to renegotiate but tossed the guy in jail even though he begged for time to repay."

"To whom much has been forgiven, much is required."

The coffeepot bubbled and spat like an enraged cat. Doreen stood and pulled two mugs from the cupboard.

Gabe snapped off a piece of half-frozen cookie and ate it. Why had he demanded his own life should be free of suffering? Why had he not been willing to see the pain of others? The kids in Romania — that was a different situation. Their lives were so very much worse that he could feel pious about helping.

His heart sank. He'd been there for all the wrong reasons. To run. To feel better about himself. He only hoped that even with selfish motivations, he'd been able to make a real difference to some of the orphans.

Dear Lord, I'm sorry. I'm sorry for so much.

The rich aroma of hot coffee tingled his senses when Doreen set a cup in front of him. How long since he'd relished such a simple pleasure? He had a sip.

"It's good to see you settled back into the apartment."

Doreen reseated herself. "It looks nice up there."

"The paint helps. It signals some kind of fresh start, I guess. That's what Jo said."

"I wouldn't have thought of putting those colors together."

Gabe couldn't help the chuckle. "Me, either. But it's growing on me."

"That feature wall reminds me of the verse from Psalm nineteen that says God's word is sweeter than honey in the honeycomb."

Jo had said something about the color. He'd brought a jar of Green Acres honey up to the apartment and held it against the wall. Not a bad match. And it tasted pretty good, too. Something about honey made all his taste buds come alive. Or maybe that was thinking about the beekeeper who'd handled every jar of it.

Doreen leaned forward, cradling her mug in both hands. "May I speak frankly with you, Gabe?"

He eyed her uncertainly.

"I've wondered if... maybe... you might be developing feelings for Sierra."

His heart lurched. That obvious, huh?

"It may be none of my business." She shot him a quick glance then refocused on the coffee. "Like I said before, you'll always be my son, no matter what. You have been for almost two-thirds of your life."

He couldn't help the smile that pulled at the corner of his mouth. "That's true."

"But, anyway. I like Sierra. She's got a heart of gold, and I know she wants to serve the Lord. And, well, you should move forward, Gabe. You should remarry and give me some grandkids to spoil."

Gabe opened his mouth and closed it again.

"I know how much you were anticipating our little ray of

sunshine. I know losing that baby heaped even more grief onto Bethany's death. Remarrying won't replace them, for either of us. I realize that. But it's okay to move into the future. I want you to know that from me. I won't hold you back."

The memory of the little paint fight with Sierra surfaced. "You know she's dating Tyrell Burke."

Doreen's hand swept the words away. "She doesn't love him."

Gabe hoped that was true. "Then why go out with him?"

"I think she needs to be needed. The girls say Sierra always had a boyfriend in school. I'm sure they all expected her to be first to the altar." She shook her head. "It didn't work out that way."

"So you're saying she's seeing Burke because she's desperate?" The thought mixed both derision and hope.

"No…" The word dragged out.

"Then what?"

"She's looking. Tyrell isn't the right man for her. I think she knows."

Gabe pushed the memory of the painting day away. Sierra had all but ignored him the next day at the farm. She didn't owe him a reason, did she? She was obviously torn between him and Burke. Or maybe she was a player, wanting to keep her options open.

"I'm not sure I'm the right guy for her, either. Or that she's right for me."

Doreen raised her eyebrows over her coffee mug.

o0o

Sierra zipped the hood of her bee suit and rubbed the Velcro tight. It was one thing to sting Doreen on purpose and something else entirely to work among the hives without protection.

Tyrell grinned at her from behind the black screen on his hood. "Ready?"

She nodded as she pulled the gloves up to her elbows. The elastic at the bottom of each pant leg covered her boot tops. A bee would have some major work to get inside anywhere but, as she knew from past experience, one occasionally managed.

"Okay, first we have to check the situation inside each hive." Tyrell pried the wooden top from the box then removed the outermost frame. "See here? This one is full of honey. That's good." He dropped it back into place and pried out one from the middle, tilting it toward her. "Honey. Some pollen." He tapped his hive tool against a darker section. "Brood. Looks healthy."

"So we don't need to add feed for the winter?"

He pursed his lips. "I've put a pollen patty and syrup pack in each of mine, but I think yours will do okay. We'll look in each one and make sure they have enough honey to see them through the winter. If not, I brought a box of feeders. I'll sell them to you at cost." He shook his head. "You could've extracted more of the honey than this, you know."

Sierra resisted the urge to do a victory dance as he dropped the lid back into place. "I know. But it doesn't seem fair to steal all their food when they worked so hard for it."

"Doesn't matter. That's why we feed them the syrup. It does the trick, and it's a lot cheaper than honey." He opened the next hive.

Sierra gritted her teeth and shrugged. "It's the model I want to follow." They'd had this conversation earlier in the fall when he'd helped her pull the heavy supers for extraction. "I'd rather allow them their own high-quality feed."

"You're leaving money on the table." He pried a frame out of the super with his hive tool and held it up to observe.

The aroma of sun-warmed honey wasn't as strong as over the summer, but it still drove straight to Sierra's nose. Worker bees crawled all over the honeycomb. More took flight around them, the air humming.

"You've got some mites in this one." He pulled an acid-soaked pad from a plastic bag in his cargo pocket.

"Wait. What are you using?"

"Sierra, it's one thing to indulge you with your chosen feeding method, but you can't let mites get established. They'll kill off the whole hive and go looking for the next one."

Yeah, she knew they were serious. "I still want to know what is in those. Are they natural or chemical?"

Tyrell shook his head. Even behind the black screen, she could sense his annoyance. Well, she was staying firm on this one.

"Who says chemicals aren't natural? They aren't derived from thin air, you know."

"I've just heard horror stories about mites becoming resistant to the increased chemicals. We want the treatment to kill the mites, not make them bigger and stronger." The same argument could be used against antibiotics in humans.

"Yeah, well, these are fine. Really, Sierra. Show a guy some trust here."

"I'll rotate to a different type next year." She'd need to order her own supplies in advance. Act like she was in charge of her hives' health. She could do that.

They treated several more hives for mites then wound a length of hot-water-tank insulation around each, careful to leave the entrances open.

Tyrell surveyed the neat rows of wrapped boxes. "You sure you don't want to send your hives south with mine? Easy greenbacks."

"Nope. There's more to life than money."

Tyrell laughed as though she'd told the best joke ever. "Maybe, but it sure does grease the wheels. Have you ever lived in short supply?"

He had her there. "Not really. My folks have a decent income." At least her mom did as an optometrist with a major eye care clinic in Portland, which allowed Dad the freedom of the open road as a truck driver.

"Stick with me, doll, and you'll have all you could ever want." He gave her a side squeeze and grin. "I might even let you keep a few pet hives on the side to run your own way."

He likely figured he was indulging her. She shrugged away. "These hives are owned by our cooperative, not by me. I'm just the beekeeper."

Tyrell chuckled. "It's not like any of them knows how to take care of them, doll. It's all up to you… and me."

He needed to stop calling her that. "Claire helped with extracting the honey."

"Yeah, she did."

"Zach found an old set of extraction equipment on a farm call the other day, so I guess next year we'll be doing ours at Green Acres."

"Old stuff can be more trouble than it's worth, especially if it's galvanized."

"Noel says the tank can be painted with epoxy and it will be as good as stainless." She hoped he'd done his research.

"Well, it will be good for them to have their own when you join up with me." He winked.

Days like this, Tyrell irritated her more than he stirred up any longing. Good thing she wasn't tied to him for more, but he knew a lot about beekeeping from his dad as well as from the commercial apiary he'd worked on in California for several years. Sierra could be thankful he was willing to mentor her in turn.

"There you go." Tyrell connected the mesh electric fence around the small bee yard and tested the voltage from the solar charger. "That should keep the bears out until they den up for the winter." He looked up the hillside where the fire had been a couple of years before.

"Thanks, Tyrell. I appreciate it."

They walked a short distance from the hives before stripping off their gloves. Sierra unzipped her hood, letting it fall back as she ran her fingers through her hair.

"There's something I wanted to talk to you about," Tyrell said as they approached his truck.

"Oh? What's that?"

He reached for both her hands. "I'm concerned about how much Rubachuk is hanging around here with you. He's not a very stable sort. You shouldn't be encouraging him." He laughed. "Though I'm sure you're not doing so intentionally, doll. You can't help being so gorgeous."

"You mean Gabe? He has a first name." So did she, and it wasn't Doll.

"Yeah, him. Just watch out for him. He doesn't have much business sense." Tyrell cupped her face in both his hands. "He doesn't have the means to take care of a pretty girl like you." He leaned in and kissed her.

If she thought Tyrell Burke was marriage material, she would be kissing him back. There would be lightning flashes or sizzling emotions or something.

All there was were two sets of lips meeting for a brief moment. Sierra was pretty sure Gabe could do better than that if he ever put his mind to it.

Chapter 15 --

*S*urprise!"

Sierra skidded to a stop at the doorway of the big house, and Chelsea walked right into her.

Many voices chimed together. "Happy birthday!"

She spun around and grabbed her sister's arm. "You knew! How did you ever keep it a secret?" More to the point, how had Chelsea convinced her to get the paint off her arms, do her hair, and put on nice clothes before they crossed to the main house for just an ordinary dinner?

Chelsea laughed. "Hey, you're the one who decided to put me to work painting your spare room while I was here. It was easy enough to keep you focused at the back of the duplex."

"Stations, guys." Jo turned from the front window and waved her hands.

"Wha—?" Sierra began as Chelsea grabbed her arm and pulled her around the corner into the great room.

"It's Gabe's birthday the day after yours," whispered Claire. "Thought we'd get the both of you in one go."

Oh, great. She ducked behind the sofa. Finally someone threw her a surprise party like she'd been hoping for years, and she had to share it with Mr. Curmudgeon?

"Shh. He's on the deck." Jo straightened her lacy top and walked over to the door, where she waited for his knock before opening it.

"Surprise!" everyone yelled again. "Happy birthday!"

Everyone but Sierra. She leaned back against the wall, watching him from across the room. Okay, she shouldn't be a petulant child about it. By the look on his face, he'd expected this even less than she had.

The cares slid from his eyes as he smiled around at the group surging toward him. "Wow, thanks. I never expected this."

Zach chuckled. "That's why it's known as a surprise party." He looked around until his gaze caught Sierra's. "Get over here, birthday girl," he hollered. "Have we got a crown for you."

"It's Sierra's birthday tomorrow," Jo said to Gabe as everyone turned.

Sierra managed to get a smile on her face, dredged up some confidence from somewhere deep within, and strolled over to the door. "Happy birthday, Gabe."

When his eyes fixed on hers, she felt the jolt to her soul. And that Old Spice smelled better than it ever had.

"You, too, Sierra."

Before she knew it, her hand was clasped in his, held high while Claire and Jo pinned... something... in their hair.

"Lean over, girl. You're too tall," muttered Jo.

Sierra bent then realized what Jo held in her hand. "Not on your life." She pushed at the cardboard crown.

"Oh, don't be like that." Claire grabbed a few bobby pins and made short work of attaching it to Sierra's hair as cameras flashed. Great. Here came Facebook.

"But we painted it purple and everything." Jo grinned. "We even glued a few fake gems to it." She tilted her head. "You look like royalty."

Yeah, she bet. Sierra cut a quick glance at Gabe, only to realize his cardboard crown was turquoise, just like his apartment walls.

He shrugged and gave her a half-smile.

Her hand was still tucked in his. What must people think? Sierra pulled free and took a step away. She hadn't even taken time to figure out who all was present.

Besides the Green Acres gang and Chelsea and Allison, Sierra counted a bunch of twenty-somethings from the church and community, some pairs and some singles. She did a longer look, waving and smiling at individuals.

She turned and whispered to Jo, "Didn't you invite Tyrell?"

Jo's brows came together. "Um, no. Never even thought of it."

Sierra dragged Jo off to the side. "Never even thought of it? He's my boyfriend!"

"Hey, I'm sorry. It's just that you never bring him around, and it honestly never crossed my mind." Jo's chin poked toward the people noisily surrounding Gabe. "He doesn't hang around with this bunch. I'm sure he has something special planned for your birthday, just the two of you."

Mixed emotions surged through Sierra. She should be furious with Jo. On the one hand, she was. But having Tyrell and Gabe in the same room would not be a good idea. Though, frankly, not as stupid as throwing a joint surprise party.

Tyrell didn't do well not being the center of attention. It was probably for the best. And besides, did he even know it was her birthday tomorrow? She couldn't remember a conversation where they'd shared such things.

Oh man. What was her relationship with Tyrell based on, anyway?

"Look, I'm sorry." Jo patted Sierra's arm. "I didn't mean to ruin your party. We just thought it would be fun to invite a bunch of friends over, have some finger food, and crank the tunes. We told them not to bring gifts. We'll do ours tomorrow when it's really your birthday."

"It's okay." Sierra blinked and gave her head a shake. "Sorry for being a spoil sport." Hip-hop music blasted behind her. She couldn't stay grouchy. "It will be fun."

Jo met her gaze. "Promise?"

"Promise." An evening where Gabe had already snagged her hand once, in front of everyone? Sure it had been for birthday solidarity, but he'd still done it. The guy she'd known before the day they'd painted his apartment would never have done that.

Was it possible Gabe was finding his way back to the land of the living? Did she really want her hand in Tyrell's when — or if — Gabe came calling?

There he stood, a silly turquoise painted cardboard crown tilted on his blond hair, laughing with Noel and Robert, a guy from church. He glanced her way and their eyes caught from across the room. Something softened in his and he quirked a grin just before Zach thumped him on the back.

Time to throw caution to the wind and, along with it, Tyrell. She just needed to give Gabe a bit more time to come around.

o0o

"So you're Gabe." A woman with curly blond hair dropped into the chair beside his.

She looked a little familiar, but he couldn't place her. "Yes. And you are…?"

"Sierra's sister Chelsea. I'm just up for the weekend from Portland with my friend Allison." She pointed out the tall slender woman talking to Jo.

Gabe stifled a grin. Poor Jo, with her neck kinked back. It must be a pain — literally — to be short in a world of tall.

"Allison is thinking of moving here. She helped out with the party today while Sierra and I painted her spare room." Chelsea tilted her head toward Gabe. "I hear we have you to thank for a few buckets of pink paint."

"Yeah, it had been sitting on a shelf for several years. I'm glad someone could make use of it." For the first time, he managed to think of Bethany and the baby without his throat choking up. Progress? He'd take it.

"Anyway, it looks good on the wall. I wish I had something to offer here at Green Acres myself. I'm jealous Allison might get to move here, and I'll be stuck in Portland forever."

Gabe watched Allison, her hands gesturing all over the place as she talked to Jo. "What does she do?" She was a bit skinny for his taste. Was thinking about women's shapes as though it mattered to him a good sign or a bad sign? *I'm sorry, Bethany. I'll always love you, but it's time to live in the present.*

The present.

Sierra joined Jo and Allison. Now there was a woman with a few curves. Not too many, but just the right amount. If they really did clear the floor later for dancing, he might brave up and ask her for one.

Gabe became aware Chelsea was talking. "I'm sorry. What was that again?"

She followed his gaze with a knowing grin. "Allison is certified to teach organic farming. She's looking forward to moving out of the city so she can put it into practice. You know, help people get their hands in the dirt rather than sit in a classroom and take notes."

If Chelsea thought his eye had swung to Allison, so much the better.

She bounced out of her chair. "Do you want to meet her?"

"Uh, sure." An excuse to join the group where Sierra laughed and talked? Looked like she and Allison would smack each other the way both sets of hands moved, but so far, they'd missed. He stood and followed Chelsea over.

"Hey, Allison! I'd like you to meet Gabe." Chelsea turned to him. "Sorry, I missed your last name."

"Rubachuk," he supplied.

"Wow, that's a mouthful." She grinned up at him. "This is my friend Allison Hart. Allison, I was telling Gabe all about your work. He owns a health food store here in town."

"Hi, Gabe." Allison turned to him and wrapped his proffered hand in both of hers. Long nails, painted black. Yeah, she hadn't had those in dirt any time recently.

"Nice to meet you, Allison. Chelsea says you're thinking of moving here?"

"Yes, it's just the opportunity I've been looking for. I'll be spending all day Monday in meetings with Jo, Claire, and Sierra to see how it might work out."

"Sounds great." Gabe's gaze slid to Sierra and that crazy crown, now sitting at a rakish angle. "Here, let me fix that." He tugged out the bobby pin that lay askew, straightened the crown, and repinned it, her hair silky under his fingers.

He shouldn't stare into her eyes for too long, not with so many interested in their exchange. He grinned. "Allison must have knocked into it. I notice she talks with her hands."

Sierra's gaze narrowed for a second, so quickly Gabe might've imagined it. Then she looked at Allison as though through a new lens. "Yes, she does. Thanks for adjusting it."

"No problem." Was it possible Sierra thought him interested in Allison? Man, he'd never had to play this game. He and

Bethany had been an item since their early teens. There'd never been anyone else in his life. What was a guy supposed to do in a situation like this?

"Anyone want to dance?" Zach called as the music changed. "We've cleared the furniture."

Allison grabbed Gabe's hand. "Come on! Let's give it a whirl."

On the other hand, giving Sierra a taste of her own medicine didn't sound so bad. Much as he'd tried to accept Burke in her life, the guy rankled him. He couldn't help thinking she shouldn't look at him the way she did if she were serious about Burke. Maybe she wanted Gabe to be jealous?

He took Allison in his arms and tried the quick, unfamiliar steps she obviously knew well.

Maybe two could play Sierra's game.

o0o

Way to make her feel like an outsider at her own party. Not that she was the only one on the sidelines, but that didn't reduce the pang of watching Gabe grin at Allison, so near his own height and skinny to boot, as they shimmied across the floor.

Okay, Allison shimmied. Gabe looked unsteady on his feet. Was it because he wasn't a dancer or because he had the every-guy's-dream-come-true woman in his arms?

And why did she care? Because no matter how hard she'd tried, she couldn't help but think of Gabriel Rubachuk that way. She'd always liked him, even when he was married to Bethany. It'd been a good kind of friendship back then. Nothing inappropriate.

But now. What was he thinking as he looked deep into Allison's eyes? A reason to stay in Galena Landing? All this time

Sierra'd thought he was leaving the area, and the only way he'd stay was if he fell in love with her and changed his mind.

The idea that another woman might be the one to keep him here had never crossed her thoughts until this moment, and it was most definitely unwelcome.

The song came to an end. Gabe and Allison parted, though Allison hung onto his hand for a few seconds longer than necessary.

Gabe's gaze swung straight for Sierra, and her heart lifted. Maybe it wasn't game over after all. He raised his eyebrows and held out his hand.

Everyone else in the room faded away. His eyes never wavered from hers as she walked straight into his arms.

o0o

Too bad this wasn't a slow dance. Gabe could've held Sierra close for a long time if the music allowed. Instead, they wove in and out among the other dancers, pulling close, then separating.

Not fully separating. He kept her hand in his, kept his eyes on hers as though they were the only ones in the room. Of course, they weren't. In fact, people would probably be talking about them tomorrow, if they hadn't started already.

As of this moment, he didn't care. In two days he'd be thirty. He wasn't a teen who needed to worry about what the other kids thought. He was a man.

The next step flung her into his arms for a brief moment, his nostrils catching the light floral scent she favored, and his hand tightened at her waist, pulling her closer.

No resistance. "Having fun?" he murmured.

She nodded against his shirt.

He'd rest his cheek on her head if it weren't for that silly crown. Maybe it was a good thing, as public as this was.

The next move pushed them apart, with Sierra twirling under his raised hand, the skirts of her lilac dress swishing around her knees. Once again their eyes caught and held.

Maybe being thirty wouldn't be so bad. Maybe he still had something to look forward to.

Chapter 16 --

*G*abe glanced around the foyer at Galena Gospel Church. No Sierra.

He'd been awake most of the night trying to make sense of his feelings. Was he being disloyal to Bethany? Did he really want to pursue Sierra Riehl? Could he handle declaring his intentions — whatever those were — and having her choose Burke over him?

She wouldn't have nestled into his arms so comfortably at the party last night if she wished he were Burke, would she? Nah. Burke was a big guy. He was muscular, confident, and good-looking. All the things Gabe was not. Even Sierra's imagination couldn't pretend that well.

But Burke hadn't been at the party. Why not, Gabe had no idea. Sierra hadn't been consulted about the guest list, as it had been a surprise for both of them. No doubt the Green Acres crew was rooting for Gabe over Tyrell. The thought brought heat to his cheeks. Like it was any of their business.

If only she were here, so he could analyze what he saw on her face. Would she welcome him with a bright smile, or would she turn for the other guy? Gabe had seen the powerful black truck in the parking lot. Burke was here. Somewhere.

The double doors opened and Zach and Jo entered, followed by Claire, Noel, and Allison. The doors shut. Where were Sierra and her sister?

Gabe started forward, but a clamp on his shoulder prevented it. He swiveled.

"Rubachuk, Graysen tells me you used to teach the junior high Sunday school class. You can have it back, dude." Burke rolled his eyes. "We were never that young and stupid, were we?"

Gabe opened his mouth and shut it again, his brain scrambling for words. "Pretty sure we were, Burke. The arrogance of youth didn't start with this generation." His memories of the other guy as a teenager made these church kids look like a row of pious angels. With harps.

Burke roared as though Gabe'd spouted the best joke ever. "Well, I'll drop the curriculum off to you this week. You're living in that dinky apartment above the health food store?"

"I never agreed to take the class back on, Burke. It's certainly something I'll need to pray about. Not sure about my long-term plans." Gabe became aware of someone at his right elbow. Zach must've heard that last bit.

"What's to pray about? Teach the kids! They need somebody to set them on the straight and narrow. I don't have the time to dump into doing this like you do."

Gabe's ire surged, but he fought it back. "Burke, I assume someone asked you to teach the class, or else you volunteered. Either way, you agreed to do it, and I'm not obligated to take it off your hands on a whim." Though the kids sure deserved better than a reluctant and arrogant teacher.

"What else are you going to do? That store can't take up much time. You could study your lesson at work." The big guy winked. "Your boss won't fire you."

Gabe tried for a casual chuckle. "You'd be surprised. Nature's

Pantry is a happening place. Look, thanks for the offer. I'll get back to you on it. Okay?"

"But—"

Gabe turned his back on the guy and focused on his buddy. "Nemesek!"

Zach bumped his fist then glanced back and forth between him and Burke. "Didn't mean to interrupt."

"No problem. The conversation was over." Gabe took a few steps away, relieved to find Zach beside him, not Tyrell. He lowered his voice. "Why does he think he's so special?"

Zach chuckled quietly. "An ego the size of Alaska. Not sure what Sierra sees in him."

Gabe shot him a hard look.

"Saw in him, I mean. Past tense. I don't think she's looking his way anymore. At least not after last night." Zach's elbow caught Gabe's ribs, and he tossed a knowing grin. "What's your opinion?"

Gabe glanced around to make sure no one seemed interested in their conversation. "Not sure." He took a deep breath. "Where is she, anyway?"

"She and her sister popped over to the house earlier and said they were heading out for a girl day."

He needed to see her. Needed to know if he'd imagined the party. Those blue eyes and pink lips had haunted him all night while the questions whirled. "Uh, that's great. I guess."

"Want my advice?" Zach's voice was so low Gabe barely heard him.

"Probably not."

"I'll ignore that. You and Sierra. You'd make a good pair, so go after her. Don't let Burke get in the way."

"That'll be her choice, won't it?"

Zach chuckled and dropped a wink. "Sounds like you've been

giving it some thought."

A flush crept up Gabe's cheeks. "Maybe."

"Well, make a move. Don't wait around on the sidelines to see where the chips fall."

Big words from a guy who'd taken his own sweet time pursuing Jo, even after he'd figured out she was worth the effort. Didn't make the advice bad, though.

o0o

The relaxing day with her sister evaporated when Sierra saw Gabe's car parked at Green Acres Sunday late afternoon. For someone who worried about never getting married, why was she so panicked now that two men vied for her attention?

Chelsea pulled in beside Gabe's car and cut the engine to her own. "Well, there you go," she said quietly. "Why else would he come around today, if he wasn't falling in love with you?"

Sierra poked her jaw in the direction of the lawn beside the deck. "To hang out with Zach, obviously. They've been best friends since they were little kids. Or maybe he's here because of Allison."

Gabe nudged a soccer ball toward Madelynn with a gentle kick, his back to the car. Maddie ran at the ball, tripped over it, and fell into a pile of golden leaves. Gabe scooped her up in the air and twirled her.

Even through the closed car window, Sierra could hear the toddler shriek in glee.

Gabe caught sight of them, flipped Maddie over his shoulder, and strode toward Sierra's side of the car.

"I don't understand you," Chelsea mumbled, opening the driver's side door.

Sierra didn't understand herself. After three years of building up a relationship with Gabe in her mind, why was she shying away now that he seemed interested?

Gabe pulled the car door open then swept a bow, which tumbled Maddie into his hands. He made a production of nearly dropping her. "Hey Maddie-girl. Say hi to your Auntie Sierra."

Madelynn's curls tickled the ground as she gazed at Sierra from upside down. "Auntie Sera!" She struggled for freedom.

Gabe flipped her right side up and released her.

"Hi, baby girl." Sierra caught the little cannonball and swept her up. After a quick, tight hug, she set the child down again. Maddie didn't like to be contained for long.

Gabe glanced over at Chelsea before settling his gaze back on Sierra. "We missed you today."

That's what she was afraid of. The royal we. The Green Acres Farm we. What about the Gabe in there?

She mustered up a smile. "Chelsea's only around for a few days. I never get to spend enough time with her."

He grinned. "It's great you love your sister that much. So many siblings don't get along."

"We've always been close, even though she's nearly three years younger than I am." Clinging to her sister at the moment seemed like a barricade blocking things she didn't want to think about. Like how mushy her gut had been all yesterday evening. The queasiness hadn't left, even with all the hiking they'd done that day.

"Where'd you guys go? There's not that much shopping open on a Sunday in the grand metropolis of Galena Landing."

"Ha! I reserve my shopping for trips to Coeur d'Alene, thanks anyway. Or at least Wynnton. Actually, Chelsea recently took up geocaching, so she was showing me the ropes. We found a couple of caches near the highway up at the pass."

"That's cool."

Gabe sounded like he knew what it was. He shoved both hands deep into his pockets as she fell into step beside him on the way to the house.

So much for retreating to her duplex and hiding out until he left. Besides, Chelsea-the-traitor had already joined the others on the deck, bending to pat Domino, who lay at Jo's feet. The steps were plenty wide enough for her and Gabe to walk up side-by-side... and far apart.

Jo glanced from one to the other, her eyebrows high.

Sierra lifted a shoulder and let it drop. How was she supposed to know? Man, she ought to have been a lot kinder to her roommates when they were dating.

Not that she was in a relationship with anyone.

Unless she counted Tyrell. And she ought to. Her gaze slipped to Gabe, who leaned against the railing talking to Noel. As though feeling her eyes on him, he glanced her way with a little smile.

Her gut flipped. Tyrell didn't have that effect on her, if she were really being honest.

"I love that jacket of Maddie's," Chelsea said to Jo.

Jo laughed. "It was a gift from your sister."

Sierra stepped closer to join them. Finally a safe subject. "I told you about all our mouse trouble when we first moved here, didn't I?"

"In the old trailer." Claire shuddered. "Brazen beasts."

"I just had to buy that jacket when I saw it." Sierra chuckled. "What could be more apropos for Jo and Zach's kid than a gray hoodie with mouse ears and a mouse face screen-printed across the front?"

"Those mice brought us together." Jo looked over at Zach. She shook her head and leaned down to rub Domino's ears. "Almost tore us apart, too. Good thing this dog survived the poison I accidentally left where he could get into it."

"Oh, no," Allison said. "That's horrible."

"It was a near thing." Jo focused on Sierra. "The road to true love is often paved with obstacles that seem insurmountable at the time."

She was preaching to the choir.

"Well, I don't plan on ever getting married." Allison gathered her long hair over her shoulder. "Watching the guys my sister has messed around with makes me doubt there are many men worth the effort. I'm so thankful that my parents left me well set up, so I don't actually need to get married to survive."

Sierra sank onto an Adirondack chair and tucked her knees up under her chin. This crew lived on the huge deck, even into winter, but the November chill already seeped into her bones. She turned to Allison. "What was your parents' relationship like?"

"All about appearances. They both had affairs on more than one occasion, and they both knew it. The only thing that mattered was keeping the big house, the fancy cars, the whole image of wealth and gentility." She shrugged. "Honesty played very little role in their lives."

"Wow, our parents modeled a really great marriage for us kids." Chelsea pointed to Sierra then back to herself. "I can't imagine not wanting what they've got. Right, sis?"

Death by slow torture. That's what her sister deserved for putting her on the spot like this.

"My parents separated when I was in high school." Claire, sitting next to Allison, nudged the swing into motion. "And Noel's dad walked out when his kids were really young. There's a lot of mess out there."

"Yet you guys figured it was worth it, I guess." Allison turned sideways in the swing, facing Claire. "Divorce stats are so high. I just don't see adding to them, especially when so many of the couples that stay married seem miserable."

"You need to hang around with different people," Jo said. "Even if your parents were poor role models, two people committed to each other and to God can make this gig work. And not just in the survivor sense, but in the true-love-is-worth-it sense."

"Twuuuue wuuuuuv…" Chelsea dragged out the line from *The Princess Bride*.

Jo laughed, locking her gaze on Sierra. "Yeah, well, true love is a pretty cool thing. It's worth every sacrifice."

Sending telepathic messages again? Sierra looked away, hugging her knees against her chest. From where Jo sat, it probably all looked good.

"Hey, Maddie's freezing out here. Let's move this party inside." Zach scooped his daughter up into his arms, but she immediately squirmed to get down. He laughed and released her as he opened the door. She ran inside ahead of him then tripped and fell to the concrete floor, wailing until Zach picked her up again.

The kid didn't know how good she had it. So many people willing to show her love, to play with her, tickle her, read to her. She careened from one to the other, protesting loudly when anyone tried to contain her for even a second. She caused most of her own harm.

Truth hit Sierra below the belt. Was she holding back like Maddie? Were her reasons any better?

The gang left the deck for the house, chattering and laughing as they shifted venues. Probably no one but Domino noticed she was still outside. He nuzzled her hand.

Sierra dropped her forehead to her knees for a moment. "Lord, help me," she breathed. *I want to trust You for the best, but it's so hard.*

"You okay?" Gabe's voice, so soft. So gentle.

So unexpected. Sierra jerked to look at him.

He crouched beside the arm of her chair, eyes filled with… what? "Sierra, I-I've been trying to get my nerve together to talk to you."

She bit her lip but couldn't break eye contact. "Oh?" The word came out just above a squeak.

"I've been thinking about last night. And, um, some of the things we've talked about over the past few weeks." Making crazy eights, he ran a finger over the back of her hand where she clung to her knees.

Warmth spread from that spot throughout her body like she'd been zapped by a lightning bolt.

"I don't know why we're always arguing, but I prefer it when we're not. Like dancing with you last night."

"I liked that, too," she managed to get out.

"I think I've been afraid to get close to you."

"Oh?" He didn't look afraid now, what she could see of his face in the November dusk. It filled her vision.

"Can I take you out tomorrow? Let's do our birthday dinner in style, just you and me. I'd like to know where this might take us."

All the reasons she'd been holding back evaporated like mist in the sunlight. None of them could be that serious, not the way his eyes darkened as his hands came up to her shoulders. She should probably move. Become more embraceable than the ball she'd curled into on the cold chair. She lowered her feet to the planks, and Gabe shifted aside as he reached for her hands.

A second later he'd pulled her to her feet and wrapped both arms around her. The dances of the evening before supplied unheard music as she slipped her arms around his waist and settled into his embrace.

"Sierra? Will you go out with me? You haven't answered."

"I'd love to." She tipped her head to meet his gaze. "Thanks."

He quirked a grin. "No thanks required. I'm not doing you a favor. I wouldn't blame you if you wanted to run."

"No running."

His hands tightened on her back as his gaze slid to her lips and back to her eyes. "Sierra, I—"

She held her breath. Was he going to kiss her? Then she'd know for sure if he was the right guy. Wouldn't she? Maybe it was silly offering her future to a man because he was a good kisser.

He leaned closer. She closed her eyes and filled her senses with Old Spice, willing him to close the few inches between their mouths.

The outside light flared and the door creaked open. "Oops. Sorry for interrupting." Chelsea's voice. And she didn't sound all that apologetic. "Just needed to grab my camera from the duplex. Don't mind me. I'm not even here." She clattered down the steps.

The moment was broken. Gabe kissed the top of Sierra's head and released her. "I don't want to make things awkward for you with this gang."

"It's okay." For an instant she considered grabbing his head and pulling him back to finish what he'd almost started, but no. Tomorrow they were going on a real date, away from Green Acres. Far enough away that no one, not even her sister, would interrupt them.

Tomorrow she'd be kissed.

Chapter 17

*I*t didn't seem right driving all the way to Wynnton for a date, especially not with Chelsea and Allison back at the farm. Jo and Claire would be great hostesses, of course. And Sierra had spent the entire day showing both of them around, detailing the history, hopes, and dreams of Green Acres.

But, well, it felt awkward sitting in the passenger seat of Gabe's old car. The guy didn't have much to say, and she didn't know what conversations were safe to start and which should be avoided. Like Bethany. Should they talk about her? At some point they'd have to, wouldn't they?

In all her fairy tale dreams growing up, getting involved with a widower and the extra baggage he came with — there, she'd admitted it to herself — hadn't been one of them. Didn't every girl dream of being number one? The one and only forever love?

"Having second thoughts?" Gabe asked softly.

"Of course not." She didn't dare look at him. "Where are you taking me?"

"I've heard good things about the Bluebell. Though, as far as I know, they don't get their beef from a ranch in Oregon."

Okay, that helped. She gave him a quick grin. "Even Oregon

has a finite amount of cattle."

"And then there's a high school basketball game we can go to, if you want."

High school sports? In a town she hadn't grown up in?

"I guess I should have asked you first if you liked basketball." He sounded apologetic.

"We can give it a try." But seriously?

"It's not like there's a whole lot to do in Wynnton on a Monday night in November."

She managed a chuckle. "We could try the mall."

Gabe grinned. "Just like a girl. More into clothes than sports. I should've known."

He sounded dejected, like he was sure he'd blown things permanently. But didn't most guys just want to watch sports on TV with junk food and drinks at hand? She could probably handle that. Minus the junk food, of course. It wasn't like she didn't have hobbies of her own.

"My brother loves soccer," she said at last. "We used to go to a lot of his games."

"Tell me about your family. Chelsea seems great, but I didn't even know you had a brother. Any other siblings?"

Finally a safe topic. "No, that's it. I'm the oldest, Chelsea turned twenty-five this summer, and Jacob is just graduating from college with a degree in architecture."

"And your parents? From what Chelsea said, you had a good home."

She nodded. "Very much so. Dad was gone a lot, driving truck..." Her voice faded as she remembered what Gabe knew about that.

"Does he — does he still drive up here?"

"Gabe." She twisted in her seat as much as the seatbelt would allow so she could see his face. "Dad was so sorry about what happened. It's haunted him ever since."

Gabe's hands tightened on the wheel. His jaw clenched as he focused on the road, and he closed his eyes for a second.

Any longer and she'd need to reach for the wheel.

Then he glanced her way with a rueful look. "I know. It took me a long time to forgive him, even though the police and rescue personnel said it wasn't his fault. She'd been working long hours and, when that deer jumped out in front of her car, she swerved. It's not your dad's fault he and his big truck were exactly in her way."

"But he was. They were."

He took a deep breath and let it out slowly. "Yes, he was. Even if he hadn't been, she might've hit the deer. Might've rolled the car. Who knows? For some reason — some unknown reason — God called her home that night."

"I can't imagine the pain you've been through."

He glanced her way, compassion glinting in his damp eyes. "I'm glad you can't. I wouldn't wish it on anyone."

Was that supposed to make it easier to take? It wasn't working. "I know I said some rough things to you when you first got back home. Pushing you to move forward. I didn't expect..." She gestured between herself and him. "I didn't mean you had to ask me out." Well, she'd kind of hoped, but he didn't need to know.

Gabe chuckled. "I know. And that's not why. Honestly."

She leaned back. "Just a random twist of fate?"

"I'd never say that. I've come to believe God's got it. Whatever happens, whatever good things and things that don't seem so good at the time, He's got it. It's been a tough journey, and I don't always remember. But underneath everything, I do believe it."

Sierra ran her hands down the thighs of her jeans. These were discussions they had to have, if they were ever to have a relationship. But was that really where they were headed? He'd almost kissed her last night... also possibly the night before.

"What about you, Sierra? You know so much about me. Tell me about a rough spot in your life."

She took a deep breath. "I've got nothing compared to you."

"Then don't compare to me. I doubt everything in your life has gone according to your initial plan." He glanced her way. "Has it?"

"Not exactly. But there's not much to complain about. I had loving parents, siblings I didn't fight with too often. Got decent grades. Although we didn't live in Irvington, we had a big house, several cars... no shortage of money."

"What did you want to do with your life that you haven't accomplished?"

She gave a sharp laugh. "Get married and have a family, I guess."

The words hung in the air. *Way to circle back to his pain, girl.* Still, it was true, and wasn't that what this talk was all about? Getting to know each other?

"I guess that's a normal desire." He was trying so hard to keep emotion out of his voice.

"Yeah. Other than Allison, apparently."

"She just doesn't know what she's missing."

Was it Gabe Allison was missing? But no. He'd invited Sierra on a date while Allison was in the house. The dances those two had shared Saturday evening hadn't meant anything. The ones between her and Gabe, though... maybe those did.

"I always wanted a houseful of kids," Gabe mused.

She'd guessed as much, watching him with Maddie. Strange that he was so much the opposite of Tyrell, who thought only of himself. Not completely fair. Tyrell thought about her, too.

Didn't he? "How come?"

"Who knows?" He grinned at her. "My brother is so much older than I am, I might as well have been an only child. But I liked kids even then. When the extended family got together, the little cousins followed me around like I was some sort of hero, while my brother listened in on adult conversations. I began to realize I had a lot of influence on those kids and I could use it for good or bad."

"That's cool. I don't have many cousins."

"So I was the strange guy that helped out with kids' clubs at church when I was a teen. Maybe some of it was Bethany. She loved kids, too. By default, I loved everything she did."

Gabe's hand captured hers where it rested on her jeans. "But I have other dreams, too, now. Dreams of my own."

The warmth of his grasp went a long way to making her believe him. Other dreams. New dreams. She could do that. She turned her hand to embrace his and caught his gaze for a few seconds before he looked back to the highway.

Yes, these dreams had possibilities.

oOo

Gabe inhaled the sharp tang of snow in the air. "Winter's coming." With any luck it would hold off until later. Or maybe tomorrow.

"I love snow. We didn't get much of it in Portland."

He grabbed her hand and took off at a run across the mall parking lot. If they were going to do this shopping thing, he'd be a good sport. Besides, he didn't have a birthday present for her yet. What would be appropriate?

They blasted through the automatic doors, out of the nippy wind. A jewelry shop loomed in front of them. Whoa. Definitely not appropriate, unless he got her a necklace or something. He kept a firm grip on her hand, liking the feel of its warmth clasped in his. *Take it slow, Rubachuk.* He steered her across the corridor past a hair salon.

They ambled down the concourse hand in hand, stopping to buy poppies from a veteran amid workers setting up a wintry North Pole display.

"It's easy to forget how little the kids in countries like Romania have." Gabe pointed out a toy store window display. "Christmas celebrations are big, but not as focused on... on junk."

"Here kids expect everything from computers to unicorns." Sierra laughed, shaking her head. "And that's just in their stockings."

Whew. He should've known she'd see through the commercialism.

"It's nice to give kids a treat," she went on. "But people buy random stuff they know will quickly break, just to make up a certain number of gifts or dollars spent. It's stupid, really."

He swung her hand. "I agree. Children need their parents' love more than anything. Time spent together, doing stuff. Working together. Games and challenges to learn to think."

"Those things don't fill up our landfills. Taking care of the Earth starts with reducing waste before worrying about reusing or recycling."

"Right. No junk for our kids. Only well-made stuff that will last and..." Oh, man. What was he saying?

Sierra pulled her hand from his and wrapped both arms around her middle. She always did that when she was uncomfortable, he'd noticed.

"I'm sorry. I spoke without thinking. I don't want to rush you."

She bit her lip... those pink lips... and glanced at him through long lashes.

Shoppers scurried past them carrying bags from all the stores in the mall. Hammers clanged as workers continued to assemble the North Pole. Sierra's scent still filled his senses. He stepped closer. "I'm sorry, Sierra. You know I want a family. We don't know each other all that well yet, but I guess I said what I'm thinking. We might be a good fit for each other, but it's too early to know for sure."

She stayed still.

Gabe shoved his hands in his pockets. "Can we just focus, for now, on getting to know each other? I agree with you about reducing waste. Not much goes to waste at the orphanage." Man, he knew he was begging. He'd really said the wrong stuff there. Just blurted it out as though she were Bethany.

She wasn't. Beth was forever gone, and he was left trying to make sense of another woman's emotions and thoughts. "Truce? I want to buy you a birthday present." He held out his hand. "Not some junk you'll throw away, but something special." He swallowed hard. "Like you."

Sierra accepted his hand as they walked toward the anchor store at the end of the concourse. "I don't really need anything, but thanks."

What would a woman like her appreciate? He swung her hand, and her fingernails caught his eye. "Maybe a bottle of nail polish?"

She shot him a glance and started to laugh.

Whew. "Maybe pink?"

She rolled her eyes.

"I know. Turquoise."

"That's best left to walls."

"Um. Black seems a little somber for you."

"Rather. That's Allison's style, not mine."

"Haven't seen many orange nails lately. Well, except for trick-or-treaters coming into the store at Halloween."

"No orange."

"You know what they ought to make? Yellow. What could be more sunshiny than yellow nails?"

"You're crazy."

But she was talking to him. Laughing with him. "Yeah, maybe. You're not the first person to mention it."

Sierra dragged him into the home goods section of the department store. "I know what I'm getting you for your birthday."

"Hey wait, no fair turning the table."

"Uh-uh. I know exactly what you need." She tugged him down an aisle overflowing with sheets and duvets.

He tried to dig in his heels, but she didn't seem to notice.

"I saw that ratty set on your bed when we painted." Sierra came to a stop so suddenly he nearly bowled her over.

That only made it easier to catch her in his arms. And keep holding her, being as she didn't fight him. "Uh, yeah. It's old." It had been Bethany's long before they'd been married. They'd never gotten around to replacing it.

Sierra pointed at a set showing a Navajo pattern of several shades of gold with turquoise designs. "There. That's perfect for your place."

It did look pretty nice, but the price tag — wow, he couldn't let her spend that much on him. "Is that stuff made of real gold?"

She laughed. "Don't worry about the price. It's 600-thread count. Worth every penny."

Considering he'd nearly put his foot through a threadbare part of the bottom sheet the other night, she was certainly correct that he needed something new. But could he accept a gift this expensive — and personal — from her? It was way more personal than the jewelry he'd avoided at the onset.

He tightened his grip, her hair tickling his jaw as he burrowed his face into her floral scent. Maybe he could look at it like an investment. An investment into their future.

Gabe turned her to face him. "Sierra? Are you sure?" He knew he was asking something more than a set of sheets could answer.

Those blue eyes with a hint of turquoise gazed directly back at him as she contemplated the question. She'd caught the levels of it, he was certain. She nodded as she slid her arms around him, her hands inside his open jacket.

Gabe caught his breath as she nestled close. He barely dared to rock the moment, but he needed to know. Needed to kiss her and feel her response. His hands roamed her back before one tangled in her hair and moved up until he cupped her face.

"Sierra…" He bent and met her lips with his, hungry for something the Bluebell Restaurant would not ever be able to fill. Hungry for this woman. For Sierra.

Chapter 18 --

*H*ey, Sierra! Time to wake up, sleepyhead."

Sierra tried to blink, but the gunk in her eyes prevented it. She groaned but didn't roll over. Her gut... oh, man. She wanted to stay curled up in a ball forever. Or possibly die. That might be the better option. Except then when could Gabe kiss her again?

"You okay?" Chelsea's voice was closer now, and the bed sank where she settled on the edge.

The slight shift caught Sierra off guard and she gasped from the additional pain.

"Hey, sis." Chelsea's hand rested on her shoulder. "You're scaring me here."

Not half as much as she was scaring herself. Hadn't she just endured the world's worst menstrual cycle ever a week or two ago? Wasn't it a bit soon to have another? She needed to get to the bathroom pronto.

If she lived that long.

"I'll be right out, Chels." Sierra shifted her legs to prepare for standing. This was going to be brutal. "Mind fixing me a cup of tea? And maybe fill the hot water bottle from the hall closet." Good thing this hadn't hit yesterday when she was out with Gabe.

"Ah, it's that time, is it? You'll survive. We always do." The mattress shifted as Chelsea stood. "See you in the kitchen."

If her sister hadn't been in the duplex, Sierra might've crawled to the bathroom, but that would evoke more reaction than she was willing to handle. She got herself as upright as she could manage and shuffled across the hall.

A few minutes later, bathrobe tucked securely around her, Sierra made her way into the living room and into the comfy chair her parents had bought her for a housewarming gift. She tucked her legs up under her, accepted the hot water bottle from her sister, and wedged it against her belly. "Thanks."

"Want honey in your tea?"

Sierra mustered a grin. "Of course. Don't you know everything should be sweetened with honey?"

Chelsea poured boiling water into the teapot. "You always had a sweet tooth."

Impossible to deny. "Ever since we saw *Mary Poppins*, remember? Just a spoonful of sugar…"

"Speaking of medicine going down, what do you usually take for pain?" Chelsea peered into the cupboard. "You look like you need some help there."

Black cohosh had done little to alleviate the cramps last time. "I don't keep anything like that in the house."

Chelsea turned, hands on her hips. "You don't believe in pain killers? Look, I know you're all into that natural medicine thing, but when it's not working, it's not working. I've got some ibuprofen along, and you are going to take it."

She grabbed a purse the size of a briefcase from a hook behind the kitchen door, opened it, and began to dig around in its vast but crowded interior. After a moment, she pulled a bottle out. "There. I'll get you a glass of water, and you will swallow these."

"Ibuprofen?" It seemed Sierra should argue more, but she couldn't summon the energy or clarity from anywhere.

"Yes." Chelsea set a glass on the side table, opened the bottle, and poured three little brown pills into Sierra's hand. "Swallow."

When did her little sister get so bossy? Sierra obeyed. Just once wouldn't kill her. Or so she hoped.

A moment later Chelsea returned with two cups of tea. After setting one down for Sierra, she curled up on the end of the old leather love seat Sierra had nabbed when they'd bought new furniture for the straw bale house.

Chelsea raised the teacup to her lips. "When did this start happening?"

"What?"

"Oh, don't play dumb with me. These heavy-duty cramps. You always had them worse than I did, but this seems like an extra notch."

"They've gotten worse in the last few months." Maybe longer? Sierra frowned, trying to remember.

"Have you seen a doctor?"

Sierra glared at her over the teacup.

Chelsea rolled her eyes. "Honestly, the medical profession is no more a bunch of whackos than you are. A doctor just might know something that could help. Don't you want answers?"

She'd barely had time to surf her naturopathy sites looking for those elusive answers. Or maybe it was that she didn't like the direction her research was taking her. The shrug she managed seemed petulant, even to her.

"That's it. Does this one-horse town have a medical clinic? I'm getting you in to see somebody." Chelsea pulled out her smart phone.

"There's a clinic," Sierra ground out. How could she go, though? She'd prided herself in doing things her way, keeping as close to nature as possible. Those little brown pills were hardened chemical sludge. Maybe she'd forgive them if they worked. It wasn't their fault they weren't real.

"Landing Walk-In?" Chelsea scrolled down her phone. "Looks like there are three doctors. With a walk-in I doubt you have a choice of whom to see."

It would probably be Sharp, who hadn't lived up to his name in decades, or that snooty Wilburn who thought she was a flake.

"Once you've finished your tea, get dressed, and I'll drive you down there. They open at ten."

Sierra should mind more than she did, but it was nice someone finally cared enough about her to take charge.

Maybe.

oOo

Gabe whistled as he wiped down shelves in Nature's Pantry, rotating stock so everything looked fresh. All he could think of was Sierra's hand in his, her body pressed against his... and her lips responding to his kisses. It seemed her floral perfume had followed him home to the turquoise and gold apartment that seemed much warmer than it had before. More like a home.

He'd tossed those 600-count sheets into the washer before he came down to the store this morning. If they felt half as good on his skin as Sierra claimed, he'd be in heaven tonight when he slid between them. Maybe one day he'd share his bed with Sierra. Now that would be heaven indeed.

The bell above the door jangled as someone came in.

Gabe rounded the end of the shelves to greet his first customer of the day.

Tyrell Burke filled the doorway in black jeans and a leather jacket. He tipped his black cowboy hat at Gabe then glanced around. "It sure does look busy to me, Rubachuk."

"Hey, Burke." He'd let that remark slide. "What can I do for you today?"

Burke lifted a manila envelope and dropped it on the counter beside him. "Just brought you the stuff for Sunday school. Glad to give it up to you."

The guy made it nearly impossible for Gabe to hold his tongue. "Might as well take it right back with you, man. I never said I'd do it."

The bigger man shrugged. "Well, who else?"

"You? You're the one who agreed."

Burke shook his head. "Temporary fill-in is all. I've been away a lot, and that doesn't make old man Graysen very happy, I can tell you. But I'm a busy guy, and when the weather's right for bees, I need to be out there working them."

The window behind the counter framed a gray sky that hadn't bothered to lighten up much for daytime. Unrelenting rain blasted by all but horizontally. Gabe might not know a lot about bees, but this didn't look like a day for outside work. Besides, hadn't Sierra said something about getting the hives ready for winter last week?

Sierra. When Burke had tried to pin this on Gabe before, he'd been unsure of his long-term plans. Now he was dreaming of making a home in the apartment upstairs with Sierra. She had picked him over Burke. He could afford to be magnanimous to the loser.

Besides, he liked the kids. They deserved better than Burke.

Gabe jutted his chin toward the manila envelope. "What're you guys studying these days?"

"Bunch of stuff from Paul's letters. Themes more than stories."

"Like?"

Burke shrugged. "Forgiveness. Seeking God's will. That sort of thing."

At least he'd read the material. Probably.

"Look, Rubachuk. It's not that I don't believe this stuff, but it's kind of new to me. Found out about Jesus a couple of years ago. I'm really not knowledgeable enough to answer these kids' questions."

Gabe's heart softened a little. "They ask some doozies all right."

"I don't know where they get them from."

"You must've had a lot of questions, too. That's what sent you searching for God, right?"

Burke's eyebrows pulled together. "Yeah. I guess."

"Who answered yours?"

"Preacher dude in California. Pastor Ron at the church here, somewhat."

"But you had someone."

"Your point?"

"My point is that these questions the kids ask, they're real. And if you don't know the answers, go searching. Ask Pastor Ron, or maybe the other guy via email. Or Ed Graysen. You'll learn a lot and be able to help the kids."

Burke stared at him for a long moment before slowly shaking his head. "I get what you're saying, Rubachuk, but it's not working. Some of these kids were practically born in that church building. They haven't missed a Sunday in their entire lives. They're way ahead of me."

Gabe had so not seen this conversation coming. "You can teach them to be real. Where the rubber meets the road. It's a genuine problem for kids who've been sheltered. Some of them are totally unprepared to make their own decisions."

"Nice try, Rubachuk. I'm not convinced. I still need you to

take it over again. Think of it as a favor I did you for a while."

"Uh." But he did have a heart for those tweens, and he wasn't really thinking of leaving town anymore, right? Not with things looking good with Sierra and his business solidly in the black? "Well, okay, Burke. One condition."

Those bushy brows rode up into the cowboy hat's brim. "What's that?"

"I'll need a substitute occasionally myself. Can I call on you?"

"Yeah. Maybe." Burke stared hard at him. "There might be a condition to that, too."

"Oh?"

"I've seen how you look at my girl, Rubachuk. Time to forget those thoughts. She's mine. I can offer her way more than you ever will." He glanced around the old store again, shook his head, and reached for the door handle behind him.

A threat? Or what? A multitude of reactions raced through Gabe, hot and cold. But it didn't matter what Burke said. It was Sierra who'd made the decision, and she'd chosen Gabe. He couldn't imagine her kissing Burke the way she'd kissed him. Nor did he want to.

o0o

Sierra shook her head and stalked straight across the waiting room and out the clinic doors, Chelsea scrambling to catch up.

"I was right in the middle of a Reader's Digest joke. Couldn't you have waited three seconds?"

Sierra bit the inside of her lip. "No."

"Hey, I was kidding. Wait up."

Why did she have Chelsea along when all she wanted was to process the information Dr. Wilburn had given her after that horrid pelvic exam? Yeah, she knew. Because she'd never have come if her sister hadn't pretty much forced her. But now. Oh man. But now...

She jerked the passenger door of Chelsea's car open and slid inside. If she'd had waves of pain before, this was a tsunami. A lot of it was in her gut, but much was in her heart, surging up her throat, pouring out her eyes.

Chelsea climbed in on the other side. "Talk to me. What'd he say?"

"He's sending me for an ultrasound to be sure."

"Okay." Chelsea sounded less certain. "What does he suspect? Sierra, you haven't been sleeping with that beekeeper guy, have you?"

"No!" The word sprang from Sierra's lips. She stared at her sister. "How can you even think that?"

"Well, aren't ultrasounds for keeping an eye on a developing baby?"

"Not only. They can see lots of other issues in the abdominal area with them, too."

"Like..."

"Like endometriosis. For instance."

"What's that?"

"It's when cells normally found inside the uterus are outside, so instead of being flushed away, they build up and cause issues."

"What kind of problems?"

Sierra shrugged. "He said the scar tissue on my uterus was among the worst he's seen."

"So he's seen this before?"

"Oh yeah. I'm not unusual. Just at the bad end of a nasty spectrum."

"So if he's sure that's what it is, what will the ultrasound prove?" Chelsea shot her a worried glance. "Does he think it's cancer?"

Sierra took a deep shaky breath and let it out as slowly as she could. "I'm not sure." But it was the first place her brain had slid, too. "Auntie Pam."

"Mom's sister?"

"Yeah. She had a hysterectomy because of uterine cancer, but it had gotten elsewhere, too."

"She died."

Sierra nodded. "About a year later. I was twelve."

"So I was nine. No wonder I don't remember it as much. Well, we can beat this thing, sis. We just need to trust God and do our part. Stay positive." She quirked a grin. "Trust the doctors."

"Yeah." Sierra found no enthusiasm to pour into the word.

"I hate returning to Portland with things the way they are, but it can't be helped. I'll come back as soon as I can, but at least you have really good friends here. We'll let everyone know so they can pray and support you."

"No." Some things were meant to stay private.

"What do you mean, no? I thought you guys told each other everything. It's one of the things I envy most about your set-up here. How close you all are."

"I need time to process this. Don't tell." Gabe. Oh, Gabe. He wanted a family so badly.

A puzzled frown crossed Chelsea's face. "Well, they all know we went to the clinic. They'll ask."

"Promise me you won't tell." Sierra choked on the words.

Chelsea put the car in gear. "For now."

Chapter 19

Sierra sat at the head of the long farmhouse table on Wednesday morning with Jo and Claire on one side and Allison and Chelsea on the other. It still seemed strange not to be at Nature's Pantry most days, especially now that most of the garden produce had been brought in and processed for winter. What was she going to do with all her free time once the sauerkraut crocks were full? She'd always meant to take up quilting...

"I really like what I've seen around here the past few days." Allison set her iPad on its Bluetooth keyboard. "You've been here for three and a half years now, and you've accomplished a lot."

"Our initial hopes were to do more." Claire took a sip of hot mint tea. "But life has a way of taking over."

"We weren't expecting Zach and Noel," Jo put in with a grin.

Thanks for the reminder Sierra was the only single one. Maybe that would change, and maybe it wouldn't. It might be nice having Allison around, just in case.

"They did bring in some different dimensions," Claire agreed. "Zach came with more land to work, which is both a pro and a con. And Noel's idea of guiding fishing and hunting tours in the mountains has changed things, too."

"As well as helping with the farm's bottom line," said Jo.

Claire nodded. "So we're in a more solid financial situation than we were, but still having trouble forging ahead to the next stage of the dream."

"But you did run some weekend workshops this past summer?" Allison's fingers poised over the miniscule keyboard.

"Three," said Sierra. "Plus the longer one that got the duplex mostly erected. We hosted several weddings and one family reunion. It seems there's always plenty to do without taking the big plunge."

Chelsea laughed. "Sounds like you guys need me as much as you need Allison. I live to organize." She batted her eyelashes at Sierra.

Sierra smirked. "She does, at that. However, she's actually good at it."

Jo and Claire exchanged a glance before Jo leaned forward. "Allison, what do you see going forward? What can you offer?"

The young woman tucked a strand of long black hair behind her ear and tapped her screen. "I'd like to offer several four-week modules. Principles of organic farming and gardening, managing the soil, selecting and seeding crops, food preservation. That kind of thing." She glanced up. "We can train people to run market gardens. I bet we can even hook up with the woofer program."

"The what?" Claire looked as perplexed as Sierra felt.

"Woofer. It stands for worldwide opportunities on organic farms. It's a volunteer program where people interested in learning the lifestyle can work on a farm in exchange for room and board."

"Wow, I didn't know anything like that existed," said Jo. "Is it new?"

"Not new, but gaining ground." Allison grinned. "No pun intended. I woofed one winter on an Argentinean farm and spent another summer in California. It was a great experience, and I see no reason we couldn't implement it here. We have a lot to offer. Or I should say, you do…"

Her voice trailed away.

Sierra thought for a moment. "We can offer other things, too. The workshop on straw bale building was well received. We actually had more interest than we could capitalize on. And people are interested in solar power and unconventional water systems." She shot a glance at her sister. "We didn't make the best of the opportunity. Didn't stay focused. Part of that was my fault, I guess. I got so busy working with Doreen at Nature's Pantry, I kind of ignored work at the farm. Though it did help pay the bills."

"Here's the thing. I can invest this much money into something." Allison looked at each of them in turn and named a generous figure. "Would I be able to build a home and classroom here? In keeping with the over-all ideology of the place, of course."

"Our zoning does allow it," Claire said slowly, glancing from Jo to Sierra.

They were obviously going to need a discussion between the three of them, as well as Zach and Noel, but the potential seemed clear.

"You laid out good possibilities in the email," Sierra said. "Very in line with our original plans."

"There's a level area beside the driveway right beside Thompson Road," Jo put in. "We run the chickens there now, but that's only because we can't be bothered to mow it."

"We meant to get a goat," said Claire.

Jo rolled her eyes. "The chicken coop is easily moved,

remember? We put that on skids so we could drag it with the tractor."

"That's a good spot," Sierra ventured. "And, um, if we go forward with this, I've got a spare room you can stay in until your place goes up."

"Hey, don't give away my pink room," protested Chelsea. "I want in on this, too."

"It'd be nice to have someone administer the whole thing," Jo agreed, eyeing Chelsea. "I'm best at just digging in and doing the work. Being polite to idiots has never been my strong suit."

Chelsea chuckled. "Most of them aren't idiots. They just need a gentle touch."

"Yeah, well. That's not me. Ask Maddie, even."

The little girl was scooting a toy bike around the great room, contented for once, if not exactly quiet. Maybe it helped that Domino was outside. She had a hard time leaving the dog alone.

"This seems as good a time to mention it as any." Jo leaned forward, her fingers twined around her mug of chamomile tea. "We're expecting again."

Sierra didn't miss the glance between Jo and Claire. She hated feeling left out. Were Claire and Noel trying? She didn't even know.

The rampant cells on her uterus clenched. Lots of women with endometriosis had trouble conceiving. Some never could. Which would be her kind of luck, especially with the strong desire Gabe had for a family.

On the other hand, Tyrell didn't. And he was a nice guy, too. She could be really happy with him. Without kids. Couldn't she?

"Congratulations!" The word came from all the other mouths.

Claire reached over and hugged Jo.

Sierra managed a smile. Hopefully it looked genuine. "That's great!" If only she could be truly happy for her friends. She wanted to be.

oOo

Gabe thumbed through his mail as he walked from the post office to the store. A few bills, a couple of cards — birthday cards? — and a large manila envelope. He stared at the yellow paper for a moment, his eyes finally registering the mark in the top left corner.

North Idaho College.

He'd almost forgotten requesting a catalog. He'd gone online since then and perused their offerings, but hadn't immediately thought to go that route on the heels of three years in Eastern Europe.

Gabe stuck his key in the lock of Nature's Pantry before realizing the door was unlocked and the lights were on.

His heart leaped. Sierra? He hadn't seen her since Monday evening when he'd kissed her goodnight.

"Hi, Gabe."

Doreen, not Sierra. He managed a smile for the woman who'd meant so much to him for years. "Good morning, Doreen. I didn't expect you in today."

She shrugged. "The bee stings have helped my rheumatoid arthritis so much I got bored sitting at home. I thought I'd come down and see what I could do to help."

"I hate to take advan—"

"Oh, you're not. Find me a task. Please."

Deep in thought, Gabe set his mail down on the counter. What could he get Doreen to do? She might be feeling better, but that didn't mean she was up for moving shelving or restocking the shelves with yesterday's freight delivery. Hmm.

171

"What's this?" Doreen fingered the college envelope. "Is there something you forgot to tell me?"

He pushed it aside. "Not really." Not anymore.

Doreen raised her eyebrows. "They don't send these out to every mailbox. How did you get on their mailing list? Are you thinking of going back to school?"

She wasn't going to let it go.

"I wasn't sure what I was planning to do when I first got back. Thought I'd analyze some options." He'd actually moved on from the local college system and looked in greater depth at larger universities in far-off cities. Places with no ties to memories of Bethany. Good thing a catalog for Oregon State or UCLA hadn't shown up under Doreen's watchful eye.

She crossed her arms. "Gabe, I thought we were passed this point. You know I can't take care of the store. Why didn't you even talk to me about this?"

Gabe's jaw tightened. "I was looking into options, I said. This has nothing to do with you."

"Nothing to do with me? When I've run this store for you for three years? How can you say that?"

"Look, Doreen. I've got no plans to go back to school, okay? I wasn't running on the assumption I could ask you to stay here forever."

"Who else? Sierra has her own... wait a minute. I get it."

Gabe looked at her hopefully. He didn't really want to talk about his relationship with Sierra yet. Not with Doreen of all people. This town contained far too many people interested in his future.

"You are going to sell Nature's Pantry." She pressed her hand to her chest. "I can't believe it. Oh, Gabe."

That was last month. Not now. "Doreen, honestly. I ordered this ages ago, on a whim. There's no need to read so much into it.

I'm not going anywhere."

"Really? But all you and Sierra seem to do is fight."

Okay, he could not keep the grin from his face anymore. "Not quite all."

Doreen studied his face while her hand slid back and forth on the envelope. "What do you mean?"

"I'm not selling the store, Doreen. I'm not going away to school. I'm not hiring a manager, temporarily or permanently. I might do a distance education course or two, but that's it. Okay?" He rounded the counter and dropped the packet into the recycling bin.

Her gaze went from his face to the envelope and back again. "About Sierra…"

Gabe could see the wheels turning. He held his smile in place as he raised his eyebrows. "Yes?"

"She's the key to all this, isn't she?"

She was the key to everything in his future. Even though Doreen had nudged him in Sierra's direction like everyone else they knew, he wasn't ready to tell her the details of their evening.

It was still too early to be certain, but the direction looked positive. At least he was pretty sure he wouldn't need that college information. He got the smirk off his face. "You want a project? I've been too busy to properly organize that office under the stairs. We just stacked everything in boxes and hauled them down, but I bet some of the musty paperwork can go into storage. Old brochures from companies we don't deal with anymore can be recycled. We could probably make better use of the filing cabinet."

It took a minute before she nodded. "If you lift the boxes, I can sort."

Gabe let out a breath he hadn't realized he was holding. "Lifting I can do."

Chapter 20 --

A lanky boy skidded to a stop in the threshold of the junior youth Sunday school room, bracing a hand on each side of the doorframe. "You're not Mr. Burke at all."

Gabe grinned at the kid. "Great observation. I'm Mr. Rubachuk. Guess I'm your teacher for a while."

The boy moved into the room, a dozen or so other tweens pouring in behind him as though he'd been the plug holding them back. "What happened to Mr. Burke?"

"This time…"

Gabe couldn't spot who'd added those words. "Hey now. I taught this class for five years. Just because I've been out of town for the last three is no reason to assume I'm not able to handle you guys."

The boy raised his eyebrows.

Gabe mimicked him. "Your name is?"

"He's Mark Kestrel," another kid chimed in.

Gabe nodded his thanks to the spokesman. "Kestrel. Any relation to Dustin?"

"Yeah, he's my brother."

If this boy was half as much trouble as his older brother had been, Gabe would have his hands full. "Dustin was in my class for a couple of years. We both survived. Might even have learned something."

"You or him?"

Gabe laughed. The kid was quick with his tongue. "Both of us." He took a good look at each pre-teen as they settled into chairs around the long table. What he'd liked best about teaching this age group had been the questions that made him dig. Rote didn't work. They needed reality and depth. Gabe breathed a prayer. Was he ready to guide them?

Did he have a choice?

He slid his Bible and the curriculum to one side. "Let's get to know one another today. What have you been studying with, ah, Mr. Burke?"

Mark leaned back in his chair. "Not much."

Gabe kept a grin in place. "Then it's time we got digging into God's word, don't you think?"

The kid shrugged. "Why bother? We're only here because our parents make us come."

"Not all of us." A girl across the table made a face at Mark before beaming at Gabe.

Gabe wasn't sure if she was here to study the Bible or ogle a male teacher. He'd make no bets yet. "Your name?"

"Samantha. Or just Sam."

He asked the others for names. When introductions had been made, he asked, "What do you think about Jesus?"

"He's God."

"He died to save us."

"He's ancient history."

Who'd said that? It hadn't sounded like Mark. "So you don't think Jesus is relevant?"

"How could He be? He died thousands of years ago."

"And rose again," Sam piped up.

The boy — Austin? — shrugged. "So they say. But what good is it now? I mean, I don't see Him here, walking around and doing miracles like He did in the Bible."

Once Gabe had begged God for an old-fashioned sign of His attention — Bethany raised from the dead. "You're right. We don't see many flashy miracles these days." He took a deep breath. "Which doesn't mean Jesus isn't real."

"Even if He is, it doesn't much matter." Mark slouched down in his seat and motioned around the table. "We're young. We're not going to die for a long time, so why worry about stuff like God now?"

"Actually, nobody knows how long they have." Gabe silently begged God for words. "My wife was only twenty-six when she died in a car crash."

The kids stared at him. Even Sam had no more than a flicker of sympathy. Did they have hearts of stone?

"I guess she wasn't that old," Sam said at last.

"It's pretty old," another girl said.

Oh, for the perspective of pre-teens.

"It may seem ancient to you," Gabe said, "but it isn't really. Who is the youngest person you know who died?"

The youth glanced at each other.

Was this groupthink? Could they not form opinions without confirmation?

"My neighbor drowned in the creek when she was two," Sam said.

"Jenkins got killed driving drunk."

"That was stupid." Mark gave his head a quick shake.

"My cousin had cancer. She was eight."

Gabe leaned his elbows on the table. "So not only old people die." That these kids thought of Bethany as old still rankled. She'd been in her prime.

Mark shook his head. "Mostly old people though. Like my great-grandmother. I think she's ninety or a hundred. She's gonna die soon, Dad said."

"The thing is, we don't know for sure, do we?" Gabe tried to meet the kids' eyes, one by one. "And eternity lasts a whole lot longer than even your great-grandmother. Whether you live to be nine or ninety—"

"We've already got nine beat," Austin interrupted with a laugh.

"So you do. But the point is, whether you live to be nine or ninety, it's barely a drop in the bucket of time. Eternity is so huge that it's worth thinking about, even when it feels a long way off."

They didn't look convinced.

"But you know, forever isn't the only reason to get to know Jesus and live for Him. It's worth it every single day."

The most response was a few raised eyebrows. Gabe had his work cut out for him.

oOo

"Hey, Sierra." Gabe smiled at her in the foyer after church.

She'd made sure she was wedged in the middle of a pew between Jo and Claire, the guys flanking them. She hadn't been ready to talk to Gabe. He'd texted her a couple of times this week, and she'd claimed busyness with Chelsea and Allison's visit. Of course, they'd been gone a few days now.

And she still wasn't ready to talk to Gabe but, at some point, she'd have to come up with words.

She managed a smile for him, her heart breaking. How was she going to live without him, just when it seemed like things were coming together for them as a couple? But he kept talking about having kids as though it were a given. Maybe it was. For other people.

"Rubachuk." Zach's fist came past Sierra's shoulder and

collided with Gabe's.

"Nemesek."

"Lunch?"

Gabe's eyes caught Sierra's for a second. "Sure, why not?"

"Why not, indeed." Zach chuckled as he turned away.

Gabe lowered his voice. "I've missed you this week."

She studied his shoes. Brown, in need of polishing. "Yeah, me too."

"Have a good visit with your sister?"

She nodded.

"That's good." He hesitated for a second. "Everything all right? You seem kind of quiet."

She blinked moisture from her eyes and looked up at him. Blue eyes with little wrinkle lines around them met hers. "I'm okay." It was a bit of a lie, probably, but they were too new to talk about this kind of thing. Maybe she could keep their relationship in limbo until after the ultrasound, after she knew for sure what she was up against. It might prove to be nothing.

It wasn't nothing. She knew it. Those painful periods had a reason for their increasing frequency.

"Hey, Rubachuk!" This time the voice was Noel's. "How are you at chopping vegetables? If you're up for it, you can come for lunch."

Claire swatted Noel's arm and winked at Sierra. "He can come anyway."

Noel grinned. "He who doesn't work shouldn't eat," he quoted, tugging Claire against his side.

Claire rolled her eyes.

Sierra backed up a step. She wanted what they had. She wanted it with Gabe.

"I can do the chopping thing." But Gabe's eyes didn't go to Noel. They seemed pinned on her.

He'd chop her from his life when he found out. Even now, he suspected something. He was reading her better than Jo or Claire. If that wasn't scary, nothing was. Her girlfriends were too wrapped up in their own lives to notice anything wrong in Sierra's. Yeah, she'd made no announcements, but shouldn't they have been more in tune with her moods?

Sierra turned and headed for the big double doors before Gabe decided to ask her if she'd ride out to the farm with him. In front of everyone.

oOo

All through lunch Gabe kept an eye on Sierra. How could no one else notice how quiet she was? Probably Jo and Claire knew what the problem was and just didn't want to make an issue of it in front of him. But if he felt like an outsider, what about Sierra? Was the pulling back on purpose or not?

The group lingered over coffee in the great room after Sunday lunch — all except Jo, who always drank chamomile or mint tea from the farm's own herb patches.

Gabe couldn't spend all his time worrying about Sierra. He dropped on the floor beside Maddie's toy box and took out a little car. He set it on the top level of the play garage and gave it a nudge.

Maddie squealed as it zipped down the ramp. She scampered after the runaway and brought it back to him. "Again!"

Jo chuckled. "She likes you, Gabe."

"Why wouldn't she?" asked Zach.

Gabe grinned. Being around this little monkey wasn't as painful as it had been a few weeks before. She was her own person, not a whisper of the babe Bethany had carried. He let the car go down the ramp again, to Maddie's glee.

Chapter 21 --

S ierra's phone beeped with an incoming text. Chelsea. *You up? Call me.*

What if Sierra didn't want to? What if the things that were happening to her were not something to share? What could Chelsea do about the technician's clinical observations, anyway?

The phone beeped again. *Got yr test results yet?*

Her sister wasn't going to let up.

Sierra hauled herself out of bed and shrugged into her bathrobe. It was midmorning. She should shower. Do something useful. Lying in the semi-darkness staring at the ceiling and thinking melancholy thoughts was not good for her.

Melancholy thoughts about Auntie Pam.

Her phone beeped. *Sis? U there?*

Sierra jabbed her finger on the button. *Later.*

Why? What happened? Call me.

First she'd spent an evening and night moping that no one cared. Jo and Claire hadn't caught on that something was wrong. Yeah, she could tell them, but she wanted them to notice.

Now she was frustrated because her sister wouldn't leave her alone.

Perverse hormonal emotions. Sierra took a deep breath and plodded into the bathroom. She scrubbed her face and brushed her teeth and hair before making her way to the kitchenette and flipping on the coffee pot she'd set up the previous evening, as always.

She stared, mesmerized, as the coffee began to drip and hiss. The fragrance began to tantalize her senses. Maybe life was worth living, after all.

Not that she had much choice. Auntie Pam hadn't. Sure, she'd fought the cancer, but to no avail.

The cell phone rang. Chelsea.

Sierra let it go three rings before she answered. "Hey."

"Hey yourself. Talk to me. You had your ultrasound yesterday?"

"Yeah."

Silence for a few seconds. "Are you going to make me drag every sentence out of you?"

It was a temptation. A childish one. "The endometriosis is pretty bad. The doctor scheduled a biopsy for next week."

"Oh, no."

Sierra could echo the dread in Chelsea's voice. "Probably surgery after that."

"Doctors can do a lot in surgery these days. Keep your chin up."

Chelsea's brain had gone straight for a bad-result biopsy, too. Interesting.

"Yes, they can. In this case, it would probably mean a hysterectomy."

"A hys — oh, no." Her sister's voice deflated. "I wanted to be an aunt some day."

Like it was all about Chelsea. "There's still Jacob." Sierra hadn't seen her little brother in nearly a year, but surely he was turning into a responsible human being that a female would someday find attractive.

Chelsea's sniff gave her opinion.

"Besides, it's not for sure yet. The results might come back negative." Why put an effort into convincing her sister when she didn't believe it herself? "I'm trying not to borrow trouble."

"That's good. I'll keep praying for you. And good news! I got Thanksgiving off, so I'll be coming up to see you with Mom and Dad and Jakey."

Sierra tried to put some enthusiasm in her voice. "Awesome!" Only two weeks away. The biopsy would be over. Maybe she'd know whether she had good news or bad before she had to pretend to give thanks for the bad.

Her conscience smote her.

People had far worse things happen to them than uterine cancer. Or even than not being able to have kids.

"What day is the biopsy?"

"Thursday."

Chelsea took in a sharp breath. "This week?"

"Yeah."

"Wow, they're not wasting any time, are they?"

The coffee pot finally beeped that it was done brewing. Sierra poured a cup. She'd need the whole pot today. "I noticed that, too."

"I'd be far more likely to just book off work and head for Idaho if you didn't have your girlfriends there to talk to."

About them. How did a gal bring up this kind of conversation? Better to wait until she knew what she was dealing with.

"Sierra?"

"What? No need to worry about me. I'll be fine." She stirred a little honey into her mug.

"You have talked to Claire and Jo already, haven't you? You promised me you would."

"Um, not yet? Things have been kind of busy."

"Sierra Ann Riehl! That's no excuse. You know it. I know it."

"Don't get all bossy on me, little sister."

"You can give that up, too. We're both adults, and you know you're being ridiculous about this. It's what friends are for."

Sierra tasted her coffee and added a dollop more honey.

"Do I need to call Jo myself? I will, you know."

Pretty sure her sister didn't have Jo's number, but there were ways to find it. Zach was the only veterinarian in town, for instance. A call to his office would get instant attention. "I'll tell them."

"When?"

Sierra sighed. "Soon."

"Define soon."

"In the next day or two." Or possibly three. Or after the biopsy results.

Chelsea was quiet for a few seconds. "Promise?"

"Sure. Soon. I just need the right time." Like when Zach and Noel weren't around, but both Jo and Claire were. And they weren't busy with other things.

"I'll be checking up on you. What time will you be home Thursday?"

"I don't know. The biopsy is scheduled for ten in Wynnton."

"Kay. Text me when you're done, or I'll call in the evening."

Sierra sighed. "Fine."

The call ended. Why couldn't she be happier that someone cared enough to push past the barrier?

She'd erected it. She knew it, even if her best friends hadn't seemed to notice. Gabe had, but he didn't know what to do about it. She didn't, either. All she wanted was for the hurt to go away.

The physical pain, the emotional pain... and the pain she was causing Gabe.

She had to wait until she knew the answers so she could lay them out in front of him. It wasn't fair to make him walk through this uncertainty with her. Really, they barely knew each other. He'd run away for sure.

He would anyway. At least, if she didn't push him away first.

o0o

The door of Nature's Pantry jangled.

Gabe looked up to see two of the rowdies from his Sunday school class. Two twelve-year-olds interested in health food? Possible, but unlikely. "Hi, guys. What's up?"

Austin elbowed Mark. "Just checking out your place, man."

"Oh, yeah? It's a health food store." He grinned at the boys. "Not what I expected to do with my life when I was your age."

Mark looked around, nodding coolly. "I bet. I doubt we want anything from here. You got any junk food?"

"Healthy junk food."

The kid quirked his eyebrows. "That doesn't make sense."

"There are chips flavored with real ingredients rather than chemicals. Candy bars and pop without weird additives." Gabe paused, unable to resist pouring as much excitement into his next words as he could muster. "Even rice cakes!"

The two guys glanced at each other, clearly not getting the joke.

"Rice cakes?" asked Mark at last. "I don't even know what those are."

Gabe chuckled. "Here, I'll show you." He led the way to the aisle where the packages were arrayed in all their flavors.

Mark picked up a tube and turned it over. "Weird. Like

puffed rice cereal stuck together with… what?"

"Different things. This one has cheese. That one has a kind of caramel sauce." But it was a good question. What did hold together the plain ones?

The boy's eyes brightened. "I like sweet stuff. Do they taste good?"

"Not really."

"Uh…" Mark handed the package to Gabe. "Then why do you sell them?"

"Because some other people think so, and they come here to buy them." Gabe could only hope he hadn't just placed an order for plain when Mrs. Bowerchuk died. No one else bought the things.

"Weird." Mark's gaze took in nearby products. "I haven't seen this kind of macaroni before. Who's Cora?"

"It's an organic brand. It doesn't have colored dyes in it, or a bunch of chemicals. The packet of cheese included really is cheese."

Mark continued to question him about a bunch of other products in that aisle, like he was interested. But what twelve-year-old boy actually cared about this kind of stuff? Gabe sure hadn't, and there had been no reason in Sunday school to think Mark was anything but a mouthier-than-average tween who sought the other kids' attention. He'd kept glancing around the group after every comment to judge reactions.

Wait a minute. Where was Austin?

Gabe knew he shouldn't have started playing CDs in the store. Even on low volume, they muffled other sounds.

He set the box back on the shelf and strode to the end of the aisle then looked both ways.

Austin stood in front of the candy, hands in his slightly bulging pockets. The boy seemed startled to see him.

"Whatcha got in your pockets, Austin?"

The kid's eyes narrowed. "My hands."

"Take them out."

The hands slowly withdrew. A bulge was still visible. "Turn your pockets inside out, please."

"I don't have to." The boy started for the exit.

Gabe stepped in front of the door and leaned against it, crossing his arms. "If there isn't anything in them I'd have a problem with, then why the reluctance?"

"What happened to innocent until proven guilty?"

Gabe grinned. "I haven't accused you of anything. I simply would like to see the insides of your pockets." It was hard to maintain his casual pose. In five years running the store, he'd never once suspected a shoplifter. Except for the time he'd found some empty packaging, but whoever had done that had been long gone before Gabe noticed anything amiss.

Mark came into view at the end of the aisle where they'd been talking.

Accomplices? Almost certainly. "How about you, Mark? Are you willing to show me what's inside your pockets?"

The two boys exchanged a glance. Mark patted the front of his jeans. They were smooth.

So Mark's job had been simply to keep Gabe occupied. Figured. Now what was he supposed to do? He hadn't caught the kid secreting anything, but evidence was stacked against him. Still, did Gabe know for certain the boy's pockets had been flat when he came in? If he didn't have anything to hide, though, Austin would probably be willing to show him the contents.

God? I could use an idea here.

Gabe pushed off the door and strolled toward the healthy junk food aisle. "You know what? I'd like to give you guys a gift. Why don't you come over here and pick out a few snacks you'd like to try? Say, maybe five or even ten dollars' worth for each of you?"

Mark's mouth dropped open.

Gabe gestured to Austin. "Come here. It's on me."

The kid glanced at the door. He might make a run for it yet.

"Oh, don't leave before you get your gift, Austin. Unless you're happy with what's in your pockets now. I wasn't sure if you'd prefer to try some of the chips, or another bulkier item." Gabe winked at Mark. "Or maybe rice cakes."

"R-rice cakes?" Austin glanced from Gabe to Mark.

Mark's eyebrows pulled together. "I don't get why you're doing this."

"Doing what?"

"You obviously suspect him of stealing."

"Is it that easy to tell?" Suddenly Gabe was enjoying himself. "But hey, I suspect *you* of collusion."

"Of what?"

"Keeping me occupied so I wouldn't notice. I bet you guys agreed to share whatever he nabbed."

Austin's chin came up. "Who says I took anything?"

Gabe grinned. "Nobody. I'm offering you a gift. You can keep what's in your pockets, or you can trade it in for something different if you like. Totally up to you."

"So you're not gonna stop me leaving this store?"

Gabe swept a bow toward the exit. "Go for it."

Austin took a couple of steps then bolted. A moment later the door jangled behind him. Hopefully he didn't have much more than the ten bucks' worth Gabe had offered him.

"I don't get you." Mark looked at him, head angled to one side.

"Why not?"

"You coulda had him there."

"Maybe."

The boy shook his head.

"Look, will Austin think twice about coming in here and pinching things again?"

"Yeah, I guess so."

"Will he think twice about doing it elsewhere?" Because it was unlikely Gabe had been selected as the one and only target.

"Maybe."

"How about you?"

Mark straightened. "What about me?"

"Were you in on the scheme, or really interested in rice cakes?"

"Uh…"

"You can take a few packages home if you want. Or pick something else. What's your fancy?"

"My what?"

"Your fancy. What do you want for a snack?"

"Are you really going to give me something?"

Gabe shrugged. "Just said I would, didn't I?"

"But why?"

"Look, there are lots of things more important in life than a few dollars' worth of food. One of them is relationships. I'm gonna be you guys' Sunday school teacher for a while, and I want you to know you can trust me. I care about what happens to you. Coming down hard might bring some justice, but I don't think it would help you or Austin trust me, would it?"

"Weird."

"Maybe. Now, want some rice cakes?"

Chapter 22

A soft rap sounded against Sierra's door. For a second she waited for Jo or Claire to simply stroll in, but no one did. Who could it be, then? Doreen? But they'd done the bee venom therapy the day before. Doreen hadn't reacted badly to any of them since the first.

Sierra set her mug of mocha on the side table next to her open Bible and walked to the door. Thankfully she'd bothered to get showered and dressed today. Unlike yesterday.

She pulled the door open.

Gabe stood outside, his hand poised to knock again.

Man, he looked good. Relaxed. Jeans and a fleece jacket to counteract the crisp November air, which smelled of snow.

"Sierra? You okay?" Gabe stepped nearer, and Old Spice pushed the snow scent away.

"Gabe!"

He enfolded her in his arms.

For a second, she relaxed against him, breathing him in, feeling safe. Wanted. Loved.

She pushed away gently. "Come on in." What else could she say? She'd fill her eyes and heart with him now, while she could.

Before she had to walk away and hurt him. She'd hurt him either way. There was no easy path through this one.

Gabe followed her into her little home and glanced around.

Hadn't he been in here before? Probably not. She smiled up at him. Later was soon enough for the pain. "Welcome to my humble abode." She swept her hand to indicate the space.

He looked around, smiling and nodding.

What did he see?

Concrete floors, etched in a deep golden brown, peeked between several turquoise throw rugs, and the pine cupboard in her kitchenette had been stained a lighter version. The walls were honey except for the purple feature wall across from the door.

Her cheeks warmed. Would he notice the common palette with his own apartment?

He slid his arm around her and winked. "Hmm, I wonder why this place seems so homey to me. Maybe it's the colors?"

"Maybe. But Jo picked yours, and they're a few shades different." She stepped out of his embrace. "Would you like some coffee? Or I could fix you a cup of mocha. I was just sitting down with mine." She indicated her steaming mug.

"Mocha? Sounds good. I didn't even know you could make that at home."

Sierra reached in the cupboard for a mug. When she turned around, he was right there, like he belonged. Too close. "Excuse me," she whispered as she stepped around him to the coffee pot.

He peered over her shoulder, his presence warming her back while chilling her heart. How could she let this man go? But it wouldn't be her choice. It would be his, as soon as he knew. Was today the day to talk about it? No. She needed the rest of her facts. In a few days. Soon.

"It's not exactly like a coffee shop, but I like to control the quality of my ingredients. Plus, I can't afford five bucks every day." Or double, if she wished to indulge in a second cup. "To say nothing of driving to town for it."

"Right." He watched her spoon in honey and add a pinch of salt and a dash of cinnamon. Then she put in a rounded teaspoon of cocoa.

"I recognize that can!"

"Yep, I buy my organic fair trade cocoa at Nature's Pantry." She stirred then opened her under-counter fridge to add a good slosh of cream. She handed the mug to Gabe. "Give that a try. I can add more honey if you like."

Gabe inhaled the fragrance. "Smells great." He took a sip. "That's really good. I'd probably go with a bit less sweetener if I were making it myself, but I'm surprised how full the flavor is this way."

And she'd given him only half as much as in her cup. Her cheeks flushed. Claire always teased her about how much she used. "It's the salt that rounds out the taste. Everything we buy ready-made is loaded with sodium, even something like hot chocolate mix, which I might use for this in a pinch. So adding a controlled amount helps it taste normal."

He settled himself in the loveseat, but Sierra tucked into her favorite chair around the corner from him. Hey, it's where her drink was.

Gabe looked about to say something several times but stopped himself.

She couldn't come up with a good starter, either. All that came to mind were things she wasn't ready to mention.

Finally he took a sip of his mocha and set it on the side table between them. "Did you and Doreen ever have much trouble with shoplifters in the store?"

Sierra blinked. So not what she expected to talk about, but a welcome diversion. She pulled her features into a studied frown.

"No, I can't say we did. Occasionally our count on a product would be low or we'd find an empty package, but it was never anything pricey. And it happened rarely."

"I had a couple of boys from my Sunday school class come into the store today." He gave a wry grin. "Did you know that Tyrell Burke handed it off to me as though he couldn't wait to be rid of it?"

She hadn't followed that. "Handed what off?"

"The junior youth class."

"Oh." In the months Tyrell had been in charge, he'd often needed a substitute. She'd managed to avoid being tagged for that hormone-driven bunch. "That used to be your class, didn't it?"

"Well, yes. But he didn't really ask if I wanted it back. He just dropped off the material."

That sounded like Tyrell. Always assuming and moving forward. It wasn't an altogether bad trait, though. Some people could never make up their minds. Her conscience bit. Some people like her.

When she focused back on Gabe's face, he averted his eyes and sighed deeply.

"Some of the kids came into Nature's Pantry?" Seemed like a better conversation than talking about Tyrell to Gabe.

"Right. Mark Kestrel and Austin Sharp. They'd planned this thing whereby Mark would keep me busy in one aisle while Austin stuffed candy in his pockets."

"Oh, no. But you caught them?"

Gabe grimaced. "Kind of. Short of frisking Austin or calling the police, I don't have solid proof."

"Probably wouldn't have gone over so well."

"No, that's what I figured. Even with Sharp standing there with bulging pockets and a guilty face, and Kestrel not looking any too innocent himself."

What would she have done if that had happened when she was at the store? She shuddered. Thankfully, it hadn't.

"So, I prayed." Gabe grinned. "And then I had this great idea." He told her what he'd done.

"Genius!" Sierra nodded in approval. "Great thinking."

"Yeah, I believe God really came through for me on that one." He smoothed Sierra's open Bible. "Where are you reading these days?"

"Psalms." Where David talked about the anguish of having so many enemies. Also not a topic to discuss with Gabe. "Austin Sharp comes from a good home, from what I know. I wonder what makes a kid do that kind of thing?"

Gabe shrugged. "It's not uncommon. Which definitely doesn't mean it's okay to experiment. The Kestrel boys haven't had it so easy, though. Dustin was a handful when he was that age, too."

"Dustin Kestrel? That name sounds familiar. I think he was involved in a drug bust a year or so ago."

"Oh, man. Those poor kids."

Sierra blinked. "Poor kids? They've made their choices, don't you think?"

"They haven't had the greatest example at home, though. Seems like their dad just lets them run wild. He's got a bit of a record himself. I'm impressed those kids come to church at all."

Oh. Obviously Gabe knew a whole lot more about the family than she did, even if he'd been away for three years. "Sounds rough."

Gabe's grin slid to one side and he shook his head. "Lots of kids struggle. From orphans in Romania to street urchins in Manila to kids shuffled from parent to parent here. Solid homes are rare. Moms and dads both present. Love. Education. Boundaries." He smoothed her Bible's pages again. "God's word.

Prayer."

Sierra's gut clenched. How had they gotten back to this topic? "There are kids in slavery, too. I've always bought fair-trade cocoa since I heard how kids in the Ivory Coast are sold to work on the cocoa plantations there. That way I can be sure my dollars support good living conditions and education."

"I've heard that about Africa, too. And that the big chocolate companies know it and don't care, because they don't want the price of their ingredients to go up."

"Yeah. It makes me really mad. Not that they notice the few people who boycott their stuff."

"It's hard to know what to do about a situation like that." Gabe took another swallow of his mocha. "Kids here in Galena Landing, though. We can help with that."

Her mouth dried and her heart sped up. "Oh? Like what?"

"Starting with my Sunday school class. Not sure how, yet, but I'll think of something."

oOo

Gabe pulled Sierra close as he stood in the doorway of her duplex, ready to leave. She came willingly enough, but didn't relax against him. He rubbed her back and nuzzled into her neck.

Was she trembling?

"Hey, Sierra, what's wrong?"

Something had to be. Today had been a guarded chat between almost-friends, like they'd been weeks ago. They'd progressed since then. Hadn't they? Surely he hadn't made up memories of their kisses and harmony the night of their date.

"Oh, it's nothing."

Alarm bells rang in Gabe's head. He hadn't done everything right in his marriage to Bethany. He knew that. But when a woman said it was nothing, it was a cry for help every single time.

"Is it something I said?" His mind roved over conversations before things had gone sour. A week ago. He couldn't put a finger on anything.

"No, really. Everything's fine."

He tucked a finger under her chin and lifted her face. Her eyes caught on his for an instant before she looked away. He swept both hands through her hair — oh, the glory of it! Long and full and silky — and cradled her face. "Sierra."

She smiled, but it seemed tremulous.

He bent and kissed her lips, gently, then with hunger. At first they lay passive beneath his, but it didn't take long for her to return the passion he felt soaring through him. "Sierra," he murmured again. It was like a man thirsting in the desert and coming at long last upon an oasis. It was like a man living in a slow motion, black-and-white world and suddenly finding himself in a colorful action flick. It was like a man falling in love. Again.

Her arms tightened around him as her lips and body responded to his.

How long did it take to know he'd fallen in love? That he'd met the woman who would be at his side for the rest of their lives? They might not make it to a hundred. Experience had taught him that. But what time he had, he needed to spend it with Sierra. She'd been created for him.

He held her face in his hands and looked deep into her blue eyes from a mere inch or two away.

She bit her lip.

He kissed it gently. If only he could kiss everything better, all the time. Maybe he could. "Sierra, I love you."

She pulled away, right out of his hands, which dropped slowly to his sides. She took a step back, then another, her head shaking from side to side. Her arm came up to wipe tears from her face.

Tears?

"What is it, sweetheart? Am I pushing you? I don't mean to." But hadn't it been mutual? If anything, she'd been ready for him when he came home from Romania. It had taken longer for him to see who she really was.

He was thirty. He'd known the joys of marriage. How long was he supposed to wait to declare himself? He hadn't misread the signs. He hadn't. And yet, this past week, she'd been avoiding him. Why? And why wouldn't she say?

"I-I'm not ready, Gabe. I just need a little time." Her gaze lifted somewhere in the neighborhood of his chest then flicked to his eyes and away. "Please," she whispered.

His hands, his arms, indeed, his whole body yearned toward her. To hold her, more gently this time, and tell her it was all right. But was it?

"I'm going now." His voice sounded scratchy, even to himself. He cleared his throat. "But that doesn't change how I feel about you. I believe God has brought us together." He saw that with blinding clarity.

She backed up another step. A tear trickled down her cheek. Why wouldn't she let him wipe it away?

"I love you, Sierra." And he slipped out into the frigid November night with little to keep him warm.

Chapter 23 --

*J*o sent me in for some groceries," Zach announced from the doorway of Nature's Pantry.

"Nemesek!" Gabe crossed the space to fist bump his buddy.

"Rubachuk!"

"Now that we've got that out of the way, did she send a list?"

Zach pulled out his phone and opened a shopping app. He shook his head and held it out to Gabe with a little grin.

Gabe burst out laughing. "This looks like pregnancy cravings to me."

"Oh yeah." Zach sighed. "With Maddie she just tamped them down, but this time, she doesn't care who knows she needs salt and vinegar potato chips. She's a desperate woman."

"No pickles? That's what Bethany craved." Gabe swallowed the twinge the memory gave him as he handed Zach a grocery basket.

"Nah, she and the girls canned dozens of jars in August. Jo's definitely going through more than our share at the moment, but I think stock will hold out. It's the chips she's frantic for." Zach rolled his eyes. "Never saw that one coming."

Gabe chuckled. "Well, you came to the right place. We have organic ones and a couple of other kinds with all natural ingredients. Do you know what brand she prefers?" He led the way to the junk food aisle. "I don't remember if she sampled any the day we painted upstairs."

"She didn't. I doubt she's eaten potato chips in ten years. I'm surprised she can remember what salt and vinegar even taste like." Zach perused the rack and picked two different bags. "Let's try those. Next we need a bag of frozen burritos. Seems like I remember you had those here."

"Yeah, I do, but why doesn't she make her own and freeze them? I shouldn't be talking myself out of a sale, but buying them seems totally out of character for Jo."

"Trust me, she plans on doing just that as soon as she isn't so tired. Maddie saps about all the energy Jo can muster." He leaned closer to Gabe. "I'll tell you how exhausted she is. She's this close to using disposable diapers on Maddie, but Claire and I got the cloth ones washed and put away yesterday, so I think we're good for a bit."

"Whoa. Jo using disposables?" Things at the Nemeseks were worse than Gabe had imagined.

"It was a close call." Zach opened the freezer case and grabbed a package of burritos with a four-chili grade.

"She likes heat? Those would scorch my throat all the way down and set off an inferno once they got to the bottom."

"She specifically said the hotter the better. Who am I to argue?"

Gabe held up both hands in surrender. "I get it. No problem."

"Now it's just a few candy bars." Zach peered at his list. "I'm surprised she didn't make me go to Wynnton for all this. I mean, she can't have wanted word to get out of all the junk she wants to eat."

Gabe laughed. "Probably more like she couldn't wait the

couple of extra hours for the return trip. Or justify the fuel expenditure."

"Good point." Zach slid three bars into the basket. "That should do for now."

"At least for a day or two." Back behind the counter, Gabe rang up the order.

"So, how are things going with Sierra since your hot date last week?"

Surely his buddy would notice the hesitation. But wasn't this what friends were for? "I don't know," Gabe said slowly. "Something seems to be upsetting her, but I don't know what it is. She doesn't want to talk about it."

"Uh oh." Zach pushed the bag of food to one side and leaned forward on the counter. "That doesn't sound good."

"Has she seemed quiet to you? Has Jo said anything? I've gone over and over what we talked about and I just can't see where I went wrong." Except for those few moments in the mall. But everything had seemed fine after that.

"I can't say I've noticed. But then I have enough trouble figuring out what makes Jo tick half the time. And pregnancy changes everything."

"Yeah." Well, Sierra wasn't pregnant, so that couldn't be the problem. But other hormonal issues? Maybe. "She's telling me she needs more time."

Zach's eyes twinkled. "Ah, so you have talked about serious matters then. It's not just my imagination what direction things were going."

"*Were* going. That's the operative word." Might as well give Zach all the details. He hadn't been able to figure things out on his own, so maybe an impartial set of ears would help. "When I got back home, you know I wasn't ready for a relationship, but I got the feeling early on that Sierra was interested. Maybe it was my imagination, but I don't think so."

"Yeah, I don't think you were making it up. She didn't seem pushy to me, but Jo and I both definitely noticed."

"Okay, that helps." Gabe nodded. "I'd planned to sell the store and move away, but she challenged me to face the past and give myself six months before I made a final decision."

Zach let out a low whistle. "It never occurred to me you might sell out. I guess it should have."

"At first I didn't intend to accept her challenge but, as a bit of time went on, I saw how much having my friends and hometown around me was good, even though it hurt. And I began to see something in Sierra, too."

"The weekend we painted your apartment?" Zach winked.

"That might've been the start. I'm not sure. But no sooner did we seem to come to an agreement than she started pulling away again." Gabe frowned. "That weekend her sister was here started it. I wonder if Chelsea doesn't like me for some reason?"

"I think you're reading too much into it."

Gabe thought back to dancing with Sierra in his arms, to kissing her a few days later, then to her perplexing rejection of him last night. "I don't think so." He shook his head slowly. "It doesn't make sense. We were past that stage."

"Hmm."

Gabe spread his hands wide. "I don't have that much experience with women. All I cared about since I was a kid was making Bethany happy. I don't know how other women think."

"They're not all alike. Take it from a guy with three sisters and a bad relationship before Jo. But you have to trust your instincts. If they're telling you something is wrong, you have to figure it out. Just up and ask her, maybe?"

"I tried. She said it was nothing, but she didn't look me in the eye while saying it."

"Oh man. I hate those words. They don't give a guy much to go on."

"Yeah." Had he really expected Zach to be able to help? Not really. Still, it felt better to get it off his chest a bit. "Well, thanks. Tell Jo I hope this hits the spot." He nudged the bag toward his buddy.

"I will. And I'll ask her if she's talked to Sierra lately. Either way, praying for you."

And to think being in Galena Landing, away from his supportive friends, had seemed attractive.

o0o

Sierra tasted the mega-batch of soup she and Claire had been working on all morning. "More oregano definitely helped. What do you think?"

Claire ran her tongue over her lips, her head tilted to one side. "Still missing something. I'm not sure I want twenty quarts of this in the larder."

"Good point." Sierra tightened the elastic holding her hair back and scrolled down the recipe they'd been using as a foundation. "How about a dab of honey?"

"Not everything needs to be sweetened with honey." Claire bumped her shoulder against Sierra's. "Especially not a savory soup."

"You'd be surprised." Sierra reached for her old recipe box on the back corner of the peninsula then flipped through it. "My grandmother put a pinch of sugar into nearly everything."

"Hmm. Not sure I can be convinced that would improve things."

Sierra pulled out several cards. "See here? Tomato-based recipes, like this soup. Take out a cup or so and add a teeny bit.

Besides, it's nearly lunch time and I want more than a spoonful of taste test every half hour."

"Good point."

A thud and a shriek pulled Sierra's attention to the door just as Jo walked in, Maddie careening around her.

"Clay! Sera!"

Sierra knelt to capture the tyke in a quick hug before Maddie charged off for the toy box in the great room, Domino romping behind her.

"Hiya, Jo." She gave her friend the once-over. "You look terrible, if you don't mind my saying so."

Jo grimaced. "I suspected as much. Maybe because I *feel* terrible. Think there might be a correlation?"

"It's possible. Have you eaten today?"

"I managed to keep breakfast down, if that's what you're asking."

And Sierra wanted to have kids? Wanted to experience pregnancy? Maybe she should be thankful it didn't look like an option. Her heart clenched. Except for Gabe. And, well, yes, motherhood was something she'd always desired.

Claire turned from the stove with two bowls. "Want to do a taste test for us? We're trying to finalize the seasoning in this soup before we start canning."

Jo eyed the bowls uncertainly. "Sure. What kind?"

"A beef-based tomato soup." Sierra turned her back on Jo to hide the addition of honey.

"Smells good. Is this what's for lunch? I was hoping there might be food over here."

"If it doesn't hit the spot for you, I'm sure we can find something else." Sierra set both bowls on the peninsula and indicated Jo should have a seat. "Is Maddie hungry? I can get a bowl with less broth for her."

"She might be. Thanks."

Sierra high-graded bits of meat, potatoes, and vegetables into one of Maddie's metal bowls. The child couldn't be trusted with regular dishes. "Hey, kiddo, want some soup?" She peered around the corner.

"Soup?" Maddie clambered into her high chair. "Tanku."

Sierra pulled Maddie's t-shirt off and buckled the tot in before setting the bowl on the tray in front of her. "Do you want help, or do you want to do it by yourself?"

"Self." Maddie nodded enthusiastically and dug her spoon in.

"Which do you prefer?" Claire asked Jo. "Can you taste a difference?"

Jo took a teensy bite from each bowl again before pushing the one on the right across the counter toward Claire. She encircled the other with her hand. "I'll keep this one. Though it could use a shot of hot pepper or Tabasco sauce, I think."

The chagrined look on Claire's face told Sierra Jo had preferred the dribble of honey. She grinned. "So, we're sweetening the whole batch with honey, then?"

Jo's spoon stopped halfway to her mouth. "Is that the difference? Now that you mention it, I can taste it. Very subtle though. But seriously, add some zing."

"You want heat in everything right now. Not sure the rest of us are up for your standards." Claire reached for a jar of hot pepper flakes and slid it to Jo. "Try it out before I start dumping them into the big pot."

Jo tilted the shaker and dumped a good dose into her bowl. She gave it a stir before tasting. "Kazam. That is a winner."

"Zam," echoed Maddie. Chunks of tomato already littered her tray.

"Is that good, Maddie?" asked Claire.

"Good." Maddie nodded so enthusiastically Sierra feared for

her neck.

Claire added a dollop of honey to the over-sized stockpot and stirred it in before giving another taste. "I hate to admit it, but this does bring out the flavors a bit more."

"Ha! Told you so." Sierra smiled smugly. "But the pepper flakes will offset it perfectly. Nice call, Jo. Good thing we dried so many of them a few weeks ago." She rummaged in the corner cupboard for a large jar.

"Trust Sierra to think of putting honey in the soup." Jo chuckled as she twisted her spoon around.

"You haven't eaten more than three bites." Claire's hands found her hips. "How do you hope to grow that baby? On love and air?"

"I'll have a bit more, I promise. It doesn't help the kiddo any if I throw it up the minute it hits my stomach, either."

"True. Sorry this is being such a rough pregnancy."

A few weeks ago Sierra wished she were part of the camaraderie her friends shared. Now she only wanted them to talk about something else. Anything else.

"Hey, Sierra, how are things going with Gabe?" Jo looked up from her bowl.

They could go back to discussing Jo's pregnancy, after all. How could Sierra possibly answer without giving away too much? "Not sure." Okay, that was a bald-faced lie. "We have some issues to work out."

By the expressions on her friends' faces, that had sounded as lame to them as it did to her.

"Issues?" Claire asked. "What kinds of issues?"

"Just... stuff. Don't worry about it. I'm sure things will become clear in the end." Guess that depended on one's definition of clear.

"After all the interfering you did when Noel and I were

sorting things out? And now you won't confide in us?"

"Yeah." Jo pointed her spoon at Sierra. "You didn't exactly allow me any peace early in Zach's and my relationship, either."

"That was different."

Claire raised her eyebrows. "How so?"

"I don't want to talk about it, okay?"

Jo shook her head. "Do you remember when I blocked out everything you said because I'd decided you were trying to steal Zach out from under my nose?"

"That was different."

"Yeah, it was different all right. You can be quite certain neither Claire nor I have any designs on Gabe. We're happily married and all that."

Claire leaned back on the counter and crossed her arms. "And I know the problem isn't Gabe's lack of faith. We've had enough visits around the Sunday dinner table to know his walk with God is genuine."

Sierra couldn't think of a reply. "Look, I really don't want to talk about it, okay? Maybe later, but not right now."

Maddie shrieked from behind Jo and threw her bowl. It bounced a few times, probably gaining a new dent or two in the process. Domino sniffed the remains and picked out the beef, leaving the vegetables on the floor for someone else to clean up.

Claire waved Jo back to the counter stool before she could slide off. "I've got it." She dampened a washcloth and headed for Maddie. As she passed Sierra, she glowered. "Don't think this is over. It isn't."

Inexplicably, those words made Sierra feel better. "I'll be honest. We could use some prayers for God's wisdom."

"Consider it done." Jo's eyes met hers for a long moment before turning to scoop up Maddie.

She'd left most of the soup in her bowl.

Chapter 24 --

*W*hat would Sierra do without her sister?

Chelsea rose as the gurney returned Sierra to the outpatient area. "You okay?" Chelsea glanced between Sierra and the nurse.

Not that the nurse would tell them anything. She wouldn't even leak any opinions to Sierra as to what the biopsy had looked like. Maybe she didn't know.

"She'll be just fine," the nurse said cheerfully, wheeling her into another one of those curtained off compartments.

Sierra bet she hadn't seen the last of those spaces. Why did hospitals insist on blue curtains? They weren't soothing. They were depressing.

"Sis?" Chelsea loomed over the stretcher, forehead furrowed with a frown.

Sierra turned toward the nurse. "Can I get another painkiller?" She couldn't believe she was asking for chemical sludge, but man, she needed something. Just the thought of that little corkscrew scraping around inside her uterus made her want to pass out all over again.

"I'll find you something." The nurse whisked out of the cubicle.

"That bad, huh?" Chelsea's voice oozed sympathy.

Sierra tried for a deep breath but she hurt too much. "Brutal. They say it's worse for women who've never given birth, and I believe them." At least the pain of childbirth would be worth it. This? Cancer, cancer, cancer. The refrain refused to die in her mind.

"How long until you get the results?"

"I don't know. A few days, at least. Probably everything takes longer over the holiday weekend."

The nurse bustled back in with a prescription for a painkiller. "One for the road," she announced, handing over a cup of water and a wee paper container with one tablet.

Sierra took both and dashed them back. It was way too late to turn down medical technology, no matter how Chelsea's eyebrows rose.

"You're free to leave whenever you're ready." The nurse set the bag containing Sierra's clothes beside her feet.

The loudspeaker called for Doctor Seeley, stat. The nurse whisked back out.

Chelsea opened the bag and pulled out Sierra's sweats. "Not feeling that great, huh?"

Understatement.

"Then it's a good thing I booked us a bed and breakfast for tonight. I grabbed a stack of magazines and a good selection of snacks. We're all set for some bonding time."

Her sister was enjoying this far too much. But at least Sierra wouldn't have to face her friends when she was in this much pain. It would be hard to dissemble.

o0o

"Good to see you back in town, Gabe!" Tammy Stephenson picked up a grocery basket beside the entrance to Nature's

Pantry.

"Tammy! How's business?"

She grimaced. "It's been slow since the economy tanked, but there have been just enough properties turning over to keep me hopeful."

"That's great. Good thing Matt has a job then."

"Oh, definitely. We'd have a hard time living off realty alone these days. How are things with you?"

Gabe shrugged. "Pretty good. Doreen and Sierra grew the business while I was away."

"You thinking of selling? When you were out of town so long, I began to wonder."

He eyed her. "It's crossed my mind a time or two, but I'm not sure that's a step I want to take."

"I told Matt I could see your heart wasn't in the store anymore, not since Bethany passed on. It must be rough here with all her memories."

And everyone else encouraged him to leave the past behind. What was Tammy doing, dredging up history?

"It's got its tough times, for sure." Bethany had never kept him guessing the way Sierra did. Yeah, he'd sometimes had to wheedle information out of her, but in the end, she'd always capitulated. Sierra was a fortress. No amount of siege had enabled him to breach her defenses.

"Well, if you decide you want to sell out, let me know. The market is soft right now, but I did have an inquiry the other day from someone looking for a small business to buy in the area. I might be able to pull a deal together for you."

Did he want to leave town? Not really. Not now that he'd reconnected with Zach and the folks at Galena Gospel Church. His Sunday school class. On the other hand, Sierra… could he face staying with their relationship at a stalemate?

"I'll keep it in mind, Tammy. I'm not sure I want to take such a big step right now." Tempting, though. So tempting. How could he keep hanging around Green Acres, seeing Sierra all the time? Especially if she turned to Burke.

Man, that would sear him to the core.

"I understand. But once this couple finds what they're looking for, I can't guarantee there will be anyone behind them. I happen to know they joined the back-to-the-land movement in the 70s but couldn't make a go of it. They returned to Salt Lake City and held down corporate jobs, but now they want a taste of the life they had to leave behind. They're in their late fifties, so it's a bit yet before they retire. How perfect would a health food store be for someone like them?"

"They sound ideal."

"Really nice people, too. Don't think about it too long, Gabe. This might be exactly what you need to start a new life for yourself."

"Thanks, Tammy. I appreciate the tip." He did, didn't he? "Is there anything I can help you find in the store today?"

"No, I only need a bit of produce. I know where to find it."

A few minutes later he rang her order through the till.

She passed him a business card with her Visa. "Talk to you soon!"

Gabe stared after Tammy long after the door closed behind her. Was this a heaven-sent opportunity? Was God trying to tell him to let go of Nature's Pantry? Of Galena Landing? Of Sierra?

He closed his eyes. But things had been going so well. Hadn't he been certain just a week or two ago that God had brought her into his life? Not as a replacement for Bethany. Sierra was a unique woman. She matched his personality in different ways.

But she was pushing him away, for reasons he couldn't fathom.

"Gabe, I heard what that hussy had to say."

Gabe blinked Doreen's face into focus. He'd forgotten she was cataloging files in the back office. "You're calling Tammy a hussy?" That had to be a first.

Doreen's face reddened. "Okay, maybe not that. But don't listen to her, Gabe. She's just trying to make a buck. This is where you belong."

Gabe contemplated Doreen's face, trying to figure out where she was coming from. "Do you have any interest in buying Nature's Pantry back from me?"

"No! Of course not."

He hadn't thought so. "Then why—?"

"You believed God wanted you to buy it from me eight years ago. When did He tell you to sell it?"

"Doreen, I didn't invite Tammy here to sign her on as my Realtor. She came to purchase onions and squash. The other was merely a side topic."

"One it sounded like you're considering."

He hadn't been, but his former mother-in-law could drive him to it yet if she kept it up. All right, maybe he had thought of it, but not seriously. And he certainly wouldn't do something rash until he knew for certain what was bugging Sierra. Until he knew there was no hope for the two of them to reconcile.

Didn't a guy have to know what he'd done wrong so he could make things right? How could he begin to guess, when Sierra refused to say? The loop in his brain circled its now-familiar path. Round and round.

"I'm sorry, Gabe. It's none of my business."

She could say that again.

"It's just, I worry about you."

She and a hundred other people, it seemed like. Couldn't he take charge of his own life? So he was doing a lousy job of it.

That was between him and God, not between him and Doreen and Zach and Jo and Tammy and the rest of the world.

He mustered a smile. "I know, Doreen. I'm thankful you care. Really. But all I need is prayer. Ask God to help me make the best decisions. The ones that will further His kingdom, okay?"

Wow, those words simplified things a lot. A weight lifted off his shoulders. "After closing, I'm going to drive out to Green Acres. Something's up with Sierra, and I won't leave until she tells me what it is."

Doreen smiled. "That's more like it. As for praying for you, I have been every day, many times. You're my son, and I continuously bring you before God's throne."

He reached out and gave her a quick side hug. "Thanks."

"In fact, if you want to drive out to the farm now, go for it. I can keep the mobs at bay here."

"You mean it? I think I will."

Chapter 25 --

*W*hat do you mean, she's not here? Her car is outside."

After knocking repeatedly on the door to Sierra's duplex, Gabe had walked over to the big house to see if she was working with Claire and Jo.

"She and her sister headed out early this morning." Claire's eyebrows pulled together in thought. "I'm not sure where they were going, actually. Sierra said something about a little getaway and they'd be home tomorrow."

Gabe rocked back on his heels, his mind buzzing with possibilities, none of them good. Didn't Chelsea live in Portland? What brought her to the Idaho Panhandle so often? It seemed every time she came, she pulled Sierra further away from him. What did Chelsea have against him, anyway? She barely knew him. And his reputation didn't stink, at least not that he knew of.

"What's wrong, Gabe?"

He jerked his head up to look into Claire's sympathetic gaze. "I'm confused." Warning bells rang. It was one thing to confide in Zach. They'd known each other since they were toddlers. It was something else completely to air his troubles in front of Sierra's close friend.

"I don't think you're the only one."

No, he should steer clear. Gabe backed up a step. "That could be. I'll try to catch her tomorrow then." So much for his hastily conceived plan where he'd kiss her senseless and not stop until the barrier, whatever it was, had disappeared.

"What happened between you, if you don't mind my asking?"

He minded. But somehow he couldn't turn and jog down the steps to his car, either.

"Gabe? I just put on a pot of coffee. Noel is cutting firewood on the hillside, but he'll be here shortly. Come on in."

Maybe having Noel there, too, would help. Somehow Gabe found himself following Claire into the house.

The warmth immediately enfolded him as the caffeinated aroma wafted toward him. The coffee pot burbled in the kitchen. He stuffed his gloves into his pockets before hanging the coat from a hook behind the door.

"Take anything in your coffee?" called Claire from the kitchen.

"Just a slosh of cream, if you've got it."

"Yep, no problem." A minute later she came out carrying two steaming mugs. She handed one to Gabe and gestured toward the great room. "Come on in, and make yourself at home."

Flames flickered in the fireplace. Gabe took a seat in one of the easy chairs. "It can't take a lot of wood to heat this place, as well-insulated as it is."

Claire shrugged. "It doesn't. Noel's working ahead. He can't sit still for more than a few minutes, so he's stockpiling for Zach and Jo right now. This pregnancy is hitting Jo hard, and Zach's having trouble keeping up with the extra work with Maddie and the cabin while his veterinary practice is so busy, too."

Gabe hadn't even known. A flicker of jealousy reared its head. Why hadn't Zach told Gabe he needed help? He could've been here. Zach didn't need to go calling on Noel for it.

Claire curled up in the end of the love seat and cradled her mug in both hands. "I was hoping you could shed some light on what's up with Sierra these days, but it sounds like you're just as much in the dark as we are."

Gabe blinked and shook his head. No call to envy Noel. The guys had been friends for several years and lived a stone's throw apart, with wives who were close friends. He'd be right here with them if things worked out with Sierra, though they'd probably live in the apartment above the store.

"I'm at a bit of a loss," he said finally. "I really don't know what I did wrong. That may sound prideful, but I don't mean it that way. Trust me, I've gone through every conversation, every…" He felt a flush creep up his cheeks. He'd nearly said kiss. "Everything that happened," he finished lamely.

Claire's eyes twinkled.

She'd obviously caught his hesitation. Whatever.

"I want you to know something. I really believe in personal privacy, even though we live communally. When Jo, Sierra, and I cooked up this plan to buy a farm together and live this way, we promised each other we'd air the issues that came into our lives. We'd trust each other and help bear each other's burdens."

She stared into her cup as she swirled the coffee. Then she glanced back at him. "It was difficult for Jo and me, in particular. There had been no one in our lives to share with before. No one we believed had our back. But slowly, over time, we grew as close as sisters. Or what I'd imagine sisters might be like."

Sisters. Chelsea.

"For Sierra, it was different. She was an open book. I chalked it up to the fact that she had a secure family and a great relationship with her sister. She didn't feel like the whole universe was out to get her." Claire chuckled. "I also figured when she fell in love, things might change. It gets pretty intense being on the hot seat in such a close community."

"I bet." But should they have changed this much? It was true that Sierra had been devastatingly simple to read two months ago, but that ease had slowly receded. What if it wasn't him? What if it was something else?

The door swung open. A draft of chilly air swirled in with Noel before he got it shut again. Noel shed his outer gear as Claire surged to her feet. "Want a coffee?"

"Thanks, I'll get it." Noel's eyes met Gabe's. "Hey, man."

"Hi there."

Noel headed into the kitchen and came back a moment later, both hands wrapped around a steaming mug. He settled into the love seat beside Claire and rubbed his cheek against hers.

She shifted away. "You're freezing!"

"Yeah, well, it's bitterly cold out there, in case you hadn't noticed." He tucked one arm around her and pulled her close.

She wrinkled her nose at him but didn't resist.

Gabe wanted this. He'd had it before, and he wanted it again. Just the comfort of knowing there was one person who loved and accepted him.

"So what brings you out our way?" asked Noel.

He'd do it. Going it alone hadn't worked. Even telling Zach had done nothing, though that had only been a day or two ago.

Gabe stared into the creamy depths of his mug. "Worried about Sierra, actually. I came determined to talk things out, but she's not even here."

"We're all a little concerned about her," said Claire.

Noel frowned. "She's off somewhere with her sister? Christmas shopping or something?"

Right, the holidays would be here in little over a month. Gabe could think of something he'd like to get her for a gift, but not with things the way they were.

"She didn't say anything about shopping." Claire stared into the distance. "But she may not have thought she needed to. She lives to shop, so mentioning it may have seemed redundant."

"She hasn't confided in you? Whatever's bothering her?"

Claire shook her head. "We've noticed, though. Jo and I tried to get her to open up the other day, but all we got out of her in the end was that prayers would be welcome."

He'd been praying, and then praying some more. He felt like the guy in the Bible who kept knocking on his neighbor's door begging for food in the middle of the night. Didn't Jesus say the neighbor would answer if only so the pounding would stop?

"I take it we all think whatever's bothering her is between you and her." Noel nodded at Gabe. "But, radical thought here. What if it's something else entirely?"

Hmm. Was Noel implying Gabe wasn't the only star in Sierra's universe? Could he be right?

Claire snorted. "What a guy way to think."

"Hey now. I know you never think of anything but me." Noel nuzzled Claire's neck, and she didn't pull away this time. "But we've already established that Sierra isn't your clone."

"Her sister," Gabe said flatly. "It's something with Chelsea, right?" But that didn't make sense, either. "Has she always come to visit this often?"

Claire shook her head. "I've only met her a few times before the last month or two. Now she's here a lot." She narrowed her eyes at Gabe. "But you're right in one way. Every time she comes, Sierra seems farther away."

Noel frowned. "I thought Chelsea came to introduce Allison, and that she'd like to join us here for the long haul. I hadn't seen anything sinister in her visits."

"Sinister is too strong a word." Claire shook her head. "But whatever is going on, Chelsea's in the thick of it. I'm certain."

"I don't know if that's a relief or not." Gabe stared into his mug, now nearly empty. "If it were a problem with me, then presumably I could fix it once I figured it out. But if it's something else... something bigger..."

Noel grimaced. "There's a problem with your line of thinking."

Gabe reared back. "There is?"

"Whether the problem is between you and Sierra or something else, it's more than that. It's not something you can fix by saying the magic words."

Gabe stared at the other man.

Noel poked his chin toward Gabe. "We guys tend to think we can fix anything, right? But Sierra admitted to needing prayer. So that brings it out of the realm of easy guy talk to something bigger."

"I suppose." Gabe dragged the word out. "I'm not sure how I feel about that."

"I get it, man. I really do. But I've been learning a lot about God in the past few years. Learning to listen to His voice." Noel leaned forward on his knees. "Hard to do when I'd been shutting it out all my life."

Claire rested her hand on Noel's leg.

"So, yeah. I think we need to step up praying. For you guys—" and he poked his chin toward Gabe again "—and for whatever is at the root of it."

Gabe nodded. Somehow he was unprepared for Noel to set his mug on the coffee table, bow his head, and launch into a verbal prayer then and there. By the time Noel said, "amen," and Claire had added a few words, the chill had melted in Gabe's gut. He added his request to the others.

He hadn't expected this bond. This brotherhood. It salved his spirit in a way he hadn't known he was missing.

"Oh, I meant to ask you, in case Sierra hadn't done so yet." Claire got to her feet.

"Hmm?"

"Do you have any plans for Thanksgiving dinner? We're planning a feast at five, and we want you to come. Jo already invited Doreen."

For some strange reason it cheered him up that he might not be the bad guy who'd caused Sierra's reticence. "Sounds good. I'd love to come. What can I bring?"

"I think we have everything covered."

"Come early and help out in the kitchen, man." Noel grinned. "You've earned your stripes."

o0o

"No, we can't stay at the B&B any longer, silly." Chelsea threw her pillow at Sierra. "Mom and Dad and Jacob will be arriving tonight. You can't duck out on that."

"But I'm a mess. Everyone will know something is wrong." There'd be no hiding. Not with Mom and Dad in her spare room and her brother on the living room floor. Chelsea sharing her bedroom was the least of her concerns.

Her sister shrugged. "So tell them already. It's not like you've committed some crime. You had a medical procedure done and you're not up to your usual energy. That's nothing to be ashamed of."

"You don't understand."

"You're right. I don't. You're making this into some huge deal and refuse to explain it, even to me. Do you think I'm the only one wondering what in the world is wrong with you?"

Gabe had noticed. Jo and Claire had, too. Sierra cringed. "I can't. Not yet. Not until I know for sure."

Chelsea plopped on the bed and crossed her legs. "But why? You need the support now, while you're worrying, as well as later."

Something in her sister's words pushed at Sierra. "I'm sorry to be such a problem to you."

"What on earth are you talking about?"

"If I could tell Jo or Claire, you wouldn't need to come such a long way to be with me."

"Oh, good grief." Chelsea threw her hands in the air. "You think I resent it? Not in the least. I'm flattered you've allowed me in, even the little bit you have, and I had vacation days coming to me. But you can't keep hiding. For one thing, Mom will know something's up the minute she sees you."

Chelsea was right about their mother. Why did this have to happen now, with Thanksgiving in the middle? What was there to be thankful for? Surely she'd think of something.

"Get your stuff together. We need to check out before eleven." Chelsea stalked toward the bathroom door then turned and stared hard at Sierra. "You are feeling better, right? We don't need to go back to the hospital?"

"I'm fine."

"Well, you don't need to bite my head off about it."

Sierra tugged her pillow over her face. Now she was pushing her sister away, too. Who was left to stand in her court? "I'm calling Tyrell to invite him for Thanksgiving dinner."

That brought Chelsea's head around the bathroom door in a hurry. "You're what?"

"Inviting Tyrell—"

"I heard you. I just didn't believe you. Why on earth would you do that?"

"Because I might marry him."

Chapter 26 --

*T*wo cars with Oregon license plates parked beside the straw bale house stopped Gabe dead in his tracks halfway to the deck.

Why hadn't he realized Sierra's parents might be here for Thanksgiving? Why hadn't Claire warned him? Somehow his brain hadn't gotten farther than Chelsea, who only accounted for one of the beaver state plates.

Zach crossed the yard carrying Maddie as she rubbed sleep out of her eyes. "Rubachuk!"

"Nemesek." Gabe met Zach's fist with little enthusiasm. Even Maddie's shy grin as she leaned into her daddy's shoulder didn't spark any warmth.

"What's wrong?"

Gabe pointed at the cars. "Anything I should know?"

Zach's eyebrows drew together in a frown for an instant. "Oh, man. I never put two and two together."

Gabe knew he'd have to face Sierra's dad sometime if he ever hoped to marry the man's daughter. He'd figured on some privacy and a setting of his own choosing. Not at Thanksgiving with — he glanced over the assorted vehicles — at least two dozen people, some of whom he probably didn't know.

He pivoted. "I'm not doing this." If only things were sure between him and Sierra, he'd gladly face her father. But this? It was totally a mistake.

Zach grabbed his arm. "Don't go. I want you here. So do a lot of other people in that house."

Maddie reached for Gabe then pulled her hand back with a giggle.

"Even Maddie wants you to stay. To be thankful with friends." He stressed that last word. "No one here means any harm to you, man. It's just... yeah, it's unfortunate timing. But let's get it over with, okay? And if it's really that bad, you can leave early. We'll even send a plate of turkey along."

Gabe took a deep breath. He'd been invited by Noel and Claire. As friends. Not as Sierra's boyfriend. After the last ten chilly days, he had no clue if he'd dreamed the kisses, hugs, and whispered flirtations between them.

"Listen, Sierra's dad is a nice guy. You'll see."

The urge to get back into his car and drive back to his lonely apartment nearly flattened him. He could cook up a box of Cora's macaroni and cheese and eat it in the turquoise and gold haven Sierra had helped paint. So much like hers.

If he were still hungry, he could have some plain rice cakes for dessert. Live a little. Smear some of Sierra's honey on top.

"Unc Abe?"

Gabe focused on the bouncing cherub in his best friend's arms. The last vestiges of her nap had disappeared. He reached out as she flung herself toward him.

She was a delight. He squeezed her tight. As soon as he loosened his grip, she launched for Zach, who barely caught her in time. A second later she leaped back to Gabe.

How could he stay glum? How could he go back to hiding?

Zach was right. His relationship with Sierra — or lack thereof — had nothing to do with Mr. Riehl.

He gave a curt nod and followed Zach into the house, Madelynn bouncing on his arm.

"Hey, man, there you are!" called Noel from the kitchen as Gabe set Maddie down and shrugged out of his coat. "I thought I'd have to do all this prep by myself."

"As if!" Claire appeared behind the peninsula long enough to swat Noel with a tea towel.

Noel winked at Gabe. "She's a slave driver."

"And that's a recommendation?" He headed toward the kitchen. This would be immeasurably easier than the great room where Sierra's dad probably sat with a football game on. Though he couldn't remember a TV set in there.

Gabe paused in the doorway to the kitchen. Noel and Claire peered into the oven built into the rock wall as the aroma of roasting turkey puffed out. His stomach grumbled. It definitely wouldn't be satisfied with boxed pasta, organic or not.

Sierra dumped a bag of potatoes into the peninsula sink before she noticed him standing there. Something flickered in her eyes.

Pain? Remorse? He couldn't be certain. He had an instant to react, but he was too late. She'd already shut him out.

"Hi, Gabe."

"Hi, yourself. You look great today." She did, and it wasn't just that he'd missed feasting his eyes on her. A long pumpkin-colored top warmed her features. Or she was blushing. It might just be the temperature in the room.

"Thanks." She rinsed garden dirt off the potatoes with the extended faucet, pointedly ignoring him.

With a near physical wrench, he pulled his gaze over to Noel, who set the turkey baster back on the island as Claire shut the oven door. "What do you need me to do?"

"Sierra could probably use a hand peeling potatoes." Noel winked.

Gabe glanced her direction. Twin red dots rode high on her cheekbones. Noel's suggestion was going over well.

"Maybe something else?" Gabe asked uncertainly.

Sierra flashed him a look.

So... he was supposed to persist? Or not? Honestly, women. Was she really worth this much agony?

She blinked back tears. Her lip trembled as she bent over the potatoes, her hair sliding forward to hide her features.

"There's another peeler in the drawer to your right," Claire said.

Okay, fine. He'd peel potatoes beside the most beautiful woman in the universe. The one he'd kissed and dreamed about. The one who'd coldly blocked him from her life without a speck of notice.

Not quite as immune as she'd like him to think, though.

Gabe reached for a potato and brushed Sierra's hand. She jerked away as though he'd stabbed her. For all he knew, she reacted less to a bee sting.

He glanced around the room to see if anyone was in earshot before starting to peel. "I've missed you, Sierra," he began in a low tone. "I've missed how vibrant you are. How impulsive."

She stiffened beside him but continued to work.

"Man, I've even missed arguing with you." He chuckled softly. "Remember when I first got back? We fought about everything."

No response.

Gabe took a deep breath. "I'd give anything to know what you're thinking. Why you won't tell me what I did wrong. I've replayed everything, over and over. I know I'm not perfect, I really do, but what did I say? Can you never forgive me for it?"

"It's not you."

Had he really heard those quiet words? And if he had, what did they mean? His heart couldn't help doing a little dance. She'd spoken to him. Given him a clue. A clue he had no idea how to follow up on. "Then what? What happened?"

Her shoulder lifted in the barest of shrugs, but her face remained curtained off behind her hair. It was all Gabe could do not to guide the locks behind her ears. Turn her toward him. Tip her face so she'd have to meet his gaze.

Hadn't worked out so well for him the other day, had it? And that hadn't been in front of a bunch of people.

"Sierra, talk to me. Please. You're putting me through torture." Maybe his voice got a little too loud on that one.

"I'm sorry. I really am." Her voice shook. "So sorry."

What could she possibly have done that was so horrible? "Let's discuss it. It will be okay. I know it will."

Unless — what if it were a much bigger deal than he'd guessed? What if... what if she were pregnant by Burke, for instance? No, he wouldn't think such a thing. He had no evidence to support that line of thought.

"Is it Tyrell Burke?" The words slipped out before Gabe could censure them.

Sierra dropped her peeler into the sink and bolted from the kitchen.

Nice job, Rubachuk.

oOo

Sierra stuffed her feet into boots — hopefully hers — and charged across the yard to the duplex. Even the stinging cold didn't keep her face from burning and her eyes from dumping gallons of tears down her cheeks.

She slipped into the blessed quietness of her little home, ran into her bedroom, and threw herself across her bed.

Why? Why? Why, dear God, why?

Why couldn't she accept the love of a good man who patiently cared for her? Why did her stupid uterus have to act up now? Why not five years ago or three years in the future?

She'd seen Gabe enter the house carrying Maddie snuggled against his chest. Well, as snuggled as that child ever got, before she wiggled her way down and scampered into the great room.

Gabe craved a family of his own. Wanted kids so badly. There was no denying it when she watched him with Maddie.

Yeah, it was really hard for them both right now. He didn't know pursuing her would lead to heartbreak for him down the road. She was a ticking time bomb. She'd have a hysterectomy before Christmas, and there would never be a chance to conceive.

The doctor had said the diagnosis wasn't certain, but she knew. She'd always followed God. Loved Him and served Him, confident that He had her best in mind. That faith had laughed in her face before fleeing from her soul. How could God do this to her?

How could He do this to Gabe? But Gabe would get over her. He'd fall in love with another woman, like maybe Allison, and have the family he'd always wanted. It would be painful to watch, exquisitely agonizing. At least if she lived long enough to see it.

Sobs choked out of her. Tears soaked her pillow. Her hair was a mess, her makeup no doubt blotchy. It didn't matter. She wasn't going back over to the big house for dinner. No one could make her. Besides, she wasn't even hungry.

"Sierra? What's wrong, sweetie?"

How had she not heard her mother come into the duplex?

She sent silent vibes to push her away, but instead felt the mattress dip as Mom sat down on the edge of it. A hand smoothed hair away from her face, just like in memories from her childhood.

Sierra cried harder. She couldn't have stopped the barrage now if she tried. Sobs convulsed her until her throat was hoarse and her eyes burned from the passage of tears.

Through it all, that hand gently massaged her back and swept her face.

Hiccups took over.

The massage stopped, the mattress lifted, and a moment later Mom said, "Here, sweetie. A drink of water will help."

Sierra took a few sips between hiccups then curled up on her side, her back to her mother. She stared dully at the dim glow the curtains made of her window.

"Tell me what's wrong."

It was a miracle Chelsea hadn't blabbed, but Sierra had made her sister promise. Good to know she'd kept it, though part of Sierra wished she didn't have to hold this in from everyone. Just for a few more days. Then, come what may, she'd tell.

"I love you, my girl. I wish you'd let me in."

Everyone said that. Jo and Claire. Gabe. Oh, Gabe. If only he loved her enough. But he wouldn't. He'd never pretended his love for her superseded his dream of having kids. But why should he? Didn't every normal red-blooded woman expect to have a family one day?

Just not her. Oh sure, she'd always dreamed it, just like all the other girls. She'd settled on names for her two boys and two girls before she was ten years old. The dream had faded over the years, only to surge with Gabe, and then be torn away forever.

"I'll leave you for a bit, sweetie. They said dinner should be ready in an hour or two, so take your time. I'll come over for you when it's time to eat if you haven't come back by then, okay? Would you like me to make you a cup of tea before I go?"

"Tea would be good."

"Okay. What kind? What would you like in it?"

"Chamomile, I think. Sweetened with honey."

"I'll get it for you."

o0o

It was a lot of potatoes to peel alone. After a bit, Doreen slipped in beside him. "Need a hand?"

"Sure. That'd be great."

This big gathering was probably as awkward for her as it was for him. Other than Sierra running out on him, of course.

"Have you met Sierra's parents?"

He shook his head. "You?"

"Not yet. I think they're here, though. I just pray that God can bless them through me."

Gabe glanced at his former mother-in-law. "That's a great way to look at it." Of course she was thinking of Bethany's death. His angle was much more complex. It included loving two women.

The outside door opened and Gabe caught a glimpse of a trim middle-aged woman slipping outside. Sierra's mom going after her daughter? Most likely. He probably knew everyone else who was present.

A shadow darkened the space in front of Gabe, and he glanced up again.

A large man pulled out a stool across the counter and settled into it.

Gabe sucked in a deep breath and released it slowly.

"Gabriel?"

At his tight nod, the other man carried on. "I'm Tim Riehl. Sierra's father." He bit his lip. "And the guy who was in the wrong place at the wrong time a few years ago."

Gabe swallowed hard. "I know the accident wasn't your fault."

"No, but that doesn't mean I don't regret it. I've prayed for you every day, asking God to restore His joy and blessings to you."

Had he known he was praying for his daughter at the same time?

Doreen reached her wet hand across the counter, a potato peel sliding off. "I'm Doreen Klimpton. Bethany's mother."

Tim took Doreen's small hand into both of his. "Doreen. I'm so sorry for your loss. I understand she was your only child."

Doreen nodded. "She was." She glanced at Gabe. "Her daddy died when she was young, and we were very close."

"I'm sorry. You, too, have been in my prayers."

"You are forgiven." Doreen picked up the next potato. "And I thank you. I've felt the prayer support of many."

"Yes, thanks." Gabe met the older man's gaze. "I'm trusting God for His answers. It's been a rough three years, but I'm beginning to see the light at the end of the tunnel."

As the old saying went, the light seemed to emanate from an oncoming train. But that wasn't any of Mr. Riehl's business at the moment.

"Thank you, son. Your forgiveness means a lot to me."

"Like Doreen said, there's nothing to forgive. Bethany's death was an accident, pure and simple." Yes, it had taken time to get that through his thick skull, but he knew it for a fact. "I'm sorry you were part of the situation."

Tim ran his fingers across his buzz cut. "I had nightmares for months. Probably not as long as either of you."

Gabe grimaced. "It's okay, man."

The outside door across from him opened once again, and Gabe glanced up. Sierra back, maybe? His gaze froze just as surely as the icy air that swirled in with the newest guest.

Tyrell Burke.

What in the name of all that was holy was that man doing here?

Chapter 27 --

Sierra was halfway across the yard before Tyrell's pickup truck leaped to her attention, parked right beside Gabe's old car.

No. No, no, no, no, no.

What had she been thinking? On the other hand, who had invited Gabe? Zach must have. She should've known.

She took a deep, shaky breath. The temptation to bolt back into the duplex was nearly unbearable. Pull the shades, turn out the lights, crawl into bed. Maybe under it.

Would it be better to face the music and see if she could pull this off, or let them all talk about her behind her back? Not just Gabe and Tyrell, but her entire family, Allison, Steve and Rosemary, Jo and Zach, Claire and Noel. Doreen. Possibly a few more strays someone had picked up.

Oh, Lord, there is no direction to turn!

Except to God Himself. She'd decided how to handle things and forged ahead. Sure, she'd prayed, but then she'd gone right back to her plan. Tomorrow she'd spend some quality time with Jesus. Today, right now, she had to face the mess she'd created.

Sierra mounted the steps, crossed the deck, and opened the door, but it didn't open fully. An instant later, she saw why.

Tyrell stood on the mat just inside, his smile widening to a cocky grin when he saw her. "There you are, doll." He tugged her to his side as the door shut. "There are a lot of people here I don't know," he stage-whispered. "How about some introductions?"

Beyond Tyrell's chest buttons Sierra focused on the view into the kitchen over the peninsula.

Gabe still stood at the sink where she'd left him, his eyes wide in shock. Then they narrowed, and he bit his lip. With a brisk headshake, he bent over his task.

She'd thought all the tears her body could produce had already flowed. She'd been wrong. Burning heat seared her eyes, and she blinked hard to gain a semblance of control.

Her dad sat on a counter stool where he'd obviously been talking with Gabe. She should've been there for that. Should've been the buffer. It was all too late. The only way out was forward.

"Dad?" She cleared her throat and tried again, a little louder. "Dad, I'd like you to meet my… friend, Tyrell Burke. Tyrell, this is my father, Tim."

Her dad stood and rounded the dining room table to shake Tyrell's hand. "Pleased to meet you, Tyrell." But then he turned slightly aside and raised his eyebrows at her.

She gave her head a slight shake. "And I know Mom is here somewhere. Mom? This is Tyrell Burke. Tyrell, this is my mom. Sandra."

Tyrell removed his arm from around Sierra's waist — thankfully — and took Mom's outstretched hand in both of his. "Pleased to meet you, Sandra. Now I see where Sierra gets her ravishing beauty."

Oh, good grief. Couldn't he manage to sound more genuine?

"My sister Chelsea is the blonde over by the window with her friend Allison Hart, who will be joining us at Green Acres next spring. And my brother Jacob is around here somewhere. I think you know everyone else." She could only hope.

Tyrell nodded toward the girls as they looked up and acknowledged the introduction with a little wave.

Mom pulled her hand out from Tyrell's grip and tossed a quizzical glance at Sierra.

"So, uh, Tyrell," Dad said. "Let's have a seat, and you can tell me a bit about yourself."

"I should help get food on the table," murmured Sierra, stepping away.

Tyrell's hand caught hers. "Looks like they've got lots of help in the kitchen, doll. I'm sure they'll excuse you." He towed her into the great room, where folding chairs had been pulled out of storage to accommodate the large group.

Sierra allowed herself to be seated next to Tyrell, with Dad on the other side of her. A buffer again. She sent up a quick prayer. She was going to need all the help she could get.

"To answer your question, I own the largest apiary in the Idaho Panhandle. You could say that sweet things rule my life." Tyrell winked broadly at Sierra.

Oh, man.

"Ah, so that must be how you met Sierra?"

"Tyrell's dad was teaching the beginning beekeeper course when I started. Tyrell bought him out since then."

"I see." Dad nodded. "I see."

"And you, Mr. Riehl?"

"The name is Tim," Dad said. "I drive a truck."

"Oh."

Couldn't Tyrell even pretend to be interested? "Dad used to drive a reefer — a refrigerated truck — but now he delivers freight for Home Depot in the Portland area."

"Do you have a flat-bed? I'm looking to hire one to haul

hives to California in a month or so."

"No. I don't have my own. I'm just a driver."

"Oh." Tyrell glanced around the room and shifted in his seat. "If you know of anyone, I'd appreciate the tip."

"Sorry. Not my area of expertise."

This was all two grown men could think of for a conversation? "When you come back in spring, Dad, you should see Tyrell's set-up. I've learned so much about beekeeping from him and his father."

Dad's brow furrowed. "Thought you said you were hauling your hives away. What will there be to see?"

Tyrell waved a hand. "Oh, they're just going south for almond pollination. I'll bring them back when it's spring here and flowers are blooming."

"That sounds... interesting." Dad glanced at Sierra.

If she was supposed to support Tyrell in this one, he was out of luck.

"Almond pollination is where the real money is with bees." Tyrell leaned forward, elbows on his knees. "I also lease hives around here to orchardists for pollination. The honey is a nice byproduct, but I sell it by the barrel to big distribution plants. Can't be bothered to do like your daughter here, bottle it all up and sell it in small lots."

"We make considerably more per pound," Sierra reminded him.

Tyrell shook his head. "But it's so labor intensive. I'd have to hire more help, and my profits would go down instead of up. Then I'd have to sell the stuff, too. Not worth the headache."

Just as well. If Tyrell got into her local markets, he'd flood them, and then where would she be?

"I see," said Dad. "I can understand you'd want to make the most profit."

Sierra cast her father a sharp look, which he ignored. It wasn't like him to put money first.

Tyrell chuckled. "Of course. That's what this life is all about, right? He who dies with the most, wins."

"Not if he dies without Jesus Christ as his Lord and Savior, Tyrell. It's a strange sort of winning that sets a man up for losing the ultimate game for eternity."

"Oh, I didn't mean it that way." Tyrell's hands swept the words away. "I was introduced to salvation just a couple of years ago. I must say it's made a big difference in my way of thinking."

Dad's eyebrows went up.

"I've even done my stint at teaching Sunday school at the local church, Mr. Riehl. Sierra knows."

And he'd dumped it back on Gabe without a second thought. How had she gotten stuck in this situation again? Why wasn't Gabe the one her dad needed to get to know? They'd been talking when she came in.

Before Tyrell.

She was to blame for Tyrell's presence. For the whole big mess. For the hurt hardening in Gabe's eyes. Would he come back and try to win her again?

Doubt it. She'd done her best to push him away. She'd never let a guy come this close before. Lots of flirtation, lots of dates, lots of easy come and go. A game for teens. For college kids. Not a game for a woman who desperately wanted to be treasured and secure.

"Even so, a man needs to plan ahead." Tyrell winked at her. "Especially when he's found a girl to impress."

Impress? He did this for looks? "Excuse me." Sierra veered through the crowded room toward the hallway and the privacy of the bathroom.

Oh, Lord, how was she going to get out of this disaster?

oOo

"I don't know what to say." Zach dumped a huge bag of salad greens into the sink Gabe had just rinsed out.

Oh yeah? Gabe's new plan was to eat alone in the kitchen and climb out the window when he was done.

"You didn't know she'd invited him?"

Zach shook his head. "No clue. I feel for you."

Like sympathy made things any better. Gabe grabbed a handful of lettuce and ripped it to smithereens. Pretending it was Burke helped. Except maybe everyone else didn't want pulverized salad. Who knew? Maybe it would be a new fad.

Zach bumped Gabe's elbow. "I think I'd better do this part."

Gabe held his ground. "There is no way I'm going out there." He grabbed more lettuce.

"Didn't say you had to. Just don't kill the food."

"Yeah. I'll try."

Rosemary breezed into the kitchen. "Someone said it was time to make gravy?"

"Want to double-check the bird, Mom? It's still in the oven. The thermometer is only up to one-sixty."

"You kids and your temperatures. Did you wiggle the drum? Press into the thigh?"

Zach laughed. "It's Claire's kitchen. I just do as I'm told."

"That'd be a first." Rosemary opened the oven and peered in. "Can someone get this out for me?"

Noel sprang to her side and lifted the huge roasting pan to the butcher-block island. "Oh, look, it's reached temperature. The turkey website says it will continue to cook a few degrees while it's resting. What do you think, Rosemary?"

She wiggled the thighbone. "I'd say it's done."

Gabe turned back to the lettuce in the sink. The last few years he'd had Thanksgiving with the orphans, his parents, and other missionaries in Romania. Mom and Jillian had prepared the fanciest spread they could afford, which hadn't included turkey. The wide eyes of all the children were still impressed.

He missed them. He should've stayed over there and never returned to Galena Landing. How could he have known he'd come back and get his heart stomped all over? It was the past he hadn't been able to face. Now he couldn't face the future either.

Zach dumped potato water into another pot in the other side of the sink then carried the liquid to Rosemary. He came back with butter and milk. "Mom's the resident gravy expert," he murmured, digging in a nearby drawer for a masher.

"I'm a fool, Nemesek."

Zach poured a good-sized glug of milk onto the potatoes. "Don't think so, man."

"I should've known better. I never intended this."

His buddy glanced his way. "A guy doesn't plan to fall in love. It just happens."

Had he fallen in love? He had. Hard. He'd told her, too. A lump formed in Gabe's throat. "Well, I shouldn't have let it happen."

"Dude." Zach shoved the masher deep into the spuds. "I know things look dismal at the moment."

Gabe barked a sharp laugh. "Understatement."

"But everyone in this house is rooting for you. Well, with the obvious exception of Burke."

"And Sierra."

"You think she looks happy?"

"No, but apparently I didn't make her happy either."

"You did at first." Zach mashed. "What happened?"

"You asked before. I still don't know. Chelsea, maybe."

"Oh, no wonder I came in here," Chelsea chirped. "I didn't

236

know you guys were talking about me."

Gabe stifled a groan as he closed his eyes. Of all things for Sierra's sister to overhear.

"Question for you, Chelsea," said Zach.

"Hmm?"

"What has turned Sierra into such a grump? Can't help but notice she hasn't been her usual sunny self the last few weeks. I thought you might know."

Gabe canted his body so he could see Chelsea without looking at her directly.

She was staring at him, eyes wide and her mouth a perfect 'o' before she snapped it shut. "There's some... stuff... going on."

"Yeah, I figured."

Thank you, Zach, for taking point on this one.

"When is she going to let the rest of us in on it?"

Chelsea's gaze shifted back and forth between the two guys. "Soon. Look, I'd tell you, but I promised to keep her confidence, okay? I can't break that."

"I guess that's reasonable." Zach glanced at Gabe.

No way was he meeting his friend's eyes. Or Chelsea's. Man. Awkward. Painful.

"So long as she isn't going to keep us in the dark forever."

"No. I promise."

Gabe pivoted. "It's Burke, isn't it? She just didn't know how to tell me she'd rather be with him than me."

Chelsea bit her lip. "That's not quite true."

He'd had enough. "Which part is true? Which part isn't? Because I assume she's the one who invited Burke to dinner today, and she certainly didn't invite me. Looks to me like she's made up her mind."

Chelsea put her hand on his arm, but he shrugged it off. "So she doesn't look happy. She chose, Chelsea. She chose Burke."

He jabbed a finger toward the great room, thankfully hidden around the corner. "That's pretty obvious."

"Give her a bit more time, Gabe. Please."

Echoes of Sierra. "I think she's had enough time, don't you? Seriously?"

Chelsea hesitated. "No. Not quite."

He laughed harshly. "Well, you're wrong."

Chapter 28 --

This was worse than sitting next to Tyrell through an interminably long and quiet Thanksgiving dinner. Worse than Gabe giving no further acknowledgment that she existed. Worse than the thought of cancer.

Maybe.

Mom paced the open area in Sierra's duplex. It didn't take very many steps before she had to pivot and start again. "We're just concerned, that's all."

"Very concerned." Dad's eyes followed Mom. Back and forth. Back and forth.

"I'm sorry you feel that way." Sierra pulled her knees up to her chest, hugging them tight.

Jacob snorted. "Dude's full of himself."

"He's really nice. I don't know why you can't see that." Maybe because it was harder and harder for Sierra to see it herself.

"He's such a new Christian," Dad said.

"You can't hold that against him. The only way that can change is for time to go by. He'll mature. He already has." Some. Not a lot.

Why did she feel like she had to stand up for Tyrell? Wouldn't it be better to be single than married to him? No. Yes. Yes?

"What about Gabriel?" Mom went on. "He seems like such a nice young man. Rather quiet, though."

"Not too quiet one on one," said Dad. "At least before dinner."

"Seriously! It's not like a woman chooses a… a man like picking one pumpkin over another. It's far more complex than that."

Mom stopped in front of Chelsea, who'd been curled up in the corner, silent. "You've been here a few times this fall. What do you think?"

If telepathy worked, her sister would hear her. *Don't tell. Don't tell. Don't tell.*

"I'd rather not get involved." Chelsea may have been speaking to their mother, but her gaze was snared on Sierra's. "Sierra is old enough to know what she's doing."

Mom threw up her hands and stalked away. "I counted on your bond to bring her to reason."

Sierra closed her eyes and took in a deep breath. Should she explain everything to her family? But she couldn't. Not yet. A few more days. Of course, they'd be back in Portland by then. This was her chance to clear the air face to face.

Mom stopped in front of Sierra, hands on her hips. "There's only one thing that comes to mind that explains all this. Are you pregnant with Tyrell Burke's baby?"

"No!" Sierra surged to her feet, eye to eye with her mother. "You know me better than that." So much for her parents giving her the benefit of the doubt.

"I thought I did." Mom waved both hands around. "But it doesn't seem true anymore. I don't know what is going on and, if you won't tell us, you leave us wide open to speculation."

"I am not pregnant. Not by Tyrell. Not by anyone."

"Fine then." Mom whirled away. "I don't know what else could be so secretive."

"I promise I'll tell you soon. It's just… I can't right now."

"See, that's the kind of thing I'm talking about. There is something behind all this. Tell me if you love Tyrell Burke."

"I do." Maybe Sierra hesitated a second too long.

Mom shook her head. "I don't believe you."

Her temper surged. "Then why did you ask?"

Dad pulled to his feet and captured Mom's hands. "Love is patient. Love is kind. Love wants the best for someone else. It endures everything for that to happen."

She watched her parents gaze deeply into each other's eyes for a few seconds. What they had. She wanted it.

Her father turned to Sierra. "When there is love, there is also evidence of love. That's what your mother is trying to say. You say you love this man, but we're not seeing the evidence of it in your relationship."

"We just don't want you to make a huge mistake." Mom sniffled.

Dad went on. "That young man is all about himself. Even when he spoke of you, it was superficial. Not what characteristics of yours drew him to you, but what you could do for him. That you turn heads wherever you go together."

"Scum," said Jacob.

Sierra turned to her sister, but Chelsea shook her head.

Great. She was on her own. Nothing new.

"We want you to be happy, Sierra," Mom said more gently. "We want you to have a marriage based on the principles in God's word, to someone who loves you and respects you."

Tyrell couldn't give that to her. Sierra knew it. She'd always known it. Why had she led him on? Why, oh why, had she perversely invited him to Thanksgiving?

She'd asked for this whole charade. For all the pain this day had caused.

"Thanks, Mom. That's what I want, too." She made a show of yawning as she stretched both arms over her head. "It's been a long day. I'm headed for bed. Coming, Chels?"

Her sister shook her head. "Not yet. I'll be quiet when I come in."

"Your dad and I will retire now as well." Mom's eyes burned Sierra. "To pray for you."

"Well, um, good night." Sierra fled to her room, thankful her sister wasn't following just yet. Praying sounded like a good idea.

o0o

Doreen's headlights glared in Gabe's rearview mirror all the way back to town. Her car pulled in beside his when he parked beside the store's back door.

Gabe sighed. How could he explain the situation to Doreen when he'd been blindsided himself?

Burke the Jerk. Smug as all get out, smirking around the Thanksgiving table. How had the loser become the winner?

Doreen leaned against the hood of her car, her breath billowing on the frigid November air. She shoved her hands in her pockets and waited.

Gabe's hands itched to shove the gearshift into reverse then peel out of here, never to return.

He would, too. Just not tonight. Sierra had asked for six months. He should've made her promise the same. With a harsh laugh, he jammed the hand brake on and climbed out of the car.

"We need to talk, Gabe."

"Not tonight. Can't you see I've had enough?"

"You're angry."

"You bet your bottom dollar I am." He could think of a few more words. Humiliated came to mind.

"I'm coming upstairs with you."

"No need."

"I think you need someone to vent on." Doreen straightened. "I'm here."

Dump his problems on Bethany's mother? Sierra's local mom-figure? Yeah, right. He stalked over to the door and wrenched it open. He'd lock her out.

"I still have keys to this building, Gabriel James. I'm coming upstairs."

"Whatever." He'd get in the shower and stay there until the hot water ran out. He could outlast Doreen.

A vestige of manners whacked him, and he stepped aside, indicating the stairway. "After you."

"Thank you, Gabriel." She made her way up the steep steps and into his kitchen. She filled his kettle and set it on the stove to heat. "I need some tea."

Tea. If he were a drinking man, tonight would be the night. Tea seemed like a granny way to deal with his problems. Gabe straddled a kitchen chair. "You know Sierra as well as anyone. What is she trying to prove?"

Doreen leaned against the cupboard by the stove and wiped a hand across her forehead. "I really don't know."

"How long has she been seeing Burke?"

"They met over a year ago, I think. When Sierra took the beekeeping course from his father."

So they'd been dating long before Gabe returned. How could he have known he shouldn't stay away from Galena Landing for three years? It had seemed the only thing he could do at the time.

Doreen poured hot water into two teacups and set one in

front of him. "But they've only been going out since spring, I think. Maybe even summer. I'm not sure. She hasn't mentioned much about him."

Gabe jabbed the teabag in his cup. "Why did she lead me on?"

Doreen shook her head. "I wish I knew."

"What does Burke have that I don't?"

"Money."

He barked a laugh. "I never thought that would matter to her. This place isn't big or fancy, but it's better than a cardboard box. It's more than what millions of people around the world have."

"I didn't say she valued it. That's not what you asked. You asked what he had that you didn't."

"Doreen, I—" Did he really want to give her the details? But what did it matter now? "I thought there was a spark between Sierra and me. We went out a few times. I — I kissed her. Told her I loved her."

Bethany's mother's face did not change expression as she squeezed out her teabag and put it in the garbage can.

"I figured on getting her a diamond for Christmas. I knew it was rather soon, but we're not teenagers. Why wait?"

Doreen nodded and added honey to her cup.

"I felt alive for the first time since Bethany died. Like I had a reason to live again. Not just a stock reason, but joy. Anticipation of what the future might bring." He glared at the insipid tea in his cup.

"I don't know what happened," Doreen said slowly. "She never seemed serious about Tyrell. She didn't glow when she talked about him. It seemed to me as though she had a friend to do things with besides her girlfriends at the farm."

"Who are both married."

"Yes." Doreen frowned. "That's why she moved in here after

Claire's wedding. She said she wanted to give them some space, but there was more to it than that."

Sierra had lived right here in his apartment. He kept forgetting. "What else?" Might as well grind some salt into his wound. Get it all over with tonight.

"Jealous isn't the right word. It's not that she'd fallen for Zachary or Noel, I mean. She just felt like a fifth wheel out there with all the lovebirds."

"So she started dating Burke."

Doreen nodded, sipping her tea. "I always kind of wondered if she... if she was waiting for you to come back."

"Me?" He didn't know whether to be flattered or horrified. "Tonight was a strange way to show it."

"Something changed in the last few weeks."

"Tell me about it." All his burgeoning happiness yanked away.

Doreen glanced at him. "But then I haven't seen her as much since you got back and took over again at the store, so it might have been my imagination. She's looked distracted. Sad."

"Why didn't she have guts enough to tell me there were problems? Maybe even tell me what they were? I could have helped. Couples talk about stuff. They share each other's burdens. I thought we were past that stage of keeping things back." Though he'd never pressed her about Burke. Should he have? But why bring the other guy into the conversation when everything looked so rosy?

He'd been a fool.

Gabe surged to his feet. "Remember when Tammy stopped by the other day and asked if I wanted to sell the business? She has someone looking for a turnkey business just like Nature's Pantry. At the time, I laughed at her, but I'm going to call her in the morning and get the ball rolling. Of course, these people may have found something else already."

"But—" Tears started down Doreen's cheeks. She didn't bother to wipe them away.

"What else can I do? I'm not sitting in Galena Landing smiling and nodding at everyone while watching Sierra and Burke's kids grow up. I can't do it, Doreen. I don't have it in me."

"I — I understand. I'll continue to pray for you, for God's leading. I've never stopped." She pushed the teacup away, still nearly full, and slipped out the back door.

It seemed so easy. He paced the floor. Did he wish Doreen would've argued? It crushed him even deeper to know she didn't think there was reason to hope, either.

Nothing. No hope.

My hope is built on nothing less than Jesus' blood and righteousness.

Gabe dropped to his knees in front of the sofa. If Jesus was all the hope he had left, wasn't it more than so many had? He'd cling. He had to.

But that didn't mean he could sleep another night between the sheets Sierra had bought for his birthday. He balled up the whole works and shoved it into the spare room closet. The room that, once upon a time, was to be his baby's room.

The death of his relationship with Sierra was just as devastating.

Gabe dug an old army sleeping bag out of storage and crawled into it. It smelled stale, but it didn't matter. He wasn't going to sleep anyway.

Chapter 29 --

*M*onday. Sierra had dreaded this day for almost a week. Her parents had finally taken off yesterday with Jacob, leaving Allison to talk business with the gals at Green Acres and return later with Chelsea.

She'd tried to tell everyone she was busy Monday, but Jo had pushed right over that. "Whatever it is, Sierra, put it off until Tuesday or Wednesday, won't you please? We need to get details finalized while Allison is here."

"I can't change the date. I'm sorry."

"Good grief, girl! What could possibly be more important for that one day?"

Sierra had stared at Jo. No doubt her misery had seeped out her eyes. "I can't tell you, but I also can't change it."

If only she could. If only she could be as happy as she'd anticipated a month ago. Thinking of dancing with Gabe at their birthday party, the kisses they'd shared in the days afterward... man, she'd give anything to erase the time since and get her hopes back.

Sure, the D&C might remove all the abnormal tissue. She might not have cancer. But somehow she'd managed to screw everything up anyway and send Gabe away. She'd only meant to slow things, not shut him down completely.

If only she hadn't invited Tyrell to Thanksgiving.

If only she hadn't made her best friends and her family furious with her.

If only.

Chelsea at her side, Sierra walked in the doors of the Wynnton Hospital ER to check in for day surgery. The smell of antiseptic once hadn't bothered her. Today she nearly gagged.

"Right this way, Ms. Riehl. The procedure room is on schedule, so we'll be taking you back there in thirty minutes." The nurse swept the curtains open to reveal a now-familiar cubicle. "First, into this gown please. I'll be back in a moment to take your vitals." She bustled back out, the curtains rattling shut behind her.

How many times had she stripped down for bodily invasions lately? Too many. Sierra pushed the thought aside and shrugged out of her purple sweats, which she'd deemed the comfiest clothes for going home later. She donned the poor excuse for a gown then folded her sweats and stacked them into Chelsea's gym bag with her wallet at the bottom.

"I'll run this out to the car." Chelsea patted the bag and turned to leave. "I'll be back before they haul you off."

"Thanks." There wasn't really anything left to say. They'd done all their arguing in the days and weeks gone by. Now Sierra just needed to get over this hurdle. Finally someone would be able to tell her the extent of the endometriosis, and do something to remove the most of it. Waiting for results was her new way of life.

"How much blood?" the nurse asked in the distance. "How far apart are the pains? You said you're thirteen weeks along?" Her voice came closer, along with her squeaky shoes and the trundle of a gurney.

"She's been spotting since late last night," a man's voice replied.

Zach?

Sierra surged upright, cocooned behind pale blue dividers no thicker than sheets. What in the world was going on?

"It was a stressful, busy weekend. She tried to get as much rest as she could, but it didn't help."

Definitely Zach.

Had she added to Jo's stress? Oh, no.

The curtains next to Sierra's cubicle rattled down the rail. Shoes appeared below the dividing curtain. "I'll get the doctor in for an exam. Here, Josephine, can you change into this gown? I'll be right back."

Sierra froze. Should she let them know she was here? Ask what was going on? Then they'd wonder why she was here in her own backless gown. Was it time to tell?

"Let me help you," came Zach's low voice.

Jo whimpered.

Sierra had never thought she'd hear a sound like that. Her heart clenched. Jo in pain? She couldn't just barge in there and intrude on their privacy. Even once Jo had donned the gown.

"Maddie will be fine with Mom. Don't worry about a thing, sweetie." Zach's soothing voice was barely discernible. "Everything will be okay."

If only Gabe were here with her, and they were facing this challenge together. With a pang, Sierra realized he would have been in a heartbeat. Before all this drama.

It would have been inappropriate in this stupid gown though. She closed her eyes. *God, are You there? I can't deal with all this on my own. I'm terrified of what the results will be. I don't want to die. I don't want to have a hysterectomy. I want a family like any woman my age wants. I want Gabe.*

Her mental prayer faltered. That would require a miracle probably beyond God's abilities.

Please be with Jo and Zach. It sounds like they might be losing their baby. Please comfort them.

"Sierra? Can I come in now?" Chelsea asked from outside the curtain.

"Shh. Come in," she whispered, and the curtain swished. The aura around her sister's head looked like a full migraine headed in. There was no way Jo and Zach hadn't heard Chelsea. It wasn't like Sierra was that common a name. It wasn't like her friends had never heard Chelsea's voice.

Sierra closed her eyes, waiting for the inevitable with her finger across her lips. Willing Chelsea to silence. Knowing it was too late.

"Sierra?" asked Zach.

Sierra stifled a groan as panic swelled through her.

"Zach?" Chelsea turned toward the curtain, her face perplexed. "What are you doing here?"

"Chelsea? Is Sierra with you?"

Chelsea turned wide eyes on Sierra and bit her lip. She spread her hands wide, the question of what to do now apparent.

Sierra took a deep breath. "Yes, I'm here, Zach. Are you guys okay?"

"Not sure. Jo might be miscarrying."

"I'm so sorry to hear that."

"What about you?"

The nurse jogged into Sierra's cubicle. "Let's get that blood pressure now, shall we? Sorry it took me so long to get back here. We're almost ready to take you into the OR." She wrapped the band around Sierra's arm and began to inflate it.

Sierra might have been saved by the nurse's return, but it definitely wasn't over.

oOo

"Gabe, I'd like you to meet Stuart and Barb Smith," Tammy said as the middle-aged couple glanced around Nature's Pantry with obvious interest.

"Nice to meet you, Gabe." Stuart shook his hand. "Thank you for allowing us to view your business so quickly."

"Uh, no problem." Actually, he could think of a bunch of problems, all with Sierra's name on them. But that meant nothing to this couple. "I'm glad I could accommodate you."

"Tammy said there are living quarters upstairs?" asked Barb.

"Yes, have a look through it as well. If you wanted to buy a house, you could always rent out the apartment."

She nodded. "Now there's an idea."

Thankfully Tammy had called him yesterday to set up this viewing and he'd done a quick blitz of the space. It irked him to remake the bed with Sierra's gift, but he didn't want to answer any questions about why his bedding was in the closet instead of where it belonged. Trying to see the apartment through strangers' eyes was weird. Would they love the turquoise and honey tones throughout? Surely the colors presented better than battered beige.

"I'll leave you with Tammy." Gabe nodded at the couple. "I'll be around, so if you have any questions she can't answer, feel free to find me." It wasn't like he could leave the building with the store open for business.

"Thanks so much." Barb twined her fingers through Stuart's as they turned toward the Realtor.

Gabe retreated behind the store's counter. He'd been meaning to sort out the shelves underneath. This would be the perfect time.

Voices rose and fell as the trio slowly walked each aisle then disappeared into the receiving bay. A few customers came and went. Eventually he heard the stairs creak as Tammy led the potential buyers upstairs.

What were they thinking? Surely if they hated it, they'd be gone by now. They'd driven all the way from Bozeman yesterday — on Thanksgiving Sunday — to view Nature's Pantry.

Did he want them to make an offer? His gut clenched. He could always refuse it. Not if it met the asking price he and Tammy had worked out on Friday, though. He'd signed a contract, but convinced Tammy not to put For Sale signs up until they saw how things panned out with the Smiths. Next week would be soon enough to answer all the curious townspeople when word got out.

To say nothing of Sierra. Would she care? Would she remind him he hadn't given it six months? She wouldn't dare.

The bell jangled and Mrs. Bowerchuk ambled in, leaning on her cane. The old woman's hunched back made it difficult for her to walk, but her face brightened at the sight of him behind the counter.

"Good morning, Mrs. Bowerchuk." The Smiths would take good care of her, wouldn't they? They wouldn't allow stock of Cora's plain rice cakes to run out.

"Good morning, Gabriel. Did you have a blessed Thanksgiving?"

The smile froze on his face. How in the world could he answer that? "I, uh, have much to be thankful for." It was true. He knew it, though it was hard to remember the details at the moment.

"Don't we all, dear boy, don't we all." She thumped her cane a few times for good measure. "I'm here for some rice cakes. Do you have any in stock?"

"I sure do. They're over here." He walked past her toward the right aisle. Not that she needed to be shown.

She peered at the shelf. "Can you spare two packages? In case that storm we're supposed to get keeps me inside a few extra days."

"No problem. Buy as many as you'd like. I think there are four on the shelf. Would you like them all?"

"Oh, no. I couldn't do that. What if someone else needs them before you can get another order in?"

"Three, then?"

She tilted her head to one side, considering.

If only the biggest problem in his life right now hinged on how many sleeves of rice cakes to buy.

"Two will be plenty, dear boy. I don't want too many lest they go stale."

As though anyone else in town bought the things. He should just give her a case lot price and drop the whole thing off at her place. "Whatever you say, Mrs. Bowerchuk. Is there anything else I can help you with today? Do you need any vitamins, maybe? Or some organic pasta?"

She blinked at him. "No, this will be fine."

Gabe tried to keep his sigh inside. "Okay, I'll carry this up to the cash register for you."

The back steps creaked and voices grew louder, though still indistinct. Nothing wrong with the old lady's ears. She turned to peer at the door to the back just as Tammy and the Smiths breezed back through.

"Well hello, Mrs. Bowerchuk," Tammy said with a big smile. "What brings you out today? It's a nippy one."

The old lady tapped the counter. "I needed my rice cakes." She lowered her voice to a stage whisper. "I'm buying two packages in case that storm is as bad as they say on TV."

"Good idea. It always pays to be stocked up." Tammy's gaze

met Gabe's as Mrs. Bowerchuk turned to the counter, fumbling with the snap-top change purse she'd pulled from her pocket.

He shrugged and grinned. What could he say? Keeping the old ladies in this town happy was part of his job. Even if they dropped less than five bucks a week into his till. He set the two tubes into her shopping bag, and she hobbled toward the door.

Gabe sprang around to open it for her, but she turned to Tammy before he could. "You here on selling business? You leave this dear boy alone. Galena Landing needs him." Then she proceeded out the door, icy wind swirling past her.

He shut the door, grimacing. "Sorry about that," he said to the Smiths.

"No problem. Loyalty is a good thing."

"Indeed it is." Tammy laughed. "It's both the beauty and the curse of small-town living, right, Gabe? Everyone knows your business." She turned to Barb. "It can take newcomers a bit of time to be made welcome, but the townspeople will come around. First out of curiosity and later because they like you and trust you."

Did that mean they were still interested?

"I grew up in a small town like this." Stuart nodded. "I know how they work. And it beats living in a high-rise and never meeting anyone else in your building at all. The more people are crammed, the less they talk to each other."

"Well, if that's everything for now?" Tammy's eyebrows rose as she looked from Barb to Stuart.

They nodded.

"I'll be in touch with you later, Gabe." Tammy waved the couple out the door in front of her then winked at Gabe as she pulled the door shut.

Another swirl of freezing air circulated the store. And maybe it did a spiral around his heart, too.

Chapter 30 --

Sierra watched Zach's truck drive past the duplex toward the log cabin they lived in. No doubt they'd picked Maddie up from Rosemary and Steve's and were busy with her. She couldn't just walk over there and intrude.

Besides, the anesthetic for the D&C had taken more out of her than she'd anticipated. The pain was considerably less than with the biopsy, but she still didn't feel all that great.

Walking to the log cabin in this icy wind? Wasn't going to happen. Chelsea had settled her with a hot water bottle, a cup of tea, and a few magazines then gone off to find Allison, who was staying in the guest room at the big house.

Guess that meeting hadn't gone off today with Sierra and Jo both missing.

She really ought to go see how Jo was doing. They hadn't seen each other again in the hospital. Jo would have questions.

It was time Sierra coughed up answers, even though she didn't really have them yet.

A tap sounded on the door and Jo's head poked around. "Can I come in?"

Sierra tried to scramble to her feet but reality set in as a cramp clenched her abdomen. "Yes, sure. Can I make you tea?" If she could just get upright and move slowly.

"Sounds good." Pale and exhausted, Jo sank into the other deep chair.

"What did the doctor say?" Sierra put the kettle on. Anything to keep attention on Jo rather than herself. She'd become adept at it over the past weeks. Years, maybe. "Is the baby okay?"

Jo took in a deep breath and let it out slowly. "No. The baby... I miscarried."

Sierra hobbled over and knelt by Jo's chair. "I'm so sorry." She wrapped her arms around her friend, unable to hold back tears.

Jo sniffled and tugged a tissue from the box on the end table. "Me, too. We were so looking forward to another little one. But I guess it wasn't meant to be. At least not now."

The whistle of the kettle called Sierra back to the kitchenette. A moment later she returned with Jo's tea, done up with just the right amount of honey and cream. She gave her friend a wan smile. "Want a hot water bottle?" She passed over the still-warm rubber bladder.

Jo's eyebrows popped up. "You were using it. Go ahead."

"I have a heating pad, too." She lifted it from the floor as she sank into her own seat again, tucking the heating pad and a quilt around herself.

"So you know why I was in Wynnton today. They did a D&C and told me to wait a few months before getting pregnant again." Jo sipped the chamomile tea, watching Sierra over the rim. "How about you? I think it's time to come clean."

"Probably." She'd guarded her secret so long she wasn't sure she could get it out even now. "I, um, had a D&C today, too."

"Oh no." Jo set her teacup down. "Those horrible periods you were having?"

"They turned out to be a result of endometriosis, so the doctor did a biopsy last week." Sierra grimaced. "Today they removed as much of the mass as possible. Once all the results are back, we'll see what I'm up against."

"Up against?"

Sierra met Jo's gaze. "He suspects uterine cancer." Okay, maybe suspect was too strong a word for the doctor's opinion. He'd only mentioned it as a possibility.

"So that's why Chelsea has been here so much. To help you with this stuff."

Sierra nodded.

"Why didn't you tell us? Or did you tell Claire and not me?" Hurt blazed out of Jo's eyes.

"No. I... I just couldn't talk to either of you."

"But why? We've been there for each other for ten years. What was so dreadful about this that you couldn't share?"

"My mom's sister died of this kind of cancer. It went quickly."

Jo swept her hand down, barely missing the teacup. "That's no excuse. In fact, it's even more reason to talk to the people who care about you. Good grief, Sierra! We're your best friends. We've vowed to share everything with each other. This definitely should have been kept in the open."

She deserved the sting of Jo's caustic words. Totally. "It's just that you're both married."

"So? How did that come between us as friends? Have I ever pushed you away on account of Zach or Maddie? Ever?"

"Relax, Jo. Getting all worked up isn't going to help your body heal any." She should take her own advice.

"I'm serious, girl. I can't believe I didn't bully you and make you tell me what was going on. Of all the stupid reasons to keep me in the dark. Just because I'm married."

Sierra bit her lip. "You were so excited about being pregnant."

"Well, of course." A shadow crossed Jo's face. "But one doesn't cancel the other." She stared at Sierra. "Wait a minute. You think it does, somehow?"

Sierra clenched her teacup in both hands. That porcelain better not be as fragile as it looked. "I can't have kids."

"What do you mean, you can't have kids? Have you ever tried?" Jo's eyes blazed at her.

"Of course not."

"Then you don't know."

"Endometri—"

Jo's hand cut through the word. "Millions of women are told they will probably not conceive because of it. Some of them still do. Yeah, it makes it less likely, but it's not a foregone conclusion."

"If it's cancer, they'll do a hysterectomy."

"And if it isn't, they won't. When did you turn into a hypochondriac?"

The words stung. "I resent that."

"You sound like you're borrowing trouble. It just doesn't seem like your personality. You've always been the most upbeat and positive one of us. Trust me, we've noticed the doom and gloom."

Borrowing trouble? Probably. But that didn't make the problem any smaller. Everything she'd said was true. She could practically see the gears grinding in Jo's brain as her friend's eyes narrowed.

"And what was with inviting Tyrell Burke to Thanksgiving dinner? Wow, did that cast a wet blanket on the whole affair."

Sierra stiffened her back. "Tyrell is a very nice guy."

"He hides it well. Jeepers, girl. You've got someone as

wonderful as Gabriel Rubachuk with stars in his eyes and you push him away for that pompous—"

"I *said*, Tyrell is a very nice guy. You don't know him as well as I do." She didn't need to be reminded of the differences between the two men. Especially not now.

Jo rolled her eyes. "That's for sure. And I have no desire to. Sierra, tell me. What in the world is going on? Why not Gabe? I thought you really liked him. That you were falling in love with him."

Sierra took another sip of her tea. Lukewarm. Warmer than her gut, no matter that she cradled a heating pad against it. Could she really trust Jo with this information?

Would Jo go away if she didn't tell? And Jo had already had a harrowing day. She didn't need Sierra to make it worse.

"What is the one thing Gabe wants more than anything else?"

Jo bit her lip. "Besides you?"

"Be serious. What does he always talk about?" Surely he'd mentioned his desires to Zach, and Sierra wasn't under any illusions Zach wouldn't tell Jo. Which meant anything she said here today might get back to Gabe. She'd have to swear Jo to secrecy.

"I'm not following."

"Haven't you seen him with Maddie? Haven't you seen him with his Sunday school class?" Better not get into how it came back from Tyrell to him. "Haven't you seen his face when he talks about the kids in Romania?"

Jo's mouth formed an 'o.' "Bethany was pregnant when she died."

"Exactly."

"So he wants a family. Kids."

Sierra nodded.

"And you're worried you can't have any."

Bingo.

Jo leaned forward. "Have you talked to him about it?"

"Of course not. We weren't really at that stage of our relationship when this started happening." They'd been at the kissing and dreaming stage, though.

"So instead you leave him looking miserable and parade Tyrell Burke in front of him?"

"I didn't know Gabe had been invited." Lame. Lame. *Lame.* She could have guessed.

"Oh, come on. Like we'd leave him alone on Thanksgiving of all days. We're his friends. He doesn't have family anywhere on the continent."

Sierra let out a deep breath. She'd blown it. Repeatedly. Big time.

"So why is it okay to date Tyrell and not Gabe?"

Her friend had never heard of giving up. Which didn't mean Sierra needed to respond.

Jo snapped her fingers then winced. "I bet he's too selfish to want kids."

"Hey! That's a big leap in logic."

"But I'm right, aren't I?"

"Only when you say he doesn't want a family." Why did she keep sticking up for Tyrell? She knew he was bad news. Knew he wasn't right for her. Why couldn't she admit it, even to herself, for more than a few seconds?

"Look, I need to get home to Maddie and some painkillers. Not necessarily in that order." Jo struggled to her feet. "Zach has to swing by his office yet and see how they managed today without him."

"Thanks for stopping by."

"I'm not done with you yet, girl. I'm going to pray that God will open your eyes about the men in your life. You need to ditch

Tyrell and explain things to Gabe."

Sierra chewed on the inside of her lip and stared at Jo. "I'll talk to you tomorrow. You be thinking on what I said."

Like she could block Jo's words out.

oOo

Tammy settled across Gabe's kitchen table from him, paperwork neatly stacked between them. "Wow. I don't think I've ever put together an offer this quickly."

Gabe's head swam. "I can't believe it, either." Was he making a mistake? "Tell me how they countered."

"That's it. They barely countered at all." She slid the top paper across to Gabe. "Nature's Pantry is exactly what they were looking for, and the apartment up here just clinched it."

Gabe stared at the numbers on the paper. When Tammy had guided him toward an asking price, he'd thought it way too high. These people had barely blinked. This amount of cash would get him a newer car and see him through college, with enough to get set up again afterward.

He hadn't given more thought to what his studies would entail. He'd better get on that. "What's the catch? There has to be one."

Tammy hesitated. "They want possession on December thirty-first."

Gabe reeled back in his chair so hard it tipped on its back legs. "That's barely a month."

"I know. I told them I wasn't sure you'd go for it, but they said it was a deal-breaker." Her mouth twisted to one side and she shook her head. "I don't see why, but that's what Stuart said. And I figured you might not mind."

Where would he go? Where would he live? "I hardly know

what to say. This is quite a shock." He gave his head a quick shake. "Go over everything with me. Every line of every page." He looked at the stack at Tammy's elbow. This would take a bit of time. Time he desperately needed.

"That's what I plan to do."

He wasn't ready after all. He jumped up. "Let me put on a pot of coffee."

"Sounds good." Tammy leaned back in her chair as he busied himself at the counter. "I'm really happy for you, Gabe. I hope everything works out well on your end."

He silenced his thoughts — and her words — buzzing the coffee grinder. All too soon the pot began to gurgle and he resumed his seat.

"Where will you be off to?"

"I really don't know. I didn't expect to be out on the street so soon. I thought these things took time." Visions of Sierra with Burke swirled through his mind. "But it's okay. I have a month to figure things out."

"Will you go back to Romania?"

He shook his head. That hadn't ever seemed like a permanent option, just a stopgap. Why, he didn't know. He gave a short laugh. "Time for an all new Gabe Rubachuk."

Tammy tapped the pen on the table as she stared into his eyes. "I'm looking forward to seeing what he looks like. I liked the old one pretty well, so I doubt I'll be disappointed."

He'd been looking forward to the new him, too. But that had been when it included Sierra. Now, he wasn't so sure. "Take anything in your coffee?"

"Just black, thanks."

He poured a cup, set it in front of her, and added a splash of cream to his own. Back in his chair, he nodded at her. "I'm ready." But he wasn't. Not really.

Chapter 31 --

S ierra took her place on one side of the long plank table. Today Claire sat at the head. Jo, Allison, and Chelsea pulled up seats.

"Everyone knows the reasons this meeting couldn't be held yesterday as planned." Claire looked from Jo to Sierra. "So there's no need to go into that any further."

Sierra winced. Claire had vented her worry about Jo on Sierra as well as her frustration at the way Sierra had kept things hidden. It was all out in the open now, distracting everyone a bit from Jo's miscarriage. Not that Jo wanted all the attention, but Sierra could sure do without it, too.

"We've all agreed via email to accept Allison as a full member of our Green Acres team." Claire nodded at Allison. "There will be some growing pains, I'm sure. You don't know any of us all that well, and we don't know you, other than from a few meetings and emails plus your letters of reference, which were very positive."

Allison glanced at each of them in turn, her eyes lingering on Sierra.. "I'm willing to do my part in keeping communication open."

Ouch. Now there was a jab.

Claire rubbed both temples. "You can see the difficulties that come when someone decides things are too personal to share, even though the outcome affects the entire group and the burden is too heavy to carry alone."

Sierra swallowed a sigh. How long would they make her pay for this? "Look, I apologized."

"I think we've all learned something from this. At least I hope so." Claire shook her head. "Moving forward then. Can you give us a timeline for your plans, Allison?"

"It depends on what kind of winter Idaho gets. I've talked to Patrick at Timber Framing Plus in Coeur d'Alene and I'll sign a contract with him as soon as we've cleared everything here. He said the first big hurdle is pouring the footings, and that can't be done until there are a few days of above freezing weather."

"Sometimes we get that in February," Jo offered. "But often not until March."

Allison nodded. "That's what Patrick said. Once the weather is good, he'll bring in a full crew to the project."

"Sounds positive," said Jo.

"Exactly. Patrick has a good reputation in the area. I drove down Friday and Saturday and went through a few buildings he's erected and talked to the owners. They couldn't say enough good things about Patrick and his guys."

Relief washed through Sierra. "Good to know." She'd been dubious about bringing in an out-of-town crew, but there really wasn't a contractor in Galena Landing experienced in this type of building. Nor did they have time for such a large DIY project.

"Still, it will take a few months from start to finish. They'll build my house kind of at the same time, so sub-contractors can go from one to the other."

Allison's plans for her own place looked bright yet cozy, with a steep roof and sweet decks front and back. It would be set behind the duplex, closer to Jo and Zach's cabin. They should've laid out the property for a village to start with.

"So there are four classrooms with movable partitions in the main hall." Allison unrolled the blueprints down the table and anchored her end with a coffee cup.

They all leaned in.

"A pair of bathrooms and a kitchen."

Claire frowned. "Why a full kitchen? We built the one here with group cooking in mind."

"Canning and cooking classes. We can always use the house as a backup space."

Claire grimaced but nodded.

"Above the hall, twelve dorm rooms with four additional bathrooms and a laundry facility."

"So twenty-four students can live in," Jo mused.

"We did design the building so it can easily be added onto should we outgrow the space."

"Classes will mostly be in the warmer weather, so students can also pitch tents," Claire added. "Like Noel's crew used to do. Tents and campers."

"Also true." Allison tapped the blueprint. "So as long as the classrooms are ample, we'll be fine."

This felt good. Finally taking Green Acres to the next level they'd dreamed of years ago. Sierra only hoped she'd live long enough to experience it. Groups of young people, studying organics and farming and sustainability. This was awesome.

She couldn't marry Tyrell. She was meant to be on this farm, being part of this calling, not eight miles away keeping house for someone she didn't truly love. No more sticking up for him. No more pretending. A weight slid off her shoulders.

Gabe was another matter, one not so easily decided. But she still couldn't talk to him without knowing the biopsy results. Just a few more days.

"—over here?" Jo pointed at the blueprint.

Sierra gave her head a quick shake. Time to focus.

"A small lab, so we can run tests like soil pH." Allison turned to Sierra. "Would you like to teach classes on herbal medicines? Chelsea told me about your training and the herb garden."

Sierra stared at her for a moment. "I feel like a fraud."

"Um..." Allison looked at the others then back at Sierra. "Why is that?"

"Do you know how many pharmaceuticals I've taken in the last few weeks? How many invasive procedures I've had done? How can I talk about natural healing when I went running to the doctor myself?"

Chelsea snorted. "More like you got dragged."

"Oh, good grief, Sierra." Jo shook her head. "Sometimes we need modern medicine. It's not evil just because it exists."

"I'd be blind without glasses," Chelsea put in. "I hope you don't advocate I double the carrots I eat and throw my glasses away."

"No, of course not." Sierra wrapped her arms around her middle. Shielding herself from attack, perhaps? "Sorry I mentioned it."

"Balance is always a good thing." Claire tapped her pen on the table. "We don't buy everything organic. We're not running this place perfectly. We're doing the best we can with what we have... most of the time."

"I haven't been able to cure Zach of stopping for an occasional burger at the drive-through." Jo rolled her eyes heavenward. "At least the diner in town doesn't appeal to him, so his addiction is limited to out-of-town trips."

"Now there's the pot calling the kettle black." Claire gave Jo a pointed look. "I saw those bags of chips you tried to hide when I popped by last week."

Everyone laughed, and Sierra managed a smile.

Quirking her eyebrows, Allison met Sierra's gaze across the table. "Will you? Which season would be best for that?"

Wasn't this what she'd always wanted to do? Teach others about natural medicine? She bit her lip and nodded. "Summer. Will we have a building by then?"

"If we set it for July, we should. I hate putting off our opening classes until then, but we didn't get things rolling early enough this fall to get started before freeze-up. So, there's no help for it."

"We could do something on gardening in May and June, if attendees don't mind tenting," said Jo. "A group of, say, fewer than fifteen could meet in the great room when they're not in the garden."

"Or there's always the pole barn," Claire added.

Allison nodded. "That might work. With a group like that we could even start a market garden on the premises. Maybe across the driveway from the classroom building? Or did you have other plans for that area?"

A market garden. Sierra stared at Allison. Why had it taken an outsider to get things rolling that the original trio had meant to do all along? "There's no place to sell that much produce. Gabe—" She choked on his name. "Gabe can absorb some at Nature's Pantry, if he's willing." If he were still talking to her by summer.

"You don't think a roadside stand would draw customers here?" asked Allison.

"It is rather the end of nowhere," said Claire. "Not counting the logging road up the mountain."

Allison shrugged. "But it's only five miles from town. People wouldn't come?"

"Nosiness will bring some," Chelsea put in. "I bet people in town are dying of curiosity as to what goes on out here."

Claire nodded. "True, that."

"If we had the garden and the laborers for it anyway, there's no reason not to go for the stand." Jo paced to the front window and peered out. "All it takes is a bit of lumber, a few coolers, and a cash float. No one needs to sit there if there are no customers, if it's right beside the garden itself."

They clustered around her, chattering about the possibilities.

Sierra tugged Jo back out of the group. "You doing okay?" she whispered.

Jo shrugged. "Kind of okay. It helps to have this to focus on today. How about you?"

"Same as you. Kind of okay. Where's Maddie?"

"Steve offered to sit with her for her nap. Rosemary is making Christmas crafts and wanted the house to herself."

Sierra grinned. "Maddie adores him."

"Yeah, he's a good grandpa." Jo's phone beeped, and she pulled it out. After reading the text message, she glanced at Sierra. "Gabe invited Zach to dinner at The Sizzling Skillet tonight so he won't be home."

Uh oh. What was up with the guy talk?

oOo

"So, what's up? Have you talked to Sierra lately?" Zach twisted his coffee cup in circles at The Sizzling Skillet.

Gabe snorted. "If by lately you mean a few weeks ago, sure."

"Not since yesterday, then?"

"No, why?"

Zach shrugged. "Just wondered."

His best friend had never been good at pretending. Gabe stared at him for a long moment, but Zach wouldn't meet his gaze. Whatever. Sierra wasn't why he'd called his buddy.

Not directly, anyway.

The waitress came by to take their orders. When she had gone, Gabe cleared his throat. "I've made some decisions."

That brought Zach's attention around quickly enough. "Like what?"

Gabe took a deep breath. "I'm selling the store."

"You're what?" Zach slapped the table. "You can't do that."

"It was a tough decision, but it's time."

"But—"

"But what, Nemesek? I own it free and clear. I'm a grown man. Why can't I sell it?"

"You just got back to Galena Landing. We need you here, man."

Gabe shook his head. "I've been back for over two months. Plenty long enough to realize that things have changed, and it's not in my best interests to stay."

"Is this about Sierra?"

"Partly. At least, if she hadn't cut me out of her life, I probably wouldn't have done it. But she did, so I did."

"You're making a big mistake, Rubachuk. Can you de-list it?"

Gabe leaned forward. "You didn't hear me. I didn't just list the business. I sold it."

Zach gave his head a quick shake. "You *sold* it? You never even talked to me about the possibility and now it's a done deal?"

"It happened rather quickly."

"I'll say."

"You know Tammy Stephenson?"

"Yeah, the Realtor. She and Matt go to our church."

"She stopped by last week for some groceries and asked if I'd consider selling. That she had a buyer looking for something just like Nature's Pantry."

"And you said—"

"I said I'd think about it."

The waitress set a bowl of French onion soup in front of each of them and topped off their coffee cups.

Zach leaned back in his chair, his narrowed gaze never leaving Gabe's. "That's not a final sale then."

"I called her Friday and said yes."

Zach mumbled something under his breath.

"She brought the couple by yesterday to view, they placed an offer, I accepted, and they take over at the end of the year."

"They *what?*" Zach leaned forward so suddenly his spoon went flying and his soup splattered. "Rubachuk, tell me you're pulling my leg."

"I'm not." Gabe kept his voice steady. He hadn't expected his buddy to be thrilled, but this wasn't the reaction he'd been going for, either.

"Man, you can't do this. You just can't. Find some hole in that paperwork and overturn it."

The waitress appeared to blot the soup off the table and deliver a clean spoon.

"You're missing something, Nemesek. I made a deal because I wanted to. I'm not going to appeal it. There's no point." Maybe "wanted to" was coming on a bit strong. But what choice had Sierra left him?

"It's all because of Sierra, isn't it?"

He lifted a shoulder in a resigned response.

"I never figured you'd give up on her this easily."

Gabe crashed his fist on the table. "This easily? What are you talking about? She's refused to talk to me for weeks. She's treated me like scum."

"She had reasons."

"*What?*" Gabe shot to his feet. "I did nothing to deserve it. Nothing, man."

"Sit down. I didn't mean it that way." Zach shoved his hand through his hair. "Look, there's been some stuff going on."

Gabe dropped into his chair and crossed his arms. "Oh, yeah? So now suddenly you're all privy to it?"

A dark look crossed Zach's face. "The confidence was hard-won."

"Don't speak in mysteries."

"Look, it's not my story to tell. But trust me when I say that nothing that's happened has been against you."

A sharp laugh exited Gabe's mouth. "Right. I'm supposed to believe that?"

"Have I ever lied to you?"

Gabe narrowed his eyes and thought through the many years he'd known Zach. "No."

"I'm not lying now either." Zach shook his head and pulled in a deep breath. "I sure wish you'd talked about this before signing your life away."

"You make it sound like I joined the military or something."

Zach's eyes veered back to Gabe. "Did you?"

"No, Nemesek, I did not. Figured I'd go back to college and... take something useful. Whatever that turns out to be."

Two plates with loaded burgers and fries landed on the table. Gabe stared at the food. Turned out he wasn't that hungry. He hadn't even tasted the soup. Neither had Zach.

Zach shook his head, picked up his burger, and took a big bite.

Gabe stared at his a moment longer before doing the same. A hint of appetite revived. This was a whole lot better than cooking for himself.

"What did you mean about Sierra?" he asked at last. "Is she really going to come clean with what's bugging her?" Not that he'd trust her again, but it would still be nice to know so he could close that door.

"Yeah, she is. She thinks she's had good reason for keeping her secrets."

"Right." No way was he going to start telling his buddy all the various scenarios his active mind had come up with. Not if Zach knew the truth, and apparently he did.

Why was Gabe always the last to know? Didn't he deserve better than this? He rammed a handful of home-cut fries into his mouth.

"Something else you ought to know," Zach said at last.

"Hmm?"

"Jo miscarried yesterday."

A surge of sympathy shot through Gabe. "Oh, no. That's rough." And here he was going on about his own problems.

"Yeah."

"I'm sorry I asked you to dinner tonight. You should have said no. She needs you there."

Zach shrugged. "It's okay. Jo's with the girls. They've been in a meeting all afternoon with Allison and Chelsea. That's helping take her mind off things."

Green Acres would carry on whether Gabe was in Galena Landing or not. Sierra would be just fine without him, too. She had the girls. She had the farm. She had Burke.

Obviously, she didn't need Gabe.

Chapter 32 ---

Sierra's cell phone rang. The number on the screen was Dr. Wilburn's office. She closed her eyes for a second. This was it. Now she'd know. She slid the phone on to accept the call. "Sierra Riehl here."

"Ms. Riehl? This is Donna from Dr. Wilburn's office."

Um, yeah, she already knew that. "Thanks for calling, Donna." *Now get on with it, lady.*

"I have good news for you. The biopsy results came back negative."

Sierra dropped into the nearest chair, her heart pounding so hard it hurt. "Negative? Really? No cancer?"

"None whatsoever."

"Well, that's good news." She was going to live after all. With all her girly parts intact.

"We'll continue to monitor the endometriosis, of course."

"Yes."

"Well, have a great day!"

Sierra thumbed the call off. She'd been braced for the opposite results. She'd all but felt the cancer eating through her uterus. She'd just known...

She'd been wrong. Thank the Lord, she'd been wrong.

Now what?

She was going to live long enough for it to be worth making plans. No way could she marry Tyrell. She'd been reminded again of what a loving husband was like, watching her dad. Zach and Noel. Tyrell could never compare. Could never fit into her life at Green Acres. Wouldn't even want to.

Sierra shrugged on her jacket and swept her purse and car keys together. One benefit of her friends being married was that their guys had trucks. She didn't have to ask anyone if she could use the old hatchback anymore.

Yeah, she could call Tyrell, but he wasn't the sort who would get the nuances over the phone. She needed to drive out there in person and give it to him straight. Make sure he got the message.

Then she'd call Chelsea and tell her friends the good news.

Gabe.

She sucked in a deep breath of frozen air and let it out slowly. These results made no difference with him. So her problems weren't as permanent as a hysterectomy, but her chances of conceiving were still zero to none. Dr. Wilburn had made that very clear even before the biopsy.

But still, she owed Gabe the truth.

She slid into the car, rubbing her gloved hands together. Brr. The wind had picked up, and dark, foreboding clouds hid the sun. Looked like that forecasted storm was going to hit after all. At least Chelsea and Allison had made it back to Portland yesterday before it began.

A few minutes later she pulled into the parking spot beside Tyrell's shiny truck. That guy must hit the car wash every week.

She rested her forehead on the steering wheel. *Dear Lord, give me the right words. Help Tyrell to understand.*

Did it matter if he understood, really? All she had to do was make it clear that this was the end. She took a deep breath and pushed open the car door. Snow swirled around her as she clutched her jacket tight and made her way to his door. She rang the doorbell.

A moment later it swung open and she met Tyrell's surprised gaze. "Sierra. Wow, didn't expect to see you here. Come on in."

If it had been summer, she'd have talked from the doorstep, but not in this wind. She stepped inside then leaned against the closed door.

"Let me take your coat. Can I get you something to drink? A cup of coffee, perhaps?"

Sierra blinked. "No thanks. I'm only here for a few minutes."

He leaned against the back of his leather sofa, the spotless room displayed behind him. "What's up, doll?"

"Don't call me that."

Tyrell grinned. "You know you like it."

"No, actually, I don't. I'm not someone's plaything or... or display piece."

Something hardened behind his eyes. "Never said you were."

"Look, I came here to tell you that it's over between us."

Tyrell's eyebrows shot up. "Over?"

"Yes. I know I don't love you enough to make a life with you, and I don't think you care about me that much either."

"You don't love me."

"That's right."

He laughed. "Well, Rubachuk doesn't love you, either."

Ouch, that hurt. "This isn't about Gabe."

"Right. You expect me to believe that?"

"It's the truth."

"Uh huh. Everything was going fine between us until he showed up like a lost puppy, preying on your sympathies."

Gabe? A lost puppy? Well, maybe. A bit.

"He's not man enough for you, doll. You need somebody strong."

"You mean I need someone who will walk all over me and never listen to a word I say? Like now?"

He shook his head, grinning. "I can't imagine Rubachuk dealing with your sass." Tyrell straightened and crossed the few steps to Sierra before she could react. He grabbed her by the arms and kissed her.

She tried to push him away, but he was stronger than she was. He deepened the kiss.

Sierra bit his lip.

Tyrell sprang back. "You little vixen, you!"

She wrenched the door open and escaped to the steps. "I told you it's over, Tyrell. How dare you force yourself on me after that?" Or before, for that matter. But definitely after.

He stared at her, his eyes hard. "That wasn't a very Christian thing to do."

"Give me a break. That's it, Tyrell. Over and done. Got it?"

"Oh, I've got it, all right. But don't come back begging me. I'll build that new house, and you'll never live in it."

As if she cared. "I never asked for a new house." All she'd wanted was love. Respect. A family.

"Every girl wants a big house."

"I don't. Goodbye, Tyrell." She turned to go.

"You won't be able to use my extraction equipment."

Like that was reason enough to bend to his will? Not hardly. "Thanks for the heads up. I'll have something in place by next fall." And best of all, she was going to live long enough to need it.

o0o

Gabe sat at the one and only traffic light in Galena Landing and watched Sierra drive through, going south. Probably heading to Burke's. It didn't matter what Zach said a few days back. She hadn't called him to explain. Hadn't stopped by the store. Hadn't made any effort to get in touch that he could tell.

He jammed his right turn signal on, not that there was anyone behind him to care. This was the perfect time to go out to the farm, when she wasn't there. She could come find him on her own time… if she ever got around to it.

A few minutes later he stomped the snow off his boots on the log cabin's porch. He'd parked beside Zach's truck down in the main yard. Someone would have to plow out the rest of this driveway before anything less than a 4x4 could get in the whole way.

Jo met him at the door. "Gabe!" She reached up and gave him a hug.

That was nice. He patted her back. "How are you doing?"

She grimaced. "Okay, I guess. Zach said he told you what happened."

"Yeah. I'm sorry." He'd lost a baby once, too. Sure, the circumstances had been different, but at least he had a clue.

"It's been a rough week, but God's got it." She beckoned him in. "Take your coat off and stay a while. Zach's just gone out to grab an armload of firewood."

"Toasty in here." He shrugged off his jacket and hung it up before removing his boots.

"We'd like to keep it that way with that storm brewing."

"Unc Abe!" shouted Maddie as she barreled into his legs.

Gabe reached down and swung her to his shoulder as she squealed with delight. He was going to miss watching this little rascal grow up. He was going to miss a lot of things.

"Let me get you some tea," Jo was saying as she led the way

into the compact main room.

How long did he have before Sierra returned? Probably long enough. "Sure. Thanks." He set Maddie down and tickled her. "Cold out today."

"The temperature has dropped something like twenty degrees, I think." She busied herself in the kitchenette and emerged a few minutes later with two cups of tea. "Here, Maddie, Mama will get you some juice."

"Joo?"

"Yes." Jo poured a bit of apple juice and a lot of water into a sippy cup and handed it to her daughter.

Gabe's eyebrows went up. A plastic sippy cup from Jo? Would wonders never cease?

Jo curled up in the armchair across from him, tucking her feet under herself.

"Did Zach tell you my news?" he asked when she sat silent.

She grimaced. "Yes. I wish you wouldn't have, but Zach says the sale is final, and nothing can be done."

Gabe kind of wished he hadn't, too. At least part of the time. Change was never easy. "He's right. The papers are legally binding."

"I can't believe you're leaving us again. Just when you got back." Her brown eyes darkened.

"Some things can't be helped. You know that."

"If it's Sierra…"

"Partly." Okay, totally. But no one was going to get him to admit that out loud any day soon. "But that's not why I'm here."

"I wish you'd talk to her."

He barked a sharp laugh. "I've tried, trust me. It's like talking to a brick wall."

"Things have changed."

"Not toward me, they haven't. She's the one who shut me

out, Jo. You have to understand. That means the topic is closed until she chooses to open it." He snorted. "Rather, *unless* she chooses to. No guarantees it will ever happen that I can see."

Zach came in, carrying an armload of firewood and accompanied by an icy wind. "Rubachuk! What brings you out here on this blustery day?" He kicked off his snowy boots and crossed over to the wood stove, where he lowered his burden to the hearth.

"It wasn't to tell us he and Sierra have talked to each other," Jo said tartly. She uncurled, headed to the kitchenette, and turned the kettle back on.

Zach glanced at Gabe and shook his head with a grin.

A person always knew where they stood with Jo. She called it like she saw it. "I did have a reason for making the jaunt out here. I've started packing up the apartment."

Jo glared at him from the kitchenette, her lips pursed.

Fine, he'd look at Zach while he spoke instead. "I don't know what to do with my furniture. I heard you all might be doing some building next year and thought I'd offer you first pick. Not that it's all that valuable, but most is in decent shape."

Zach and Jo exchanged a glance.

"There's the kitchen table and chairs, the living room set, and the bed, night stands, and dresser. Know anyone who can use any of that?"

"Aren't you going to need furniture where you're going?" Jo dropped her hands to her hips.

"Well, that's the thing. I don't know where I'm going, so I don't know what I'll need. Doreen is taking back the hutch we borrowed from her in the first place, along with a bookcase. Which leaves another bookcase, actually. Add that to the list."

"Gabe, you can't up and leave town like this."

He raised his eyebrows at Jo. "Oh?"

"You just can't. It isn't right."

Gabe grimaced. "It's not a question of what's right, Jo. Sometimes a man has to do what he has to do. I was lured into thinking there might be a reason to stay in Galena Landing, even though I'd planned to put the store on the market as soon as I got back stateside."

She inhaled sharply.

"So I'm simply going back to my original plan. It wasn't as spontaneous as it seems."

"Talk some sense into him, Zach." Jo spun back to the kettle.

Zach held out both hands in a helpless gesture, meeting Gabe's eyes. "I agree with her, man, even though I know it doesn't do any good."

"Too little, too late," agreed Gabe.

"Where there's life, there's hope," Jo shot back as her cell phone rang. She picked it up off the counter and glanced at it then at Gabe. "Sierra? Wonder why she's calling." She swiped the phone on. "Hey, girl, what's up?"

She listened for a moment. "No way. Are you okay?"

Gabe couldn't help leaning closer, not that he could make out Sierra's words.

"Where exactly are you at? ... Okay, sit tight. Oh, I guess you can't do anything else. ... No, you're right. It's a long time to wait for a tow truck. ... I'll talk to Zach."

"What happened?"

"She slid the car off the road turning off Cottonwood and onto Highway 95. She said the tires caught slush, and down she went."

"There's quite a ditch on that corner," Zach said.

Jo glanced from Zach to Gabe and back again. "Think you could pull her out with the pickup?"

Zach nodded. "Probably. I have a good tow rope." He bit his

lip. "Only thing is, Noel's not home. I could sure use some help." He looked at Gabe.

Sierra needed a hand, and he was in a position to provide it. No brainer. "I'll come."

"You sure? Thought you two weren't talking."

Gabe stood. "We weren't. Maybe we still aren't, but that doesn't mean I'd let her freeze to death in a ditch. Daylight's wasting, Nemesek."

Chapter 33 --

 $\mathcal{S}$ ierra rubbed her hands together, trying to stay warm. She hadn't really dressed for the weather. Yeah, she had a parka on, but yoga pants and tennis shoes were not exactly winter wear. Thin leather driving gloves. No hat.

Of course, she'd expected to drive to Tyrell's, and then home in one piece. Catching her tires in the soft snow and sliding down a four-foot embankment hadn't been part of her plans.

So much for being self-sufficient. Why did stuff like this always happen to her? Okay, maybe that was a bit melodramatic. But it seemed she'd been bouncing from one crisis to another for months.

She rubbed her hands up and down her thighs. How long did it take to get frostbite? When would Zach arrive? Would he really be able to pull her car out of this ditch or would she have to call a tow truck from Wynnton after all?

The rumble of Zach's pickup filled the air.

Sierra wiped a circle of condensation from her window and caught her breath. It might be Zach's truck on the highway, but it was Gabe sliding down the steep bank to her car. Gabe pounding on her window. Peering in through the spot she'd just cleared.

"Sierra! Are you okay?" He tugged at the car door, but it was wedged against the snow bank.

He yelled something up to Zach, who looped a thick rope from his elbow to his hand and around. Zach nodded and disappeared.

Gabe worked his way around the car and yanked the door on the passenger side open. The frigid wind blasted inside with him. He reached for her seatbelt clasp and undid it. "Are you hurt? Can you crawl out this way?"

Sierra's teeth chattered in relief. She fumbled for the lever to push her seat further back, giving herself room to climb over the console.

"Come here, sweetheart. You can make it." Gabe backed out to give her room, his hands outstretched.

The endearment melted a bit of the ice around her heart as she struggled across to the passenger seat. Those feet and legs barely felt like they belonged to her. So numb.

She stopped to catch her breath, but Gabe tucked one arm under her knees and one around her shoulders, lifting her as though she weighed nothing. She was pretty sure that wasn't true. She wrapped her arms around his neck.

"Need a hand?" hollered Zach over the wind. He waded through the snow toward them.

"I've got her!" Gabe shouted back.

If only he meant it for life. She'd done so much to keep him away, but this... this felt wonderful, being wrapped in his arms.

He stumbled up the steep incline. Zach was there to keep them both from landing in the snow then ran ahead to open the truck's passenger door.

Gabe slid her into blasting heat.

Sierra hated to let go of him, but the words he'd let slip had only been a natural reaction to aiding a damsel in distress. They weren't personal. She believed that until she got caught in his eyes. Those deep blue wells pulled her in.

His mittened hand swept her cheek. "Sierra," he groaned as he pulled away. "I'm going to give Zach a hand with the car. You sit tight." The truck door snapped shut.

Emotions whirled through Sierra's frozen gut like the blizzard outside. Too late. Too late. Too late. But was it? He'd come. For some reason, though she'd called on Zach, Gabe had come along. How had that happened?

Her toes began to tingle. She tugged off her driving gloves and, with stiff fingers, struggled to undo her laces. It took ages to get her shoes off and pull her feet up under her, cross-legged. She rubbed her hands up and down her numb legs, willing sensation to return.

The truck bounced a little, like one of the guys had jumped off the tailgate. Zach opened the driver's door and slid in, glancing her way. "How are you doing?"

"F-fine. F-frozen."

"I bet." He grinned. "Well, here is the moment of truth. We'll see if the beast has the power and traction to get the hatchback out of there." He shifted into four-wheel-drive low then first gear. "You might say a prayer."

Like she hadn't been praying nearly nonstop.

The truck eased forward and came to a stop a few seconds later. The wheels began to spin, and Zach stopped to roll down the window. "More sand under the tires, Rubachuk!"

Gabe's muffled voice replied, "Got it."

A clang.

Zach eased the truck forward again. This time the tires caught.

Sierra could almost feel the weight of the little car as inch by inch, Zach and his truck pulled it up out of the ditch, Gabe's shovel adding sand often. At long last, Zach heaved a sigh of relief and patted the dashboard. "Good job."

Gabe opened the back door and crammed in beside Maddie's car seat. He thumped his mittens together and blew out a blast of air. "Cold out there."

"But warm in here." Zach glanced in the rearview mirror. "Buckle up, man. Let's haul this baby home."

The heat blasting from the vents cocooned Sierra. Made her drowsy. The adrenaline buzz drifted away. She was safe. "Thanks, guys." Totally inadequate words, but the best she could think up at the moment.

"Just glad you're okay," came from the backseat.

oOo

Gabe watched Sierra's profile the whole way back to Green Acres as she leaned against the headrest, eyes closed. Her face seemed pale beneath her makeup.

Her nearness brought feelings of longing surging to the surface. No matter how many times in that short drive he reminded himself she'd wound up in the ditch coming from Burke's place, he still couldn't force from his memory the light in her eyes when she'd seen him sliding down the bank to rescue her.

Okay, maybe he'd imagined it. The window had been pretty fogged in. But still, she'd clung to him with a ton of strength as he carried her back up that hill.

She just didn't want to fall in the snow and get further chilled.

No, it was more than that.

But she'd been to see Burke. She'd chosen the other guy. He mustn't forget.

They'd arrived back at Green Acres. He and Zach hadn't

even checked the hatchback to see if it were drivable. Sierra certainly was in no state to have done so, and Gabe had only wanted to keep her in his line of vision.

Her eyes fluttered open as she realized they were back at the farm.

Oh, to kiss those eyelids again. To feel her eyelashes on his cheeks.

Gabe gave himself a shake and opened the back door. He made his way around to the passenger side just as Sierra slid to the ground. He stuffed his hands in his pockets. He had no right to catch her, to carry her. She glanced over at Zach, who came around the front. "Thanks, you guys. I don't know what happened."

Zach poked his chin toward the hatchback, still linked to his truck. "I should've kept an eye on things for you. That car needs new tires."

"It's not your responsibility."

Zach grinned. "Sort of yes and sort of no. Let me feel some guilt, okay?"

Sierra managed a smile. "Guess I'm grounded until the roads clear enough to get to the tire shop, then. Unless I damaged something else hitting the ditch."

"It's probably okay," Zach said. "I'll have a closer look when the weather clears."

They stood silently for a moment, snow sifting down on their shoulders. Sierra turned toward the duplex.

Could Gabe follow her? Didn't they need to talk? But was he really ready to be told a final *no*?

"Hey, come over to the log cabin, Sierra." Zach reached for her arm. "Let's get you warmed up. Jo was worried about you. She's probably watching for you out the window."

She hesitated a moment but nodded, taking a tentative step

on the path through the woods.

Zach glanced at Gabe before striding off up the path.

Nice of his buddy to give him a moment alone with Sierra. He waded through several inches of snow beside her, ready to catch her if she needed it. She came close a few times.

Finally he reached past her to open the cabin door, his arm brushing her shoulder. Even through both their winter coats, he felt the touch and stifled a groan.

She'd been to Burke's. He'd sold the store. Today would be goodbye. He needed to brace himself for the inevitable.

Gabe slid the jacket from Sierra's shoulders as Jo scurried up then enveloped Sierra in a hug.

"Are you okay? I've been so worried."

"I'm okay. Thanks to some knights in shining armor."

That sounded promising, didn't it? He hung up her jacket then his and kicked his snowy boots to the mat.

Jo wrapped a quilt around Sierra and nudged her toward a chair.

"Hey, I'm fine. Don't smother me."

"You're freezing. Do as you're told."

Life must've been entertaining when these two had been roommates. But Sierra curled up in an easy chair, tugging the quilt closer. She glanced at Gabe from beneath lowered eyelashes.

He gave her a tentative smile.

Jo turned the kettle on. "Maddie's having a nap, so keep the noise to a dull roar."

What noise? Gabe didn't have anything to say. He settled into the other easy chair. All he could do was pray and wait. The rest was up to Sierra.

Jo passed out mugs of tea. "I put lots of honey in yours," she informed Sierra.

Sierra managed a smile. "Thanks."

Jo dropped onto the love seat beside Zach. "Well, don't everyone talk at once."

Gabe bit his lip. It wasn't his place.

"Okay, fine." Sierra pushed the quilt from her shoulders and sat up straighter. "I should've been more careful on the road. I knew it was slippery, but I had to talk to Tyrell. It couldn't be done over the phone."

Interesting. Gabe kept his expression as bland as he could.

"I had to tell him everything was over." Sierra's face was turned toward Jo, leaving her profile open to Gabe's scrutiny.

Wait. She called things off with Burke? A surge of elation gushed upward. The geysers in Yellowstone had nothing on him.

"How did it go?" asked Jo.

Sierra grimaced. "He didn't take it very well, but I think he believed me in the end."

Being a fly on the wall might've been interesting. But weren't they all in hibernation by now?

"Did you tell him—" Jo shot a glance at Gabe before looking back at her friend. "—everything?"

"No." Sierra sucked in such a deep breath that Gabe could hear it several feet away. "He didn't need to know."

The two girls stared at each other. Gabe wished he could read the message that passed between them. "Is it time?" asked Jo.

Sierra nodded, almost imperceptively.

Jo surged to her feet. "Come on, Zach. Let's go in the other room."

Zach eyed each person before grasping the hand Jo held out to him. They disappeared down the short hallway to their bedroom.

Gabe studied Sierra as she stared off over the rim of her cup. Was she going to make him ask? He didn't have it in him.

"So, I... uh... I guess I owe you an explanation."

He clenched his teeth. "I'd appreciate it."

"It's not easy for me to talk about this."

He waited. *God, please give her the words. Please help me understand.* He clenched his hands together. *Help me bear it.*

"I've been having increasingly painful periods." Her cheeks flushed.

His did, too. Not the average non-married conversation.

"Chelsea finally made me go to the doctor. I've had a bunch of tests and procedures done in the last few weeks."

Gabe hadn't known. How could he? Why had she held this back? "I'm sorry to hear that."

"I have endometriosis." She glanced at him.

He shook his head. "I'm not familiar with the word."

She bit her lip. "An unnatural thickening of the uterus walls. It causes a lot of problems."

"I see." He sort of did. But there must be more.

"I found out today that it isn't cancerous."

He swung to meet her gaze full on. "Well, that's great news! Right?"

She nodded, her face still pensive. "My aunt died of uterine cancer when I was a kid. I've been really worried about it."

Gabe surged to his feet, crossed the space, and knelt by her chair. "Is that why you wouldn't talk about it?" He reached up and tangled his fingers in a curl of her hair. "I would have been there for you."

She searched his face, apparently unconvinced.

"I would have."

Sierra inhaled sharply. "There's more."

"I'm listening." He tried to capture her hands, but she pulled away.

"I know..." Her voice broke. "I know you miss Bethany. And I remember how excited you were about her pregnancy."

"It's okay, Sierra. She'll always be in my memories, but she wouldn't have wanted to hold me back. I can't live in the past for the rest of my life."

"That's not what I meant, exactly. I mean... you love kids. You're good with Maddie. You're always talking about having a family."

"Yes?" No denying that.

She unwrapped the quilt and pushed past him as she rose then crossed the room to stare out the window at the snow-covered trees. "I can't get pregnant, Gabe. I can't give you kids."

Chapter 34 --

Sierra stared out the window. Snow had built up on a bough of a nearby evergreen. Suddenly the whole mass slid off with a rumbling poof and the branch sprang upright.

Wasn't that supposed to happen? She'd dropped her biggest bomb. What would the result be?

The room lay silent behind her. She hadn't expected that. Surely Gabe had a reaction of some sort. Maybe he was tiptoeing toward the door, hoping to sneak out without talking to her. She whirled around.

Gabe sat on the floor where she'd left him, his face cradled in his hands.

Angry? Sorrowful? How could she know? "Gabe? Did you hear me?" Her voice echoed harshly in the quiet room.

"I heard you." But he didn't look up.

She took a few steps closer. "I know you told me you'd be waiting for me. I know I pushed you to your limit. I know—"

He sprang to his feet. "You don't know."

What was the look in his eyes? It changed a dozen times a second.

"You don't know what it felt like to open my heart to

someone again." The words exploded out of him. "How hard that was for me. How it felt to be pushed aside for a guy like Burke. Why him?"

Sierra searched his face then looked away. "He doesn't want kids."

He brushed her words aside with a sweep of his hand. "Why didn't you talk to me? Why did you force me to watch helpless from the sidelines while you paraded Burke in front of your family? Why didn't you trust me enough to see if I'd walk through this beside you?" He grasped her arms and gave her a little shake. "Why?"

"But you want children—"

"Why not let me decide how important that is to me compared to losing you?"

"But—"

Another shake. "Sierra, don't you see? If we don't trust each other, we have nothing."

Didn't they already have nothing? "I'm sorry."

He dropped her arms and turned away. "Not half as sorry as I am."

"You don't understand! I said I'm sorry! You're supposed to—"

Gabe pivoted. "Supposed to say it's all okay? It isn't that simple. Words don't make it fine. They don't undo what's happened."

"I was trying to protect you." Sierra wrapped both arms around her middle.

"I don't need protecting. I'm a grown man, Sierra. I'm not a kid to feed… honey to. I'll take the truth any day over processed baby food."

Moisture welled up in her eyes. "Well, then, I guess we're done. You want a family, and I can't provide that. I apologize for my actions, and you push me away. I guess we're even." Tears burned down her cheeks as she turned back to the window. "Just go away."

"How far?" His voice was low and even.

"What do you mean, how far? However far it takes."

"I sold the store."

He *what?* Sierra swung around. "Pardon me?"

"You heard me. A friend of mine who's a Realtor had a client looking for a business like Nature's Pantry. We talked, they looked, and we signed a contract a few days ago. It's theirs at the end of the year."

"But you can't do that. Why didn't you tell me?"

His jaw hardened. "Why didn't *you* tell *me?*"

She took a step closer. "I don't get it. You sold the store because of me?"

"Did you think I'd stay in Galena Landing and cheerfully watch you have a dozen of Burke's kids?"

"But I can't—"

"So you say now. But what was I supposed to think, Sierra? How on earth could I have known?"

She dropped into the nearest chair and folded her arms over her head. Oh no, no, no. What had she done? How could Gabe have yanked this away from her? It was her fault. All hers. "I'm so sorry," she choked out. "What are you going to do?"

"I don't know. It's only been a few days. I haven't come up with a plan."

Nature's Pantry in some other owner's hands? After all she'd poured into it? But Gabe was right. She'd provided so little to go on. If she'd only given him more thought, she'd have remembered his original plans were to dump the store and run.

She'd pushed him too far. How could she make it up to him? "Gabe, I—"

"Sierra, don't you see? You mean more to me than all the children we might've had, but now I have nothing to offer you. No home, no job. Nothing."

She wiped her tears away with her sleeve and looked up. He stood several feet away, right where she'd left him. She sniffled. "I have nothing to offer you, either."

They stared at each other. The hardness in his eyes had dissipated. Were those tears welling in his eyes, too? Maybe they were all hers, making everything she looked at damp. She wiped her face again and reached for a tissue from the nearest side table.

He crouched beside her. "Maybe that's the best way. It's how we come to Jesus, after all. Nothing we have is good enough to sweeten the deal for Him to love us."

Was he saying what she thought he was saying? Was forgiveness possible?

His hand swept the hair from the side of her face, and she leaned into his touch, her gaze never leaving his. "We don't always get what we deserve."

"Maybe that's a good thing." Both his hands cradled her face. "Can we start again? Can we build some trust and see where God leads us?"

"Do you mean it?" The last of the ice thawed in her belly. "Please."

His lips caressed hers.

oOo

There wasn't a better place to have a Christmas party or better people to have it with. Gabe looked around the dining room table at Green Acres at his friends. His and Sierra's. Jo had tucked Maddie into her crib in the spare room and come back with the box containing Pictionary.

Zach caught his eye and nodded. Claire winked. Noel grinned.

They were all in on it. Now if it would only go as planned.

"I'll bet anything we girls will leave you guys in the dust." Jo pulled the board out of the box.

Claire got out the game pieces. "We've been reading each others' minds for years."

"I wouldn't be so sure about that." Zach leaned back in his chair at the head of the table. "Me and Gabe go back a lot farther than you do. And I don't think Noel will be much of a hindrance."

"You're on." Gabe draped an arm around the back of Sierra's chair.

"Hope you're a good loser," she said, smirking.

"I never lose." He grinned at her.

"Neither do I."

"Not competitive much, are we?" asked Noel. "Pretty sure we guys will give you girls a run for your money."

Sierra surged out of her chair, ran into the kitchen, and came back with a jar of honey. "I bet we win. What've you got to wager?"

Gabe grinned. "I came prepared." He strolled over to where his jacket hung behind the door. Then he brought an object back and set it beside the jar.

"Cora's plain rice cakes?" Sierra sounded incredulous. "I'm not sure I want to win, if that's what the prize is."

"I think we can—" Gabe tapped the honey jar twice and waggled his eyebrows. "—sweeten the deal, if you don't mind the pun."

"I don't know if there's enough honey in the world to make those things palatable."

"Guess you'll have to lose, then, if winning is such a

problem."

She rolled her eyes and picked up the dice. "Let's get started."

The girls drew the first turn, Sierra sketching a place for her team.

"Portland!" called Jo.

Gabe leaned closer. "How could you tell?"

"We've been studying the map since you decided to go to college there." She smirked at him.

"But that doesn't look anything like a map."

Sierra dug her elbow into his ribs. "Quit making fun of my artistic skills."

"Or lack of them." Gabe turned to the guys. "Who's going first for our team?"

"You are. Pull a card already." Noel jutted his chin at the box.

The game turned out closer than Gabe had expected. After much laughter and scribbles no one should have deciphered, both teams sat within reach of the finish line.

"We are going to win," Zach informed his wife.

"Whatever." Jo waved a languid hand. "Sierra, would you mind putting the kettle on? This will soon be over, either way, and I'd like some tea."

Sierra cast Jo a quizzical look but stood. "Sure." She headed into the kitchen.

Zach grabbed the box of cards and hid it while he shuffled them.

"Hurry up," whispered Claire.

Gabe's gut took this opportunity to twist, and his hands got clammy. The teams had switched allegiance, though Sierra didn't yet realize it. Now it was everyone against her. Sort of.

Sierra slid back into her chair seconds after Zach replaced the box. "Whose turn is it to draw?"

"Gabe's," Jo replied. "Yours if it's an all-play."

Gabe pulled the front card out of the box. Zach had better have done this correctly. A glance proved the set-up was complete. He made a moue of disappointment. "It's an all-play." He slid the card to Sierra.

It was all he could do not to boldly watch her reaction. He did catch the sidelong glance she shot him, but he carefully stared off into space as though contemplating his work of art.

"Ready?" Noel had his hand on the egg timer.

"Ready." Oh, yeah, he was ready. He'd been planning for days how he could mess up a drawing as simple as this one. A stick man on one knee.

"Basketball?" said Zach.

"No." Gabe glanced at Sierra's paper. She'd drawn a circle with a little crown on one edge.

"Tiara?" asked Claire.

Sierra shook her head. She quickly drew a square at an angle, adding some facets with an arrow toward the crown.

Jo leaned closer.

Gabe added a diamond ring anyone could recognize. Noel and Zach made guesses from horses to knitting.

Finally their laughter got through to Sierra, and she glanced at his paper.

He added another stick figure, this one in a skirt, standing in front of the kneeler.

Her gaze went from the paper to his face.

"Oh, man." Zach shook his head. "Sierra was right. I'm no good at this game. I sure do hate losing though."

"No, it's my artwork," Gabe said. "Too bad I'm not a better artist." He shifted to one hip and pulled the little velvet-covered box out of his pocket. He turned to Sierra. "Let's switch to charades, so I can demonstrate instead of draw."

Her eyes widened and her hands clapped over her mouth, the

pencil skittering across the floor.

In one fluid motion, Gabe dropped to the floor on one knee and opened the box. "Sierra, will you marry me?"

"Proposal!" called Noel. "Is that what you were trying to draw?"

Sierra burst into tears and lunged at him, wrapping both arms so tightly around his neck he thought he'd choke as he rocked back on his heels.

"Hey, now." He laughed and steadied them both. "What kind of answer is that?"

"It's a yes, you crazy man. It's a yes!"

Epilogue

*S*ierra walked through the empty apartment above Nature's Pantry. She'd spent so many hours here. A few back in the early days at Green Acres when Bethany was still alive. Many more while Gabe was in Romania. And others since his return.

It was hard to say goodbye.

"You'll like the Smiths." Gabe came up behind her and slid both arms around her, nuzzling her neck.

She took a deep breath as she leaned back against him. "It won't be the same."

"No, it won't. But we don't want time to stand still. We want it to move forward."

"April seems a long way off."

"I'll be back before you know it with a fresh diploma to my name, ready to take over the management of the nonprofit you've helped set up."

Somebody to keep things pointed in one direction would be a huge relief. It had taken Allison's introduction to realize how scattered their efforts had been until now.

"Take good care of that junior youth class for me."

"About that. Are you sure?"

"It's just four months. I have faith in you. We can go over the lessons on Skype every week if you want."

She let out a long breath. "That would help."

His hands turned her around to face him. "And then June."

He rested his forehead against hers, gazing deep into her eyes. "I can't wait."

She slipped her arms around his neck. "Me, either."

"Don't let that event planner sister of yours turn this into her wedding." He kissed her temple then let his lips wander down her jawbone. "Stand your ground."

Hard to do when his touch made her bones like jelly. "I will."

"And in a year or two, if God doesn't send a surprise our way, we'll find a child who needs a home." He kissed her nose. "Maybe two or three of them."

A beautiful thought. Why hadn't she realized that biology was only part of parenting?

His lips nuzzled hers. For a long moment she reveled in the sensation. She felt his reluctance as he pulled away.

"I need to hit the road."

"I know." Sierra ran her fingers down his face. "Drive safely."

"The new car has Bluetooth." He winked. "So I can talk to you the whole way to Portland."

"At least where there's coverage." She kissed him. "Oh, Gabe, don't go."

"I have to, sweetheart. I'm doing this for us. To open the doors God has put in front of us." He pulled her tight for a moment then tugged her to start walking toward the back stairs.

She went down in front of him, aware of every footstep, aware this was the last time they'd leave the apartment behind.

Gabe walked her over to the hatchback, which looked even more decrepit sitting next to his nearly-new Accord. He'd badly needed a new set of wheels, especially for all the driving back and forth he'd promised to do in the next few months.

She might even stay down there with her parents for a week or two. That would be a good idea. Do some wedding shopping there. Her dress, maybe.

And see more of Gabe.

He opened her car door, but she flung herself back into his arms. "I love you, Gabe. I'll be counting the days."

"I love you, too, Sierra. Drive home safely. Those new tires should keep you from sliding off the road when your knight in shining armor isn't here to rescue you."

She sniffled. "That was Zach."

He laughed. "Believe what you want. I'll do anything to protect you, even if it means letting Zach and Noel take care of things for a few months."

"Not everything."

"Definitely not everything." He rested his forehead against hers, looking deep into her eyes. "Winter will soon be over. April is coming." He kissed her. "And then June."

The End

Recipe for Sierra's Mocha
A warm hug for winter days!

In your favorite coffee mug, place:
- A pinch of salt
- A rounded teaspoon of organic fair-trade cocoa
- A dash of cinnamon
- A teaspoon of local honey (or to taste)

Add hot organic fair-trade coffee until the mug is nearly full. Stir to dissolve the honey and mix all ingredients. Add a slosh of organic cream and enjoy!

Dear Reader ----------------------------

Do you share my passion for locally grown real food? No, I'm not as fanatical or fixated as our friends from Green Acres, but farming, gardening, and food processing comprise a large part of my non-writing life.

Whether you're new to the concept or a long-time advocate, I invite you to my website and blog at www.valeriecomer.com to explore God's thoughts on the junction of food and faith.

Please sign up for my monthly newsletter while you're there! My gift to all subscribers is *Peppermint Kisses: A (short) Farm Fresh Romance* that follows Wild Mint Tea in chronology. Joining my list is the best way to keep tabs on my food/farm life as well as contests, cover reveals, deals, and news about upcoming books. I welcome you!

Enjoy this Book? ----------------------

Please leave a review at any online retailer or reader site. Letting other readers know what you think about *Sweetened with Honey: A Farm Fresh Romance* helps them make a decision and means a lot to me. Thank you!

If you haven't read *Raspberries and Vinegar*, the first book in the series, with the story of Jo and Zach's romance, or *Wild Mint Tea*, the second book, containing Claire and Noel's story, I hope you will.

Keep reading for the first chapter of Allison's story, *Dandelions for Dinner: A Farm Fresh Romance 4*. Following that is the first chapter of *More Than a Tiara*, my novella in a Christmas duo entitled *Snowflake Tiara*. Both are available from most online retailers in ebook and print.

Dandelions for Dinner

A Farm Fresh Romance

Book 4

Valerie Comer

GreenWords Media

Chapter 1 --

*A*llison Hart had perfected the art of staring out the window and checking her watch simultaneously. The contractor said he'd be here by ten, and it was now quarter after. If guys could be on time driving in Portland city traffic, how hard could it be on northern Idaho's rural roads?

Waiting. Who had time for it? She tapped her foot and crossed her arms, not that there was anyone to see. No one who lived at Green Acres Farm was home today, which suited Allison just fine. She'd arrived three days earlier and had already experienced about all the togetherness she could handle.

The rumble of a vehicle grew louder, and a white pickup with the emblem of Timber Framing Plus emblazoned on the side turned into the driveway.

Finally. Allison strode for the door, buttoning her cardigan against the cold March day as she went.

The contractor slammed the truck door and turned toward her, hard hat in hand.

Wait a minute. This wasn't Patrick at all. This guy had a shock of black hair, unlike Patrick's thinning salt-and-pepper, to say nothing of dark brown eyes, slightly angled. Skin that on anyone else might look tanned but, combined with the rest, definitely tagged him of Asian descent.

She was bad at telling them apart, even with her nephew's

Korean features. This man could be anything from Japanese to Thai to Filipino. She shook her head. Didn't matter. He could be Martian for all the difference it made to her. The biggest problem was, he wasn't Patrick.

The guy tucked his hard hat under his arm and stretched out his hand. "Hi, I'm Brent Callahan from Timber Framing Plus."

Since when did a Callahan run to Asian features?

"Allison Hart."

He had a strong grip, like he knew what he was doing, even though he didn't have the other man's years of experience.

"Where's Patrick?"

"Back in the office. He sent me out to check the footings."

The wind had built up speed crossing the Galena Valley. Would it slam straight into the mountain beside the farm and come to an abrupt halt or find other some direction in which to continue? Either way, she should've worn something without the big holes in her bulky cardigan. She wrapped both arms around herself in an attempt to stay warm. "I was under the impression he was coming himself. I have a list of questions for him."

Brent grinned. "Nothing I can't answer, I'm sure. I've worked for him since high school."

Her eyebrows shot up. When was that, last week?

"Ten years, ma'am." He winked, set the hard hat on his head, and turned toward the construction site, where numerous concrete tubes stuck a few inches out of the ground.

Ten years? That made the guy something like twenty-eight. He sure didn't look it. Allison hurried after him. "I'm sorry. I didn't mean to doubt your experience. I just expected Patrick. It's his business, after all."

Brent turned to face her, dark eyes unreadable. "Timber Framing Plus is a large company. We work on more than one project at a time. Patrick oversees them all, but don't confuse yourself into thinking that means he and his two best friends put into place every piece of wood that makes each structure."

"But he said...." Allison's words trailed away as she tried to recall the exact words in their discussion.

"What did he say, ma'am?"

Her temper flared. "My name is Allison, not ma'am." It was a temptation to make him call her Ms. Hart so he'd remember which of them was the real boss on this site. Ma'am made her think of someone old with an unsavory reputation.

"Allison. " He tipped his head. "What did Patrick say, exactly?"

"He said he'd oversee the project personally."

Brent laughed and shook his head. "And he will. From his office in Coeur d'Alene, where he can keep an eye on all the structures we're erecting this season. Available to any of his foremen, day or night, with whatever questions or problems we might encounter."

"But—" Allison hated losing, but this was obviously not a battle she was going to win. If Patrick's office were any nearer, she'd march right in and give him a piece of her mind. A two-hour drive might be worth the satisfaction.

She looked at Brent, but he was striding away from her. He made a fine figure in navy work pants and shirt. Not a big guy, but not scrawny either. Good looking.

A disaster. She'd counted on Patrick. Somebody with experience. Somebody who was safe.

Not that being older made a man safe to be around. She knew that. Her dad had been nothing but trouble to any woman he came within flirting distance of. And Mom had repaid him in kind. Only a shared desire for convenience and prestige had kept the two of them married all those years.

It hadn't provided much security for her and her sister.

Thinking of Lori brought all the old aches surging to the surface. Drinking, sex, and drugs had comprised Lori's life since she was fourteen. She somehow managed to keep things just enough together to keep Child Protection Services at bay and retain custody of her little boy.

Sebastian. That poor kid. Allison soaked him up every minute she could, but Lori was always quick to move on. To another city, another man, and another addiction. The little guy deserved so much better it made Allison's heart ache. If only she'd been able to make a difference for Sebastian by staying in Portland, but her sister had screamed in her face and dragged him off to Tucson with a guy named John. Likely an apt name.

Allison blinked the tears away and straightened her spine. The man over there crouching down and poking at the footings wasn't a loser like the guys her sister hooked up with. He had a real job. She could trust him to build the farm school she'd proposed to the women of Green Acres when they met last fall.

So they might all think marriage was a great thing, but she'd watched her parents. She'd escape the curse. She was absolutely, definitely, for sure here to build herself a spinster house and get herself a big dog to guard her.

Brent Callahan stood in front of her, head angled as he looked at her.

No room for a man in her life. So totally not interested. Didn't matter if he was ugly and fifty or gorgeous and close to her age.

She met Brent's gaze evenly. "And the verdict is?"

"The verdict is I'll have a crew out here Monday to get started."

"You?"

He narrowed his eyes. "Yes, me. Didn't I just tell you that Patrick assigned me as the foreman in charge of your project?"

No. No, he had not.

oOo

Thanks, Uncle Patrick. Why couldn't Brent's first gig as foreman be for some middle-aged man? Someone who would swing by the worksite a couple of times a week? Someone who would respect Patrick's decision and trust Brent's experience? After all, his uncle had been grooming him for several years to take over the commercial projects.

He didn't need Allison Hart to question his every breath. He didn't need a female client at all, especially not one near his own age. The girl was almost as tall as he was. Her bulky black cardigan came to mid-thigh, topping black leggings and high black boots. Too skinny for his taste. She was probably anorexic. No one could possibly eat normally and look like that.

Too bad, really. She was kind of pretty under the layer of makeup, though she could do with a little color. And while he liked long hair on a girl as much as the next guy, hers swung straight nearly to her waist.

Not much softness to Allison Hart. It was like she was careful to give off the persona she wanted. Nah. Brent would bet this was who she really was underneath.

He'd been staring. He tried for a natural smile. "It looks like we'll be seeing a lot of each other for the next few months."

Her jaw twitched. "Great. Just what I needed." She glared at him through narrowed eyes.

Brent's spine straightened on its own. "I have the experience and the credentials."

She gathered her hair in both hands and flipped it over her shoulders. "I'd really rather have Patrick."

"I am his fully qualified representative." He'd nearly said nephew. Bet that wouldn't go over well with skinny Miss Priss. He'd quit calling the man uncle in public years before, when they'd begun working together so closely. It was better on the job site for the crew not to be reminded of their relationship. Most didn't even know, given that Patrick looked totally Irish and Brent...did not.

"I'll be staying at The Landing Pad." Brent thumbed toward the town of Galena Landing. "Along with the guys who will be my permanent crew here. Once we get rolling, we'll be here from eight to five Monday through Friday with an hour off for lunch." He quirked an eyebrow at her. "If that meets your expectations?"

Allison's eyes narrowed until he couldn't see the brown orbs any more. "That will be fine, so long as your crew is disciplined, experienced, and gets the job done as soon as possible." She grimaced. "I can't believe he did this to me."

She was seriously starting to get under his skin, and that took some doing. "I'm sorry Patrick didn't make it clear."

Her eyebrows rose. "*You're* sorry?"

"Indeed. Do you think I enjoy being treated like a second class citizen?" He leaned closer. "Just because I'm not who you were expecting doesn't mean I am not the right man for the job."

She took a step back.

Good. She was getting the idea. His cell phone rang with his uncle's ring tone, and he reached for it, maintaining eye contact. "Hi, Patrick. Brent here."

Allison reached for his phone, and he turned away.

"How's it going, Brent? Are the footings ready?"

"We can start Monday. Say, it seems you forgot to mention to Ms. Hart that you wouldn't be on the job here every day."

His uncle laughed, but it sounded strained. "She's not too happy, I take it?"

"You got that right."

"Well, it gets worse."

Uh oh. Brent's hand tightened on his phone as he strode

toward the truck. Better be out of earshot for this one. "How's that?"

"We ordered all the windows for her job from McGowan Windows."

No secret there. "Yes?"

"The plant burned to the ground yesterday. We have to find another manufacturer." Patrick paused. "And get in line with everyone else."

Brent closed his eyes. So many words he'd quit saying a few years ago vied to explode from his mouth. He tightened his jaw to clamp them back and took a few deep breaths.

"Brent?"

"I'm here." Inhale, exhale. "Please tell me this is your idea of an early April Fool's joke."

Patrick's chuckle had a nervous edge to it. "I wish. It's not just the Hart job affected. We've got three other clients who ordered McGowan windows. And of course we're not the only company. Everyone else is scrambling to get on some other manufacturer's list, too."

"Expected delay?"

"Several months, probably. That Hart structure has a lot of windows. But I don't have anything confirmed yet. Waiting to hear back."

"This is going to go over like a ton of bricks, you know that?"

His uncle sighed. "I know. Right this minute I have three other lines lit up with incoming calls. I need to go. I'll let you know as soon as I have some answers."

"Just a sec. I assume we're to go ahead as far as we can while we wait?"

"Yes. We'll try not to lay off any guys. It will take some juggling, but we'll make it all happen."

"Okay. Thanks, Patrick." But his uncle had already ended the call.

Now he had the joy of explaining this to his client. Brent turned slowly, but she was right there. She'd followed him to the truck and probably overheard every word.

Both hands rested on what would be hips on a woman with curves. Her dark brown eyes stared straight into his from mere inches away. "Well?"

Good thing Brent had become a praying man. He shot a plea heavenward. "We have a problem."

"So I deduced. What is it? How bad?"

"The window manufacturing plant we'd ordered your windows from burned to the ground yesterday."

Her jaw clenched and she shook her head slowly. "Right. That's too bad. Just get them from somewhere else."

Brent opened his mouth and closed it again. Another prayer winged away, this one for patience. He managed to smile, so that was progress. "Not as easy as you might expect. McGowan's plant was one of the largest in the US."

Allison raised her eyebrows. "And?"

"And there are dozens of contractors with orders placed, many of them with multiple clients. No other plant has the capacity to simply step in and meet the demand."

"So you're telling me we have no windows coming, and no idea when we can get them."

"Basically. But Patrick's on it. He'll let me know as soon as something is confirmed."

Allison jabbed her finger against his chest. "Do you know that this is supposed to be a school?" Poke. "That we have classes booked and students coming in July?" Poke.

"Hey, wait a minute." He grabbed her hand to stop the jabs, and she jerked away. "It's not like I went to Milwaukee and torched the factory to spite you. This situation is totally out of my hands. It makes no difference if Patrick was going to be onsite or me. This is bigger than Timber Framing Plus. We'll do our best, but we're not miracle workers."

If he were, he knew where he'd start, and it wouldn't be with Allison Hart.

Author Biography

Valerie Comer lives where food meets faith in her real life, her fiction, and on her blog and website. She and her husband of over 30 years farm, garden, and keep bees on a small farm in Western Canada, where they grow and preserve much of their own food.

Valerie has always been interested in real food from scratch, but her conviction has increased dramatically since God blessed her with three delightful granddaughters. In this world of rampant disease and pollution, she is compelled to do what she can to make these little girls' lives the best she can. She helps supply healthy food—local food, organic food, seasonal food—to grow strong bodies and minds.

Her experience has planted seeds for many stories rooted in the local-food movement. *Raspberries and Vinegar*, *Wild Mint Tea*, and *Sweetened with Honey* will be followed by three more books in the Farm Fresh Romance series including *Dandelions for Dinner* (early 2015) and two additional tales set on Green Acres Farm in 2015-2016.

To find out more, visit her website at www.valeriecomer.com, where you can read her blog, explore her many links, and sign up for her email newsletter to download the free short story: *Peppermint Kisses: A (short) Farm Fresh Romance 2.5*. You can also use this QR code to access the newsletter sign-up.

Made in the USA
Monee, IL
08 May 2021